TAKING CHANCES

By the Author

Where Love Leads

Taking Chances

Visit us at www.boldstrokesbooks.com

Amanda,
Thanks and
happy reading!

TAKING CHANCES

by

Erin McKenzie

2018

ISBN 13: 978-1-63555-209-6

This Trade Paperback Original Is Published By
Bold Strokes Books, Inc.
P.O. Box 249
Valley Falls, NY 12185

First Edition: December 2018

CREDITS
EDITOR: RUTH STERNGLANTZ
PRODUCTION DESIGN: STACIA SEAMAN
COVER DESIGN BY MELODY POND

Acknowledgments

Eleven years ago, Debbie and I became foster parents, and our lives were forever changed. We had the rare good fortune to adopt all three of the children placed with us. Our daughters and son are the greatest blessing of our lives.

To Monica and Renée, your professional knowledge and personal experiences were invaluable to this story. Thank you so much for sharing them with me.

Thank you to Tricia, my good friend and first reader, for your willingness to read and reread, and for your unwavering support and encouragement.

To the Bold Strokes team, thank you for giving me the chance to share my stories. Ruth, thank you for helping me to breathe more life into my manuscript, and for encouraging me to venture, finally, into the world of Skype.

Lastly, thanks to you, my reader, for choosing this book. You have given me the confidence to keep writing, and for that I am truly grateful.

To the hundreds of thousands of foster children in the U.S. and around the world: May you find healing, happiness and love in a forever family of your very own, be it biological, adoptive, or chosen. Never forget that you are special and deserving of every good thing this world has to give.

This book is also dedicated to the memory of Connie Smith, our own MAPP trainer and home finder, who led us into the world of foster parenting with humor and positivity. You were a bright and joyful part of this world, Connie, and you are deeply missed.

CHAPTER ONE

Fabulous," Valerie Cruz groaned, as she walked into the county office building and saw the packed waiting room at the DMV. This one was the closest to her Central New York home besides the Syracuse branch, which would be ten times busier. "So much for leaving work early." She pulled a ticket—C297—and looked up at the display to see that they were now serving C253. Seeing no seats available, Val sighed and stepped back out into the building's foyer.

As she watched the people coming and going, Val made up little stories in her head about their lives, like she'd done since she was a little girl. Take those two young men in their fancy suits, strutting by with briefcases in hand. She decided they were attorneys, returning from a long docket of cases at the courthouse across the street. Maybe the little old lady in the shabby threadbare coat was coming from the Medicaid office because she needed help making ends meet since her husband died. Val turned to watch another group of people exit the elevator. A well-dressed woman was carrying a toddler and whispering softly to him, followed by two young women making a show of waving good-bye to the child. Val pegged the older woman for a foster parent who had just brought the child for a visit with his birth mom. The two younger women stayed in the lobby.

"When Sammy called her *Mama* in there, I wanted to punch that bitch in the throat. I'm his mama, and no fucking stuck-up bitch is gonna raise my kid."

Val was startled by their loud conversation, which she couldn't help overhearing.

"What're you gonna do?" the mother's companion asked.

"They say I haven't been doing enough to get him back. I gotta keep Anthony away, but I didn't know the fool was a damn sex offender. And I gotta get a job and my own apartment. I've been trying, but don't they know how hard it is to get a job in this fucking town? I never even got my GED. How am I gonna do all that in ninety days?"

"I don't know, girl. Damn."

The mother pushed open the door to the sidewalk with a trembling hand, fiercely wiping her eyes. "Get me outta here. I need to smoke."

Val's stomach hurt as she watched the women leave. Her guess about the circumstances had been spot-on, but regardless of why the young woman was in this boat, it was hard to witness her pain. Val couldn't help but think about her own complicated history. She had been in seven foster homes from the age of nine until she'd aged out of the system at eighteen. Some had been okay, others hellish. Now that she'd been on her own for eleven years, Val rarely let herself dwell on the bad memories. Still, she had a soft spot for kids in need and wondered what would become of little Sammy. She silently said a prayer for the beautiful child.

A peek into the DMV told Val she had a while yet to wait, so she wandered down the hall to the vending machine to grab a drink. On the way back, she perused the community bulletin boards to pass the time. In the center of one board, on neon yellow paper, was an advertisement for an upcoming foster parent training class. Val stepped closer and read it, surprised at the name listed as the point of contact.

Connie Smart. She had to be the same one, but wouldn't she be retired by now? Val hadn't seen her in several years, but the idea of meeting up again made her smile. Connie had been the case worker on her last two foster placements and had sort of taken Val under her wing. Connie had seen through her bravado and false I-don't-give-a-shit attitude to the hurting kid underneath, and she had been a major reason why Val had taken the chance on going to college. But foster parenting? True, she had entertained the thought a time or two, figuring she knew firsthand what foster kids needed, but the idea of actually being responsible for someone else had scared her off. Some days she wasn't even sure she had her own shit together. But as she stared at the poster, she felt something tugging at her. Before she could analyze the feeling too closely, she snapped a picture of the poster with her phone and walked back to the DMV.

❖

"Ready for tomorrow night?" Joe asked as he poured a cup of coffee in the break room.

Paige Wellington looked up at her coworker and groaned. "I hope so. I've never led one of these trainings before, but Connie insists I'll be fine. She says diving in is the best way to learn. I just hope I don't drown." She'd only transferred from child protective to the foster care unit six months ago, and she was still getting her bearings.

Joe took a seat at the table where Paige sat, sipping her Matcha. "Please. You're the most organized, professional person I know. I moved over from CPS two years ago, but Connie never asked me to run a class." Joe pouted, and Paige laughed.

"That's because you'd wet yourself." Paige had known Joe ever since she'd begun working in Children and Family Services, and he was notoriously afraid of public speaking.

"True, but still," Joe huffed. "At least you've already been through MAPP training yourself."

"Thank God," Paige replied. "Can you believe that was nine years ago already?" Paige had signed up for the Model Approaches to Partnerships in Parenting foster parent training course, inspired by the heartbreaking experiences she'd had working for CPS. So many children had been placed in foster care on her recommendation, and she understood only too well the fear and uncertainty those kids had faced. "I'm grateful every day that Emma was placed with me. It makes me sick to think what could have happened to her."

"Weren't her bio parents the ones running that meth lab in their double-wide?"

"Yeah, and they were selling to a tri-county distribution ring. If someone hadn't called CPS to report that a baby was in the home, Emma might still be with them." Paige shuddered at the thought. Thankfully, they were still in jail, and since no suitable relatives turned up to take the baby, Emma had become Paige's adopted daughter just after her second birthday. It had easily been the best day of Paige's life, and she could barely remember life before Emma.

"Well, she's lucky to have you," Joe said, pulling Paige out of the past.

"I'm the lucky one. She's a terrific kid."

Joe nodded. "So, how are you liking it on this side of the hall?"

"It's definitely been a learning curve, but I'm glad I took the opportunity to leave CPS. It was getting to me, you know?"

"Yeah, I know. There's only so much negativity a person can take. I felt like it was starting to change me, and not in a good way. I had to get out of there before Charlie divorced me. I was a bitch to live with back then, or so he told me."

Paige laughed. "I didn't notice, but then again, I was probably a bitch, too."

Joe shook his head. "No way, honey. You're the sweetest person I've ever met." He stood and put a beefy hand on Paige's shoulder. "Good luck with MAPP class."

"Thanks. Guess we'll see how it goes tomorrow."

Chapter Two

Paige watched the participants of the MAPP class trickle into the conference room. She straightened the handouts and smoothed her skirt for the tenth time, then heard Connie chuckle behind her.

"Relax. I'll take the lead tonight. You'll be fine once we get started."

Paige managed a smile and nodded. Connie was a home finder for the foster care unit and had worked there for over twenty years. She was a redhead with bright blue eyes and an irreverent sense of humor, and her demeanor put nearly everyone at ease. She also had a heart of gold and was the most knowledgeable person in the whole department. Connie always wore a smile and somehow made the job look easy. Paige knew there was no one better to learn from and was happy to be paired with her.

Looking around the room, Paige saw that eleven of the twelve registered participants had arrived. Five couples of varying ages and an older woman who had come alone sat at the rectangle of tables, waiting for class to begin. Paige wondered what had brought each of them here tonight. She could feel the nervous energy in the room as the people glanced around at each other, and she hoped she wasn't giving off the same vibe.

Connie moved to the front of the room and was about to welcome everyone when the door opened. Connie's face broke into a wide grin. "Valerie! I thought I was seeing things when your name showed up on my class list."

Everyone watched as a young woman entered the room and let Connie wrap her up in a hug. The woman turned, and Paige inhaled sharply, her curiosity about the newcomer quickly shifting to attraction. The woman was stunning. Long, glossy dark hair was pulled back in a clip at the base of her neck. Her sleeveless sunflower-yellow top accentuated a lovely expanse of golden brown skin, which glowed under the fluorescent lights, making Paige's own skin look pasty by comparison. Expressive dark eyes glanced quickly around the room as she took a seat. This Valerie, whom Connie clearly knew, looked familiar, and after a moment, Paige realized why. She looked like a young Jennifer Lopez—in other words, gorgeous. Apparently she wasn't the only one who thought so—every guy in the room was now sitting up straighter, and a couple of the women, as they smoothed down their hair, were staring at the latecomer with something akin to awe. Paige smothered a grin.

"Now that we're all here," Connie said, "I'd like to welcome you to MAPP class. We will spend the next eight weeks training you in the major aspects of foster parenting, with the hope that your homes will be added to our list of good foster placements for the many needy children that come into care. But first, introductions. I'm Connie Smart, and I am a home finder for the county. My colleague here is Paige Wellington, a case worker in the foster care unit. Between us, we have over thirty years of experience working with children and families in the area."

Paige raised her hand in a wave, then proceeded to pass out folders of materials. As she passed Valerie's chair, she caught the scent of something warm and tropical, like coconut, and the voice that quietly thanked her was low and rich. Feeling silly that she'd even noticed, Paige quickly moved on.

"Now let's have you all introduce yourselves," Connie continued. "Please tell us your name and why you decided to join this class."

Paige listened carefully to the participants. Two couples who looked to be in their fifties wanted to foster now that their own kids were grown, because their homes felt too big and empty without kids around to keep them young. The older woman had been a foster parent in the past but had stopped taking in children when her husband became ill. Now a widow, she wanted to get recertified. One of the twentysomething couples was unable to have children and was hoping to use foster care as a vehicle to adoption, while the other just wanted to help children in need. While most of the group had presented as friendly and optimistic, the last couple seemed decidedly less so. The man stared impassively at the tabletop, rubbing the graying stubble on his chin, while the much younger-looking woman, straight-faced, said they were always taking in kids anyway and might as well get paid for it. Paige winced at that, but then turned her attention expectantly to the last person at the table.

"I'm Valerie Cruz," the beautiful woman said, her eyes on Connie. "I was in foster care for nine years and lived in seven different homes. I want to help make sure that any child in my care has a much better experience than I did. I just feel like it's time to step up."

Whoa. Paige felt a wave of compassion for her, as Ellen, the widow, began to clap. Connie smiled and winked at Valerie, who ducked her head in embarrassment as the others joined in the applause. Paige had a revelation as she watched Connie nod with pride. Did Valerie know Connie from when she'd been a foster kid herself?

Valerie shifted in her seat. She hated being in large groups. Thank God Connie was here to make it bearable. Scanning the room, Val focused on each person in turn, trying to get a read on them, a hard habit to break. As a child, she had learned early on to trust her instincts about people, and in some cases, those instincts are what had kept her safe. She knew from experience that Connie was as good as they came, but she wasn't so sure about the other instructor. The woman looked kind of uppity, with her silk suit and perfectly coiffed blond hair, like she was supposed to be having dinner at the country club but took a wrong turn and ended up here. Yet she had seemed interested when the other people spoke, and Paige's eyes had been kind when they'd focused on her.

Connie brought her out of her musings by announcing that they were going to be working on an exercise in pairs. Since everyone else was coupled up, that left Val with the older woman, Ellen. She scooted her chair closer to her and was greeted with a warm smile.

"Hi. Guess we're supposed to be filling in this worksheet here," Ellen said.

Val glanced at the heading on the paper: *Attachment Issues in Foster Children*. She nearly scoffed aloud. She had far too much experience with this topic.

"I bet you know a thing or two about this." Ellen apparently had picked up on her reaction. "I know I do. When my Earl was alive, we fostered seventeen children, and some of them had no idea what it meant to trust another person. Took a lot of patience to get through to those kids."

Val nodded, remembering. "Yeah, I know what you mean." She *was* one of those kids, and she'd fought and tested her foster parents at every turn, never trusting their motivations or sincerity.

"Shed a lot of tears in the beginning, until I learned not to take it personally when the kids pushed me away," Ellen said. "We stuck it out, but patience was the key."

Val felt a pang of guilt for her past behavior, but as she thought of a few of her foster placements, it evaporated. "Unfortunately, some of my foster parents never figured that out."

Ellen placed a gentle hand on Val's arm. "It's a tough business, on both sides, but you know what? You're here tonight, and I think that speaks volumes about your strength." Ellen chuckled. "Not that this old lady's opinion matters."

Val looked Ellen in the eye and smiled. "Actually, it matters a lot."

Chapter Three

Val was picking out her books for story hour when they arrived, the same two little ones that had been brought to the library every Tuesday and Thursday morning since summer began. The little girl looked to be about seven or eight, with drab blond hair and sharp hazel eyes that scanned the room thoroughly every time they were here, as if convincing herself it was safe. She held the hand of her little brother, who was maybe two or three years younger. His solemn brown eyes peeked out from beneath a shock of messy hair the color of wet sand. Their clothes were mismatched and worn, and smelled strongly of cigarette smoke. Their mother always dropped them off with the same loud, brusque directive—"Lily, Ian, sit on that rug and behave. I'll be back when you're done." The children immediately dropped down on the rug, right in front of the chair Val sat in to read to the group.

Val loved being a children's librarian and looked forward to these times when she could interact with and entertain kids. But there was something about these two that moved her, maybe because she felt like she gave them the only two hours of peace they'd get all week. Their mother always seemed angry at them, like they were too much of a bother, and it broke Val's heart. She knew that feeling, knew how much it sucked the soul out of a child.

Val shook her head, mentally chastising herself. She had a bad habit of judging others too quickly, and she shouldn't think badly of this mother when she knew nothing about her circumstances. All she could do was show these two children as much kindness as she could while they were with her.

Several other children arrived with their grown-ups, who all stayed and waited, many holding their little ones in their laps. Val sat down in the wingback reading chair with her books, all keeping to today's theme of In the Jungle. Before she began, Val glanced down at little Lily and Ian, who stared back at her with rapt attention. She smiled warmly and winked at them, then began to read.

An hour later, Lily and Ian were contentedly coloring pictures of lions at the craft table when their mother stalked into the room. She was texting rapidly on her phone, and with barely a glance at her children, she barked, "Come on, let's go."

Val immediately saw the tension return to their shoulders as they scrambled to obey. Grabbing their papers from the table, Val said, "Here, guys, don't forget to take your pretty pictures with you. And since you like animals, here's a flyer for an upcoming event we're having here at the library." She glanced at the mother, who glared back, but as Lily took the papers in one hand and Ian's hand in the other, she gave Val a ghost of a smile.

"Jeez, she's harsh," whispered Linda, Val's assistant, once they had left.

"I know, but maybe she's got a lot on her plate. At least she brings them here. She probably figures she's giving herself a break, but maybe it gives them a chance to get away, too." Val sighed. "I feel bad for them. That little Ian never talks. I don't think I've even seen him smile. But Lily, she's got some spirit. I can tell by how she takes care of her brother."

"Shouldn't the mother have to stay with them, though? They're so young."

"Maybe, but I'm afraid if I say something, she won't bring them back," Val replied. She remembered how the library had been a safe haven for her when she was young—she couldn't risk taking that away from those kids.

Linda shook her head. "My sister and her husband have tried for years to get pregnant. It's just unfair how some people would do anything to have a child, while others have kids they don't even seem to want."

Val felt the old familiar ache in her chest. "Sometimes the wanting is there, but the ability to cope just isn't," she replied with a sigh.

❖

Val unlocked her front door and closed it behind her. She tossed her keys on the kitchen counter, grabbed a hard cider from the fridge, and plopped down on her couch with a sigh. She'd been in a mood all day. Usually she was quite good at hiding her feelings behind a friendly, outgoing facade, but today, putting on a smile for the library patrons had been exhausting. She knew that she was reacting to the comment Linda had made about unwanted kids. The remark had been innocent—after all, Linda knew nothing about her past, and Val intended to keep it that way. But it always put her on edge to see parents be harsh with their kids, like that mother at story hour. Lily and Ian seemed so well behaved, but of course she knew that kids who were good in public could be hellions at home. Who knew why their mother acted that way? Val sighed. The whole day just brought her back to times and places she'd worked very hard to put behind her.

Val took a long pull from her bottle, then went into the kitchen to throw together something to eat. An unbidden image of the little girl and her brother came to mind, and she wondered what they were getting for dinner tonight. She could picture them sitting at her feet, completely engrossed in her storytelling. Ian never spoke, but his face was incredibly expressive. Lily was smart and excellent with Ian. Maybe she was reading things all wrong. Val didn't know what went on outside of the two hours a week the kids were at the library. But something about the mother just made Val uncomfortable. Whatever. Their life was none of her business.

On the counter was the folder of materials from MAPP class. They'd been given an assignment to review examples of behaviors exhibited by children in foster care and identify appropriate responses. Val flipped open the folder and began to read the examples. They were dead on: *When given a rule or direction, the child ignores you or does the opposite of what is asked.* "Yep, I did that," she said aloud. *The child frequently lies or makes up stories.* "And that." *The child shows physical aggression toward others, even when unprovoked.* "Oh my God, that, too." *The child steals from others.* "Finally, something I didn't do," Val said, chuckling.

At least the assignment was focused on the reasons why the children in the examples acted out. In her experience, most adults just labeled kids as bad or disrespectful without figuring out what was emotionally driving their behavior. She knew exactly how it felt to be in that situation, and she completed the assignment with ease.

Thursday evening rolled around, and Val was in MAPP class half listening to a lesson about reactive attachment. She'd seen many examples of attachment issues, when kids couldn't form healthy attachments to their caregivers due to prior neglect or abuse. She found herself focusing on the assistant instructor rather than the topic. Paige's blond hair was styled in a loose French twist, and she wore a cream sleeveless blouse with sage-green linen pants and sandals. Her look was much less severe than the first time she'd seen her, though her clothes were of obvious high quality, and Val couldn't deny that Paige was very attractive. She still didn't smile much, though, and she was teaching in a rapid voice, like she couldn't wait to be finished.

Maybe she isn't as uptight as I thought, just nervous. Suddenly, someone cleared their throat behind her, and she turned. Connie just winked and moved away, and Val realized she'd been caught staring at Paige. Damn it, Connie never missed a thing. Val turned back around and saw that her classmates were reading something in their packets. She glanced back at Paige, who was watching her with a curious look on her face. Had she noticed Val staring, too, or just being inattentive? Embarrassed and irritated, Val started to read the assigned page, trying to ignore the fact that her cheeks were on fire. The last thing she needed was Paige thinking she'd been checking her out.

At the break, Paige saw that Val kept to herself while the others mingled and chatted a bit. She watched as Val flipped through her notebook with one hand and twirled a strand of her dark hair around the fingers of the other. She bit her lip in concentration, and Paige wondered if she had any idea how damn sexy she looked when she did that. Wandering over, she stopped by Val's chair and peered over her shoulder at her meticulously written and highlighted notes.

"Looks like you're a model student."

Val stiffened and sat up straighter at the words, and she realized Val had taken her off-hand remark as sarcasm.

"Sorry to startle you. It's just that a three-hour class is a long time to sit without taking a break."

Val looked up at her with a small smile. "I mostly stand all day at work, so I don't mind sitting."

"What do you do for work?"

"I'm a children's librarian."

"Really? That sounds interesting. You certainly don't fit the stereotype," Paige replied with a laugh. When Val frowned, she quickly added, "You know, old lady with a bun and eyeglasses on a chain, shushing everyone."

"Oh."

Damn, now she'd insulted Val's whole profession. "Anyway, there are refreshments on the back table," Paige persisted, trying for a save.

"Thanks, I'm good," Val replied and looked back at her notebook. When Paige didn't move, she looked up again, one eyebrow raised.

Paige was usually pretty good at small talk, but this attempt had been an epic fail. "Okay, then," she said and moved away, her cheeks flaming. Back at the refreshment table, she grabbed a bottle of water and thought about the gorgeous but not so approachable Val. *An hour ago she was staring at me, but now she'll barely acknowledge that I exist. What the hell is that about?*

Chapter Four

Val stepped into Pony's and searched the dimly lit, noisy club for her friend. It wasn't her favorite scene, but it was the only mostly lesbian bar left in the area. She saw her best friend Sasha sitting at the bar and made her way over, trying to ignore the flirty looks from the half dozen women in her path. She was not in the mood to be hit on. Sasha saw her and hopped off her barstool to sweep Val up into one of her trademark bear hugs.

"Damn, girl. You're looking as fine as ever," Sasha said, holding Val by the shoulders and looking her over.

"Thanks. You're looking pretty fine yourself." Sasha's black curls were cropped military short, and her white tank accentuated the flawless dark skin Val had always envied. "You seem thinner, though."

"Trying to lay off the junk food. Gotta keep this ripped physique in tip-top shape, you know."

Val was delighted to see Sasha and couldn't keep the huge grin from her face. They hadn't seen each other in months while Sasha had been away at Senior Leader Course training, and she had just returned to her company at Fort Drum last week. "So, hotshot, what's it like to be a sergeant first class?"

"Same old shit. I'm just responsible for more of it now," Sasha replied with a groan. Val didn't fall for the grumbling—she knew how proud Sasha was to serve in the US Army and how hard she'd worked. "What about you? How's life among the stacks?"

"Enlightening. Look at us, all grown up and respectable. We've come a long way from Leigh and Jerry's, huh?"

"Damn, remember when they brought us out to the farm? We were, like, *Aw hell, no.*"

Val laughed. "They were the best foster parents, though. Didn't put up with our shit, but I knew they cared."

"I'll always be grateful for the hundreds of hay bales I had to move that year. Made basic training a hell of a lot easier," Sasha replied. She wasn't one to brag, but Val knew Sasha had bested many of the men at basic. She was smart, strong, and tough as hell.

Val ordered a Sam Adams and settled on her stool. Sasha leaned in close. "Incoming, five o'clock." A woman approached from Val's right and boldly stepped between her and Sasha.

"Hi there. I'm Steph. I couldn't help but notice you when you came in, and I told myself my night wouldn't be complete unless I got to dance with you. So how about we go on out there?"

Val plastered on a polite smile, trying not to recoil at the stench of alcohol on the woman's breath. "Thanks, but my friend and I have some catching up to do. Maybe another time?"

The woman pouted, then placed her hand on Val's leg and squeezed. "Most definitely," she said in what she must've thought was a sultry voice, but really just sounded wasted. She moved unsteadily away.

Sasha laughed. "That didn't take long. What were you here for, ten minutes?"

Val rolled her eyes. "She was pretty ballsy. What if you and I were together?"

"I'm thinking she didn't care. Lucky for her we aren't, or I might have had to sober her up." Sasha took a swig of her drink. "Anyway, we ought to be used to this by now. After all, you are all fifty shades of hot."

"Stop," Val said. "I did not come here to pick up women. I am perfectly happy to hang out with my BFF and just chill."

"In that case, we might want to go somewhere else. Two more incoming, eight o'clock."

Val burst out laughing.

❖

Sasha and Val grabbed a booth at Clara's Diner, which wouldn't be crazy busy until last call at the bars. A waitress approached, filled their water glasses, and whipped out an order pad. "What'll it be, girls?"

"I would kill for some pecan pancakes," Sasha said.

"No violence necessary," the waitress responded with a wink. "We'll just make 'em for ya." She turned to Val. "And you?"

"I'll have a piece of coconut cream pie and a coffee, decaf," Val replied.

"You got it." The waitress gave Sasha another smile and left.

"She was totally flirting with you," Val teased.

"And why shouldn't she? I'm incredibly good-looking. You and me, girl, we just break hearts everywhere we go."

Val laughed. Sasha was beautiful, and many a woman had fallen for her killer smile. "Speaking of broken hearts, whatever happened to that woman you were seeing—Mandy, right?"

"Holy crap. Train wreck, that one," Sasha replied, shaking her head. "She so didn't get me. She couldn't understand why I wouldn't leave the Army and go play housewives with her. She wanted me around constantly. When I told her I had reenlisted and was going to SLC training for five months, she went ballistic. I had to let her go. It's a damn shame, really—she was pretty feisty in bed."

"Luckily, they'll be lining up to take her place," Val replied.

"Nah, I'm swearing off women for a while. Too much drama, and I can't get shit done. You, though, could totally be holding interviews for Ms. Right. You know she's out there."

Val was saved from replying right away by the arrival of their food. Her slice of pie was a four-inch deep masterpiece of custard and whipped cream, and she dug in, moaning. "I could live on Clara's pies."

"Yeah, but you'd die of a coronary at thirty. Quit changing the subject. We were talking about you and dating."

"I date," she lied, pretending to peruse the song titles in the 1950s tabletop jukebox beside her.

Sasha snorted. "No, you don't. You occasionally scratch your itch with a one-nighter, but you haven't had a girlfriend in forever."

"You know I don't do relationships. Like you said, too much drama." Val took a sip of water, avoiding Sasha's eyes.

"Yeah, for me, but you could use a little drama in your orderly librarian life—shake things up a bit." Sasha took a huge bite of pancake, then shook a scolding fork at Val.

"I am shaking things up. Remember Connie Smart, our caseworker from the county? I'm taking a training with her."

"For what?" Sasha asked.

"To become a foster parent."

"Foster parent training? Holy shitballs, are you serious?"

"Yeah, I'm serious," Val said, a little defensively. "You know I've always loved working with kids, and you know how bad they need good foster homes. I think I'd be pretty good at it, actually."

"Hey, I'm not trying to put down the idea," Sasha said hastily. "You *would* be good at it. I just never thought you'd want anything more to do with the system. It wasn't exactly kind to you. Guess you just surprised me."

"Surprised myself. But I'm enjoying the class so far. Connie and the other trainer make it interesting, and I feel like I could really help a kid, you know?"

"I know you'd be great," Sasha said. "A lot of the kids we were placed with did better because you took an interest in them."

"Thanks," Val replied, feeling validated.

But then Sasha added, "So you're a little backward. Guess you can get a kid first, then we'll work on a girlfriend."

Val smirked and smacked Sasha in the arm. "Whatever."

CHAPTER FIVE

Val added a few more chairs to the rows in the open space of the children's section. The library was hosting *Raptors, Reptiles, and Rodents* today, and a large crowd was expected. While she waited for the presenter and her entourage of critters to arrive, Val took a moment to sit and finish her coffee. She enjoyed these animal-related events, and this was one of the reasons she loved working at this library. The board was willing to approve a diverse offering of educational events to engage children in learning and reading, and the more kids they could reach, the better.

"Look who I found," Linda said, leading two women into the room. Donna Drake, better known as the owner of the traveling exhibit *Mama Dee's Amazing Animals*, walked in with her daughter Beth, each holding pet carriers.

"Val," Donna said, setting down her load and wrapping Val in a huge hug. "How ya doin', kiddo?" Donna was in her sixties and called everyone kiddo.

"I'm doing fine, Donna. Hey, Beth." Beth was her age and was a carbon copy of her mom, in olive khaki cargo shorts and vest, hiking boots, and her blond hair in a long braid down her back.

"Hey, Val," Beth responded, with even more enthusiasm than her mom. Beth had a long-standing crush on Val, and was now looking at her with such dreamy-eyed adoration, it made Val squirm.

"Beth, honey, let's go get the rest of the animals." Donna and Beth made a few more trips out to their van, then set up the stands and perches needed for the presentation.

"Kids are coming," Linda said, as the noise in the lobby increased. "Let's get 'em seated."

For the next fifteen minutes, dozens of kids and parents came in. Val was surprised to see little Ian, followed closely by Lily, as they tried to get seats close to the front. She glanced around for their mother and saw her way in the back of the room, slouched against the wall and looking at her phone. Well, at least she was here.

"Hello, Valerie." Val turned and came face-to-face with Paige from the MAPP class. "I didn't know you worked at this library. I promise I'm not stalking you—we came for the animals." Paige was smiling and holding the hand of a little girl.

"Oh, hey," Val said, trying to hide her surprise and slight unease at seeing Paige in a different context…and on her turf.

"This is my daughter, Emma." The girl smiled shyly and waved hello. "We're trying to find a seat—you've got a full house."

"Well, if you'd like Emma to be up close, there's a seat there in the second row, right in the middle," Val said, pointing.

"Emma, are you okay sitting up there without me? I'll be right over here."

"Sure, Mommy. I wanna see up close."

"Go on, then." Paige gave her daughter a quick hug and watched her scamper off to the seat.

"How old is she?" Val asked.

"Eight going on thirty," Paige replied, with an exasperated roll of the eyes. "She loves animals and demanded that I bring her today."

"She's a cutie. Love all those dark curls."

"Thanks. I would've killed for hair like hers when I was younger—mine's as straight as a pin."

"Looks pretty good to me." Paige looked at her in surprise, and Val realized that she had spoken out loud.

"Um, thanks."

"So, yeah…thanks for coming. I've got to get ready to start the program," Val said, her cheeks hot.

"Okay," Paige replied, amused at Val's chagrin but also shocked that the usually reticent and antisocial woman had complimented her. Her surprise grew as she watched Val interacting with the children and parents. She was friendly and warm as she greeted everyone and helped kids get seated. She even cleared a space for a couple of moms to park their massive strollers. And when she smiled, she was utterly gorgeous.

At the top of the hour, Val stepped to the front of the room and got everyone's attention. "Hi, boys and girls. Thanks for coming today and bringing your grown-ups along." A few children laughed. "Make sure they behave and are really quiet during our presentation, so the animals don't get scared, okay?" The room erupted in giggles, and the kids shushed their parents and each other.

"I'd like to introduce you to Mama Dee, wildlife rehabilitator and expert. She's brought along several of her friends to show you today. Remember, listen closely, because at the end of the program, I'll be asking you some questions. There may even be prizes involved. So if you're ready, give me a silent cheer." Val pumped her arms in the air, and the audience copied her. Then she stepped aside, and the presenter took over.

Paige smiled as Val moved to stand beside her again. "Well done," she whispered. "You sure have a way with children."

Val shrugged. "Thanks. Kids are easy. It's adults who give me fits."

"Hmm. I think I know what you mean."

Do you? Val regarded Paige for a moment, then turned her attention to the animals.

❖

Val tried to focus on the kids taking turns petting a reticulated python, but her gaze kept returning to Paige. She was wearing navy shorts, a white sleeveless polo shirt, and white slip-on sandals. A single silver bangle adorned her wrist, and around her neck she wore a silver chain with a blue blown-glass pendant. Even her blond hair, pulled back into a simple ponytail at the nape of her neck, managed to look elegant. Conspicuous in its absence was any ring on her left hand, although why in the world Val was noticing that was beyond her. Paige was watching her daughter with a look of indulgent affection on her face, and she was beautiful.

Pulling her gaze away, Val looked to where Ian and Lily were sitting. Lily had her arm along the back of Ian's chair in her typical protective way, but she was chatting animatedly with the girl to her right, the one with the dark, curly hair. Paige's daughter. The girls seemed to have hit it off and were now oohing and aahing over the chinchilla Donna was showing.

Val marveled at how young children could be so accepting and without judgment—Emma, with her hair neatly contained in a sparkly headband, wearing a perfectly matched outfit and high-end sneakers, had no issue being friendly with Lily, whose hair and clothes were messy and stank of cigarette smoke. Val realized, with a pang of guilt, that she had not given the same acceptance to Paige. She had judged her based on her hair and clothes, thinking her stuck-up and rude, when in reality, Paige had been nothing but kind to her. Val looked over to Paige and caught her looking back, a smile on her lovely face. Val smiled in return, deciding that it couldn't hurt to be a little nicer.

CHAPTER SIX

By the sixth MAPP class, Paige was really beginning to enjoy the experience. Her confidence was growing, and she liked sharing her knowledge to help people. She'd been a nervous wreck initially, but Connie made everything easier, and the members of the class were, for the most part, enjoyable to work with.

Paige also noticed that Val had softened considerably and seemed to be enjoying the class as well. She had buddied up nicely with Ellen, who was happy to share her wealth of experience, along with a plate of homemade baked goods each week. Val was talking to others during breaks and even offering genuine smiles to everyone, especially, it seemed, to her. That made Val even more attractive, if that was possible.

Tonight's class had been rather emotional, as they watched video clips of interviews with actual foster children. The sadness, confusion, and anger the kids felt was painfully obvious, but so was their resilience, hopefulness and desire for a loving family and a chance to start over. She'd glanced over toward Val frequently during the presentation, and she had seen wave after wave of different emotions crossing Val's face. At one point, Val had even wiped away tears while Ellen patted her hand.

At the break, Paige went to sit by Val and offered her a brownie. "So, those videos are tough to watch, huh?"

Val looked at her sharply for a moment, then dropped her gaze. "Yeah. Brought back some memories I didn't really want to relive." She left it at that and took a bite of her brownie.

"I remember how Emma was when she came to me, like it was yesterday. She was terrified of every noise, every stranger, and it took a long time to get her to trust that I was safe. She didn't sleep through the night until she was nearly three. I can't imagine what she experienced in that first year of her life, but it must've been very traumatic."

Val nodded. "People think babies don't know what's going on and will just get over stuff quickly. That is so not true." She shook her head and sighed, then looked quickly at Paige. "Wait, your daughter was a foster kid?"

"Yep. I used to work for CPS and got really overwhelmed with all the crappy situations kids were dealing with. I wanted to do more than just be the one to remove kids or issue ultimatums to neglectful parents, so I became a foster parent. Emma was my first and only placement."

"Why only?" Val asked.

"Emma needed a lot of time and attention, and I wanted to just focus on her. I wouldn't be opposed to another foster child now, though."

"I heard that," Connie said, placing a hand on Paige's shoulder and giving Val's ponytail a tug with the other. "Anytime you're ready for more, let me know." She winked at Paige, then turned her attention to Val. "It's your turn for the home study this week. You said Wednesday afternoons were good, right?"

"Right. I get out of work at three," Val replied.

"Well, then, how about I head over to your place around three thirty this Wednesday?"

Val nodded. "Okay."

"Good. It's a date. I'll look forward to catching up with you." Connie snagged a brownie off the plate Ellen was passing around. "Aren't these things the bomb?" She grinned and flitted off to talk to someone else.

Paige smiled. "She's a trip, isn't she?"

"Yeah. That woman saved my life, in more ways than one." Val looked after Connie fondly.

"How so, if you don't mind me asking?"

"When I was a teenager, she saw past all my attitude and genuinely cared, when most people didn't want anything to do with me. I was what a polite person would call a handful."

"And an impolite person?" Paige teased.

"A royal pain in the ass," Val replied with a self-deprecating shake of her head. "I'd argue just to argue, break the rules just to get a reaction. I wasn't mean, just defiant."

"I'm guessing you had a good reason, though. Kids usually don't throw around a bad attitude for nothing."

Val looked at Paige appraisingly. "It's nice to talk to someone who gets that there is always a reason behind a kid's actions."

Paige nodded. "I've learned a lot about that over the years, from my work and even from my own childhood." She looked down at her hands. "Children are virtually powerless. When they are mistreated, they'll fight back with the only weapon they have—their behavior."

"Truer words were never spoken," Val replied. "Did you have a tough time as a kid?"

Paige shook her head, trying to remove the memories that had cropped up. "Let's just say it wasn't all sunshine and rainbows." She stood up and nodded toward Connie. "Looks like break's over."

Val had only been home for ten minutes when her doorbell rang. She gave her living room one more glance to be sure it was tidy, still in disbelief that this was happening. Connie Smart, of all people, was about to judge the suitability of her home for foster care. She ran a hand through her hair, took a deep breath, and opened the door. Connie stood there, a huge grin on her face.

"Well, hello there. This is so exciting, visiting you in your very own home," she said, as she breezed in the door and gave Val a hug. "It's an adorable little house. Ooh, I love those hardwood floors." Connie proceeded to give herself a tour, exclaiming at everything as she went. Val just grinned and followed. Once Connie had peeked in every room, they went back to the living room and sat on the couch.

"It's nice to have you here," Val said. "Bet you never thought you'd see the day that I would have my own house."

"Nonsense," Connie replied. "I always knew you had it in you to be successful and make a good life for yourself. You just had to learn to get out of your own way."

"Yeah, well, I try. Still isn't easy sometimes." Val suddenly felt like a teenager again, wanting to spill her guts to Connie. She was one of the only people she'd ever felt safe talking to about her feelings, besides Sasha.

"Tell me what you've been up to. The last time we got together, you were heading off to college," Connie said, settling in for a story with an expectant smile on her face.

Val felt a stab of guilt. Had she really gone so long without reaching out to this wonderful person who had been so important to her? "I'm sorry."

"For what, love?"

"Once I left for school, I didn't look back for a long time. I should have done a better job of keeping in touch."

"Oh, honey, of course you didn't look back. College was your ticket, your clean slate. I'm so proud of you." Connie squeezed Val's hand, and Val felt tears coming.

"How come you always make me feel good about myself when I think I'm rotten?"

"What can I say? It's a gift," Connie replied with a gentle smile. "So tell me about college."

"Ithaca was pretty amazing. When I first got there, I had a hard time. Kept to myself a lot and basically lived in the library. My roommate was nice, though, and she eventually got me to go out and meet people."

"Good for you."

"She moved in with her boyfriend after the first year, so I ended up with a new roommate. Things got really interesting then." Val felt herself blush.

"Oh, really," Connie teased. "Do tell."

"Well, she was a lesbian, and she kind of made it her mission to hook me up. If I had any doubts about being gay before meeting Dillon, I sure didn't for long." Connie laughed, and Val warmed to telling her story. "Dillon introduced me to the LGBTQ group on campus, drove us over to the gay bars in the city on weekends, and finally made me feel okay about coming out. She was pretty awesome." Val laughed aloud at a memory. "She used to tell me that if every librarian was as hot as me, all lesbians would be prolific readers."

"Sounds like she was a good person for you. Do you still see her?" Connie asked.

"Nah. She met the love of her life and moved to Seattle. Last I heard, she was on the third love of her life and living in San Francisco."

"Oh, my." Connie laughed. "Glad you weren't dating her."

"Yeah, dodged a bullet there, right? Dillon is amazing, just not the settling down type."

"So what about your studies? You know, the actual reason you went to college?" Connie teased.

"I graduated with a 3.8 GPA and was hired right out of school. Not bad, eh?" Val couldn't help but feel pride in her accomplishments.

"Not bad at all," Connie replied. "Did I mention that I'm proud of you?"

"Thanks. You helped, too. You always encouraged me. Remember when you said that if I bust my ass, I can do anything?"

Connie chuckled. "Sage advice." She glanced at her watch. "We'd better get to the home study or we'll be here all night tripping down memory lane. I can see that you have a suitable, clean home, with room for two children at a time."

Val swallowed. "Uh-huh."

"Tell me how you plan to provide childcare if young children are placed with you."

Val swallowed again. This was getting real. "Well, there's that daycare center two blocks away from work. I would contact them first."

"Good. We have lots of families that have sent their foster kids there. It's a terrific organization. What about your job? Would they be flexible if you had to miss work for a sick child, or for court?" Connie asked.

"Yes, I think so. Plus I have a great assistant who can take care of things if I'm out."

"Excellent." Connie handed Val a thick blue binder. "This has all the information you'll need about the county's requirements and policies, contact numbers, forms and such. Read through it." She sat back, crossed her legs, and looked Val in the eye. "Now, the most important thing. Why do you want to become a foster parent?"

Val took a deep breath and let it out slowly. She'd been formulating this response for weeks, and it always came down to one reason. "Megan."

"Ah." Connie knew. Everyone who had been involved in the foster care system back then knew about Megan, but Val had actually been in the same foster home and shared a room with the girl when it happened.

"She still haunts me, you know?" The beautiful, broken little girl, failed by the system, unable to escape her abuser, dead at the age of twelve. They had been in a home with too many kids, too much chaos. No one would believe that the oldest boy, their foster parents' own biological son, was a monster. He was perfect in everyone's eyes, a model student, star athlete, altar boy. Of course no one had a problem with letting him babysit some of the kids while his parents carted foster kids to appointments or ran errands. But Val had known that something wasn't quite right, that Megan was afraid of him.

"He's up for parole again soon," Val said quietly. The bastard who had raped Megan countless times, threatened to kill her if she told, could possibly walk free. Val had found the note that day fifteen years ago, just before the foster mom found Megan hanging in the basement and screamed. The words were burned in her brain forever.

You hurt me. I begged you to stop. You laughed at me. You said you'd kill me if I said anything. Well, guess what? I've had enough, and I'm going to tell. I'm going to make sure you can't touch another kid ever again. But you won't be able to kill me, because I'm going to do that part myself. Fuck you, Kevin. I hope you rot in hell.

"I went to the last hearing. I'll be at this one, too," Connie replied.

Val nodded. After Megan, Connie had gone above and beyond for Val—she'd understood why she raged against everyone, cut herself, and made it her mission to protect all the younger kids she was placed with. Connie found her the therapist who'd helped Val survive it all, placed her in the best foster homes she could find, and kept her with Sasha, her closest friend. Connie knew.

"Honey, you know you can't rescue them all, right? Lord knows I wanted to when I first started working. It's a heartbreaking business sometimes, but you can only do so much."

Val looked up at Connie with tears in her eyes. "I know. But I want to do something. Even if I can help one kid, it'll be something. Paige told me about Emma, and that little girl now has a great shot at life because of what Paige has given her. I want to try to be that person for a hurting kid, too. Trying to help matters to me."

Connie reached over and gave Val a long hug. "I know, sweetie, and I know your heart. You're going to be great."

Chapter Seven

Tonight was the final MAPP class, and Paige marveled at how quickly the weeks had flown by. Four participants were conspicuously absent. The couple she'd been uneasy about had not had a favorable home study, according to Connie, due to their harsh ideas about discipline and their aversion to therapeutic intervention for kids whose behavioral problems suggested they were hurting from unseen wounds. And the young couple who had just wanted to help kids realized, not unwisely, that they might be in over their heads when they heard all the potential difficulties of fostering. Connie had suggested that they start by volunteering, perhaps with the Big Brothers Big Sisters organization, and they had enthusiastically agreed.

Everyone else, though, had been great, and Paige was excited to have more good placement options for the steady stream of kids coming into care. As they wrapped up the evening, Ellen announced that she would be starting a support group for foster parents and hoped everyone would come.

"If you make those brownies, I'm there," Val said, and everyone laughed, nodding in agreement.

"Thank you, Ellen," Connie said. "It's very important for you all to utilize any support available to you, including Paige and me. Feel free to reach out to us with any questions or concerns. Parenting on the best of days can be quite a job, and foster children bring their own unique challenges. But I'm confident that you all will be able to meet the needs of your future placements."

Paige handed out a flyer to everyone. "Don't forget, there will be a foster care picnic at the fire hall next Saturday. Everyone is welcome, even if you do not have foster children yet. It's a great way to meet other foster parents and broaden your network of support."

When she was done, she walked back to the front of the room. "I just wanted to thank you all for making this class a great experience. I learned so much myself, and I look forward to working with you in the near future." Her gaze immediately went to Val, who was smiling warmly at her. Something tugged at Paige's chest, and she was sorry that she would no longer have these weekly meetings as a chance to see Val. How had the time passed so quickly? She realized she was staring but smiled back as the other class members clapped, then stood to offer hugs and handshakes.

A few minutes later, as Paige was packing up her things, she felt a light touch on her shoulder. Val stood there, her hands in her pockets, looking slightly uncomfortable.

"So, um, thanks. It was good to meet you," she said. The dichotomy of seeing this strong, intelligent woman apparently unsure of herself was strange, and endearing.

"I'm happy to have met you, too, Val," Paige said, genuinely meaning every word. *Wait, I never asked what you do for fun, or if you'd like to go out some time...am I imagining the connection between us, or do you feel it, too? Do you even like women?* Paige swallowed. "I'll see you at the picnic?"

"I'll be there," Val replied. She stood for a moment, looking at Paige, then her eyes widened as Paige moved in for a hug. Paige felt Val stiffen, then relax and hug her back—hard. The embrace set her whole body alight, and Paige was acutely aware of everywhere their bodies touched. She wanted everyone else in the room to disappear—now. Paige had to make herself let go, for decorum's sake, but man, that hug felt amazing. She stepped back and smiled at Val, noticing the flush on her cheeks and wondering if it was due to embarrassment, yet hoping it was something more.

"Looking forward to it. Good night." Paige watched Val walk away.

"She's a special one." She jumped at Connie's voice in her ear. "I think she'll make someone a great...foster mom." Connie winked and stepped away, leaving Paige speechless.

❖

The weather on the afternoon of the picnic was perfect, and all the kids were running around happily between the bouncy house with the huge slide and the food tables. Paige was transferring hot dogs from the grill to a serving tray when she felt eyes on her. She turned around and saw Val, holding a paper plate with a waiting hot dog bun. Damn, it was good to see her.

"Hi there. Good timing...got some nice hot ones." Val just smiled as Paige placed a hot dog on her bun, her dark eyes dancing with amusement. Paige felt a jolt somewhere low, which competed with the surge of embarrassment she felt at her own words.

"Thanks. How've you been?" Val busied herself spooning baked beans and potato salad onto her plate, then met Paige's gaze again.

"Good. You?" Paige tried unsuccessfully to calm her thumping heart.

"Can't complain. No one ever listens if I do, anyway," Val said. "You have to work the grill all afternoon?"

"Actually, I was just giving someone a bathroom break. Here he comes now." She handed her tongs back to a big guy in an apron emblazoned with the Buffalo Bills logo. "Here you go, Joe. She's all yours. Don't think I burned anything too badly."

"Thanks, kid," he said and smiled at Val. "Haven't seen you before. Foster parent or new employee?"

"Future foster parent," she replied, smiling back.

"Well, welcome aboard. I'm Joe Massey, senior caseworker and grill master. Eat up—there's plenty more."

"Thanks."

"I was just about to round up my daughter so she can eat," Paige said, searching the crowd. She spotted Emma in line, waiting to climb the bouncy house ladder. "You're welcome to join us if you'd like." *Please say yes.*

"Sure," Val replied with a grin. "I'll go snag the end of that table for us."

A few minutes later, Paige and Emma sat down across from her with their plates full of food. Emma's dark hair stuck to her sweaty forehead, and her cheeks were rosy. She was chattering away about the awesome slide when she realized Paige wasn't her only audience, that they were sitting down with Val. She immediately quieted and looked at her, scooting just a little closer to her mom.

"Emma, do you remember Miss Valerie from the library? She's going to be a foster parent."

When the child nodded but didn't speak, Val smiled at her. "Nice to see you again, Emma. That bouncy house is so cool. Wish I was a kid so I could play in it. Is it fun?"

"Yeah, it's awesome! The slide is really fast."

Just like that, ice broken. Paige was amazed at how quickly her daughter relaxed. Val was great with children. It was hard to believe that this friendly, engaging woman was the same one who had been so closed off when they'd first met. Val was like an onion, and Paige wanted to keep peeling back the layers.

Emma took a huge bite of her burger and chewed, swinging her legs under the table. "This burger is awesome, Mommy."

Paige rolled her eyes and smiled at Val. "Awesome is the adjective du jour lately." She ruffled her daughter's curls and gently admonished her to slow down lest she choke. Emma inhaled her food anyway, then begged to go back and play. "Go on, and stay where I can see you."

Val watched the girl scamper away. "She's adorable. Lots of energy."

"Oh my God, you have no idea. The only thing that slows her down is a good book. Thankfully, she loves to read."

"I knew I liked that kid for a reason," Val replied. "How come I don't see her at the library more often?"

"We've gone a few times, but always on Saturday mornings. She's just getting into chapter books, and I already have a pretty large collection for her to tackle. We read together almost every night."

"She's a happy girl. You are obviously a terrific mom." Val felt a tiny shiver of envy, thinking of all that she had missed out on as a child. Then her mind flipped to an image of herself and Paige, spending a quiet evening together...reading. Um, what?

Paige blushed. "Thanks for saying so. There are days when I wonder, but I love her to pieces."

"I can tell." Val studied Paige, taking in her shining blond ponytail and sun-kissed skin, her freckled shoulders peeking out from beneath her collared tank top. She was completely different from the women who usually hit on Val at the bar. There was something fresh and unassuming about Paige, despite her perfectly put together appearance. Val realized she was staring at the same moment she heard the words in her head. *God, she's so beautiful.* Val looked away quickly. "So, what were you like as a kid?"

Paige raised an eyebrow. "Me? I don't know. Compliant, I guess."

That was an odd descriptor, Val thought. "What do you mean?"

Paige sighed. "My parents were very strict, and I, being their only child, got the full brunt of their high expectations. I don't recall having a whole lot of fun, actually."

Val noticed the bitter tone that had crept into Paige's voice. She wanted to know more. "Was it lonely?"

Paige looked at her in surprise. "Yeah, it was. My parents are both attorneys in a huge law firm in Manhattan. They always wanted me to be perfectly dressed, perfectly behaved, and perfectly well-mannered, never an embarrassment to them. But they left the enforcement of those rules to a long succession of au pairs and nannies. I barely ever saw them."

That explained the initial vibe Val had gotten when she'd met Paige. She was so put together because as a kid she'd been forced to appear that way. "That kinda sucks."

Paige laughed. "Well put. I'm sorry if I sound like I'm throwing a pity party. Actually, I had everything I ever needed, got a top-notch education, and even traveled abroad with my parents once a year. It's just that…sometimes, I gladly would have given up all of that just to have their time and attention, you know? I kind of felt like I was invisible."

Val did know, for completely different reasons. "I get it. While your parents were cruising the Mediterranean with you in tow, my mom was dragging me around to crack houses at midnight."

"Oh, Val, I'm sorry. I really have nothing to complain about, do I?" Paige looked stricken.

"No, it's fine. We can't help who our parents are. My point is that we were both lonely and neglected, even though we came from completely different worlds."

"I guess I never thought of it like that," Paige said. "At least I had a couple of nannies who were good to me. Did you have anyone?"

"My abuelita. Sorry, my grandma. She was amazing. Tiny woman but fiercely protective. She did everything she could to take care of my brother and me." Val fingered the necklace she wore, a silver eagle. "She gave me this when I was eight. She said it meant that I was strong and could handle whatever life threw at me. She used to say *Be good, and life will be good to you.* I didn't believe life would ever be good when I was a kid, but now I know she was right."

"Where is she now?"

"She's gone. When my mother went to jail, she wanted to take us, but she was too sick. She had diabetes and was nearly blind. My brother had a different dad, so he went with him. I went into foster care. Abuelita died, and I never saw Enrique again."

Val couldn't believe how easy it was to talk to Paige. She so rarely spoke of her past to anyone, but Paige listened with such genuine interest, such a kind expression, that the words just came. Val noted the warring factions in her head, one telling her it was okay to be open, the other to get the hell up and run. Her anxiety kicked up a notch, and she pressed her sweaty palms onto her thighs. Paige looked at her with those compassionate blue eyes, and Val swallowed. *You make me want to stay.*

"I'm so sorry, Val," Paige was saying. "You haven't been able to contact your brother?"

"I don't even know if he has the same last name anymore. All I know is that he moved to the West Coast. Nobody would tell me anything else. How many Enriques do you think live over there?"

"That must have been so hard, not being able to find out more."

"Yeah, well, water under the bridge," Val replied, waving her hand dismissively. "I'm doing all right, and I have to believe he is, too."

"I'd say you are. I know plenty of kids that didn't have it half as bad as you, and they still couldn't get their act together. And here you are, a kind, independent, successful woman, despite all you've been through. You're the success story we hope for every time a kid enters the system. And you impress the hell out of me."

"Wow. Thanks."

"You're welcome." Paige bit her lip, then nodded as if she'd made a decision. "Do you get a lunch hour at work?"

"Whoa, topic change whiplash."

Paige laughed, the husky rich sound sexy as hell. "Well?"

"I do, but I rarely take the full hour," Val said.

"Would you be willing to change your ways and have lunch with me someday soon?"

Val smiled. "Sure." *I think I might be willing to change a lot of my ways for you.*

"Excellent. I'll text you. Hey, the ice cream truck we rented is here. Come on, let's beat the kids to it." Paige jumped up, and Val followed, feeling a flicker of something that seemed an awful lot like happiness.

Chapter Eight

Val smiled at the children gathered before her on the rug, waiting for her to begin story hour. She glanced at the door one more time, but her little regulars, Ian and Lily, weren't there. They hadn't come the last time, either. Val had a niggling sense of uneasiness, but she tried to push it aside as she began to read.

Afterward, she mentioned her concerns to Linda. "You know that brother and sister that always come to story hour and sit right down in front?"

"Yeah, but I didn't see them today."

"I know, or last time. They've been coming like clockwork, twice a week. Guess I'm just wondering what's up." Val fiddled with her pen as her mind started to worry.

"You think there's a problem?" Linda asked.

"I don't know. I'm pretty sure I saw their mother hanging out in the back corner of the parking lot the other day when I left. There were a couple of guys with her, but I didn't see the kids."

"You're really worried, aren't you? I'm sure they're okay. Maybe they're visiting their grandparents or something."

"Maybe."

"So, guess what?" Linda said, changing the subject. "Josh is taking me to a Syracuse game on Saturday. I've never been to a game at the Carrier Dome. Have you?"

Val could think of a dozen things she'd rather do than sit in a stadium full of thirty thousand loud, obnoxious sports fans. "Nope, never been."

Linda leaned in and lowered her voice. "We've been seeing a lot of each other lately. He could be the one." She nearly squealed with excitement.

Val smiled indulgently. Linda had met The One at least three times this year alone. They never stuck around long. Val felt bad—Linda was sweet, but way too high maintenance emotionally. "That's great."

"Hey, we should double-date sometime. You never talk about what you do outside of work. Are you seeing someone?"

"I'm not really big on dating," Val said and turned her back to grab a stack of books off the counter, hoping Linda would drop the idea.

"Ooh, I bet Josh has some single friends. I could set you up. What kind of guys are you into?"

Val sighed. *Oh, what the hell.* "The female kind."

"The female ki…wait, holy crap. You're a lesbian?" Linda's eyes widened so much, it was almost comical.

"Yep." Val waited, but all Linda did was stare at her for what seemed like an eternity.

"My cousin Gina is a lesbian," Linda said, when she finally regained her voice. "I bet she knows some single girls."

"Oh, for God's sake," Val said, exasperated. At the hurt look on Linda's face, she softened her tone. "Listen, I appreciate your interest in my social life, but really, I don't have any desire to date right now. I'm perfectly content with things as they are." An image of Paige popped into her head, and she remembered the tentative lunch plans they'd made. Now *that* she could do—just lunch, no expectations to impress anyone or hook up. Hanging out with Paige was easy.

"But don't you get lonely all by yourself?" Linda, who couldn't go a month between boyfriends, would probably never understand Val's deep need for solitude and her own space.

"I've got a couple of friends I hang out with, but I really am fine with my own company. I'm an introvert—I don't need people around me all the time."

"Wow." Linda just kept looking at her like she'd sprouted wings or something.

"What do you say we get this cart of books shelved?" Val said, trying to keep the irritation out of her voice.

"Oh, sure. And Val, if you ever change your mind about double-dating…"

"I won't." Val busied herself on the computer and didn't look up again until Linda finally walked away. Ugh. Why did people think there was something wrong with you if you didn't want to date? Val had tried when she was younger, but those experiences had just proven what she'd already known. When you let people in too far, you get hurt. Val had had enough heartbreak to last decades. No way in hell was she going to put herself out there again.

❖

Val was sitting at the bar when Sasha and her friends came in. She waved them over, noting with interest that Sasha was holding hands with a cute blonde.

"Hey, girl," Sasha said as she approached, and Val hopped off the barstool to give her a hug. "Meet my crew. This is Aaliyah, Dutch, and Jen. Crew, this is my best friend Val." The women exchanged greetings, and Val watched with amusement as Sasha and Jen leaned close together and made googly eyes at each other. Sasha's usual charismatic swagger was gone, replaced by sappy looks and giggles. Aaliyah, tall, handsome, and dark-skinned, had already caught the eye of a group of women at the pool tables.

"Mind if I go shoot a game, Sarge?"

Sasha laughed. "Nah, but be careful who you play with."

Aaliyah grinned, got herself a beer, and strutted off to meet her admirers.

"So, Val, can I get you a drink?" Val turned to Dutch, a short, stocky butch with a crew cut and multiple tattoos on her bare, muscular arms. She was looking Val up and down with undisguised interest.

"No, thanks, I'm good." Val turned to talk to Sasha and Jen. "So, Jen, you keeping my buddy here out of trouble?" Grinning, she gave Sasha a wink.

"I'm trying," Jen said, giving Sasha's arm a squeeze, "but it's tough."

"Aw, c'mon, babe, I'm a perfect angel and you know it," Sasha protested, and Jen ruffled her hair. They were so cute it was sickening.

"You didn't tell me you'd found a woman who would actually go out with you," Val teased.

"Shut up. Kind of happened fast, right, babe?" Sasha said, wrapping her arm around Jen's shoulders.

"Yeah. Once she met me, no other woman stood a chance," Jen joked and gave Sasha a peck on the lips. The peck quickly turned into a full-blown kiss, tongues included.

"Um, still standing here," Val said, and the two women broke apart, giggling with embarrassment.

"Sorry," Sasha said. "See what she does to me?"

"I'm going to find the restroom. Get me a rum and Coke?" Jen caressed Sasha's arm and walked away.

"Girl, you're so done," Val said with a grin.

"Holy fuck, Val. This woman's got me twisted. I wanna marry her and have her babies."

Val laughed out loud. "I have never seen you so caught up. Is she for real?"

"Yeah, she's amazing. I met her when we were deployed. I got it bad, Val. Never thought I'd say this, but she could change my ways."

"What, no more bar hopping with me so you can flirt with all the ladies? What am I going to do?" Val put her hand on her chest in mock distress.

"Maybe you should find yourself a good woman. You can't be alone forever."

"You, too?" Val rolled her eyes.

"What?"

"You're the second person today who's told me I need to date."

"Well, maybe it's a sign. It's been a long time since you've been with anyone. What about Dutch? She seems interested." Val turned and saw that Dutch had taken a seat farther down the bar and was still staring at her. So creepy.

"Oh, please. She's looking at me like she's starving and I'm prime rib. No, thank you."

Sasha laughed and took a swig of her beer. "Yeah, Dutch is intense, but she's a good person, though I admit, probably not your type." She laid a hand on Val's shoulder. "Seriously, though, I worry about you sometimes."

Val could feel her anxiety growing. "Sash, you know better than anyone why I don't go there." She'd had a handful of hookups over the years, but she never let anyone too close. Go to their place, leave before morning, and no exchange of personal details. That was how it had to be.

"Yeah, yeah, I know. People suck, they always end up hurting you, and they always leave. I felt that way, too, Val, but what happens when you meet someone who doesn't suck? Someone who actually wants you for you? I thought I was happy playing the game, but meeting Jen made me realize that I've just been empty, trying to fill myself up the wrong way. Now I actually feel like I can let some of that past stuff go, you know?"

Val nodded but couldn't really relate. She only trusted two people in this world, Sasha and Connie, and she didn't see how that was ever going to change. "I'm really happy for you, chica, and I hear you. I just might take a little longer to get there." Maybe her future lunch date with Paige would be a step in the right direction, but she just wasn't ready to share that with Sasha. That way, when she crashed and burned, no one would be the wiser.

"Well, I won't give up on you, woman. Somebody besides me ought to know how amazing you are. Now c'mon, let's go shoot some pool and show those amateurs over there how it's done," Sasha said.

Val gave Sasha a huge hug. "You're on."

Chapter Nine

Val was on the couch sipping her second cup of coffee when Sasha stumbled out of the guest room. She blinked in the morning sunlight shining through the sliding glass door and groaned.

"You look a little rough," Val said, chuckling.

"You should not have let me do shots with that crazy chick," Sasha accused, rubbing her head.

"Hey, you agreed to the terms. You didn't think she could beat you at eight ball. Serves you right for being cocky."

"Whatever." Sasha flopped down on the couch and flung her arm over her eyes. Val went to the kitchen and brought back a steaming cup of coffee, black.

"Here you go, soldier. Better start the recovery process, or it'll be a long drive back to Fort Drum. Jen still asleep?"

"Yeah. That woman sleeps like the dead. I'll wake her up in a bit." Sasha sipped the coffee and closed her eyes. "Oh, that's good. Thanks."

Val regarded her friend thoughtfully. "You really like her, don't you?"

Sasha opened one eye and smiled. "I really do. She's sweet, smart, tough when she needs to be, and a freaking goddess in bed." She waggled her eyebrows and grinned. "But you know what makes her so special? We can talk for hours about anything. I told her all about my past, and she gets me. She's the only person other than you that I'll go there with, you know?"

Val didn't know, but she was truly happy for her friend. Again she thought of Paige and how easy she was to talk to. She was amazed and, if she was honest, a little upset at herself for sharing as much as she had.

She barely knew Paige. Mentally shaking herself, Val tried to bring her focus back to Sasha. "I think you guys are great together. Bring her around more often so I can tell her all your embarrassing little stories."

"What stories?" Jen walked into the room, adorable in an oversized T-shirt and socks, and Sasha's face lit up. She patted her lap and Jen sat, snuggling into her lover's arms. They gazed at each other with so much emotion, it was almost hard for Val to watch.

"Listen, I'm going to go catch up on my email. Jen, there's more coffee and muffins in the kitchen, and I left you shower towels in the bathroom. What time do you have to be back, Sash?"

"I go on duty at fourteen hundred. I hate weekend shifts," Sasha whined.

"Suck it up, Sergeant," Jen commanded. "Leaders lead whenever there's a need."

"Yeah, well, all I wanna do is lead you back to bed and—"

Val stuck her fingers in her ears. "Lalalalalalalala."

The others laughed, and Jen stood. "Go get in the shower while I get my caffeine fix," she said, pulling Sasha up from the couch.

Sasha saluted, kissed Jen on the forehead, and headed off to the bathroom.

Jen rolled her eyes. "She's crazy."

Val smiled. "Crazy about you, I'm thinking." Jen seemed great, and Sasha was clearly over the moon. Val felt a little pinprick of fear that she could lose Sasha to this new relationship, then an equally sharp feeling of guilt. She would never begrudge Sasha her chance at love and happiness. Still, the sense that things were about to change was strong.

Jen blushed. "It's mutual. Sorry we didn't get to chat much last night, though. Sasha talks about you all the time."

"She does, huh?" Val said. "All good, I hope."

"Definitely. You're her family, she says. I couldn't wait to meet you."

"I'm happy to meet you, too. Anybody who makes Sasha this happy is cool with me. What happened to your other friends last night? I didn't see them leave."

"Dutch had to work this morning, so they drove separately and headed back. Next time we come down, let's do dinner."

"Good idea," Val agreed. They chatted for a few minutes, then her phone rang, so she excused herself to take the call.

"Hello?"

"Val, it's Connie. Are you home?"

"Yeah...what's up?"

"Two little ones were just removed from their mother and we need to place them. Can you take them today?"

"Whoa, really? Um, yeah, but what do I need to do?" Val's heart started racing. Things just got real.

"First, relax, then just be ready to focus on them. They're scared and the removal wasn't pretty, according to the CPS worker. She'll fill you in when they get there."

"When are they coming?" Val was pacing now, her mind a whirlwind. *Two little kids, coming to my house, relying on me for their every need. Oh my God. What if I fuck this up?*

"In about an hour," Connie said.

"Holy shit, Connie." She was close to hyperventilating.

"You've got this, kid. I have to go, so we'll talk later on, okay?"

"Okay...bye." Val dropped the phone from her ear and just stood there for several moments. Her heart was trying to pound its way out of her chest, and her hands were shaking.

"Hey, what's going on?" Sasha, freshly showered and dressed, looked at Val with concern. "You look like you're in shock."

"I think I am. That was Connie. I'm about to get my first foster kids."

"No way. Damn...you okay?"

"This is what I went to the training for, so yeah, I'm okay. Scared out of my mind, but okay." Val took a deep breath to calm her nerves. *Get it together—the kids are gonna need you to help them.* She shook herself and started picking up the kitchen.

"Can we help?" Sasha asked. "We can stick around for a little while longer."

"Nah, it's probably best if it's just me here when they come. Don't want to freak them out with too many strangers."

"Makes sense. When are they supposed to get here?"

"In an hour." Val took another deep breath and let it out with an audible whoosh.

"What's in an hour?" Jen said, entering the room with their overnight bag in hand.

"The arrival of Val's new foster kids," Sasha replied, with a slightly awed tone to her voice.

"Oh, Val, that's fantastic!" Jen dropped the bag and enveloped Val in a warm hug. Stepping back, she took Val's shoulders in her hands. "You're doing an amazing thing, you know."

"Thanks, Jen. I hope so. Right now I'm not sure if I want to jump up and down or puke."

"Well, if they're coming in an hour, you don't have time for either. Get a snack ready for them and find some kids' shows on TV. They'll need to decompress when they get here," Jen said.

"How do you know so much about foster kids?" Val asked.

"Not foster kids per se, but scared kids in general. My mom ran a daycare out of our house for years. A snack and the TV almost always helped the ones who were having separation anxiety when their moms dropped them off."

"Got it. Oh my God. I need to shower, and get the guest room ready, and…" Val spun around in circles, unsure where to start.

Sasha put her hand on Val's arm. "Breathe, woman. We already stripped and remade the bed in the guest room. And the kids, all they're really going to need is to feel welcomed and safe. You remember, don't you?"

Tears of gratitude came to Val's eyes, and she wiped them away with a smile. "Yeah, I remember. Thanks, you guys."

"Call later and fill us in, okay?" Sasha said, retrieving the dropped bag. With her other arm, she pulled Val into a hug. "Love you, chica. You're gonna be great."

Val hugged her back, then squared her shoulders with determination. Sasha's confidence in her, as well as Connie's, helped immensely. "Wish me luck."

"Already done," Sasha replied, and then they were gone.

Val checked the time—in forty-five minutes, she was going to be a foster parent.

"Abuelita, pray for me," she whispered, then she sprinted to the shower.

❖

Paige rang the doorbell as Shelly, the CPS worker, murmured reassurances to the children behind her. The door opened quickly, and Val stood there, wide-eyed and looking nervous. It was so good to see her again. Paige wished she was here on a social call, but she had a job to do. Val smiled, then glanced down at the children. Her jaw dropped for a moment, but she recovered herself quickly.

"Come on in."

Paige entered, followed by Shelly and the kids. She turned around when she heard the little girl gasp.

Val was down on her knees. "Hey, Lily, Ian," she said gently. Lily let go of Ian's hand and fell into Val's arms, sobbing. Ian stared for a moment, tightly clutching the hem of his grubby T-shirt, then promptly sat down on the floor at Val's side.

Paige exchanged glances with Shelly, who shrugged. "Val, you know these children?"

Val looked at her over the girl's head, eyes moist. "Yep. Lily and Ian are my story hour buddies at the library, huh, guys? I've been missing them lately." To the children, she said, "I'm really glad to see you. Welcome to my home."

Lily sniffled and reached out again for her brother's hand. "Look, Ian, it's Miss Valerie. We're okay now."

Paige fought valiantly to hold it together, but her eyes teared up as she watched the poignant scene before her. This had never happened before in her experience. She looked again to Shelly, who just wiped her own eyes and smiled.

Val stood then. "Come on, guys. I've got a little snack for you over there on the coffee table, and I found a good movie on Netflix. Would you like to watch it?"

Both children nodded, and Val led them into the living room. On the table, two small plates held grapes and Goldfish crackers. The children quickly moved toward the food, then stopped and looked at Val.

"It's okay. Eat," Val said, as she started the movie. The children dug in like they hadn't eaten in days. "Slow down, now. Don't want you to choke."

Paige beckoned Val over toward the kitchen. "Val, this is Shelly, from CPS." The two women shook hands. "It's unbelievable that you already know the kids. That makes things so much easier."

"I can't believe it, either. At work, we were just talking about how we hadn't seen them in a while, and I was worried. What happened?"

"Their mother was high on heroin, drove across somebody's lawn, and crashed into their front porch. The kids were in the car," Shelly said.

"Oh God," Val said, glancing at the children. "They weren't hurt?"

"No, thankfully. They were buckled in their booster seats, and the car wasn't going that fast. The mother was passed out cold, though."

"I've seen her. She hangs out at the back of the library parking lot sometimes. She would always wait outside when the kids were at story hour with me," Val said.

"Yeah, we've heard that's a known spot for dealers," Shelly said.

"What happened to her?" Val asked.

"They had to give her Narcan, so they took her to the emergency room."

"Jesus," Val said softly.

She walked over to the children. Speaking gently to them, she asked if they wanted a drink and if they liked the movie. As she went to get them some cups of water, Paige couldn't help but watch. She was touched by Val's kind attentiveness to the children, but she'd be lying if she said there wasn't more to her feelings. Val looked incredible, in worn soft-looking jeans, a light green T-shirt with a picture of a tree frog on the front, and dark brown moccasins on her feet. Her wavy black hair was pulled back into a loose braid. She looked comfortable, warm, and approachable, and Paige was drawn in. Remembering Shelly, Paige pulled her gaze away from Val and cleared her throat.

Val returned to the kitchen. "So now what happens?"

"We'll need you to come down to the county office building tomorrow morning to go over some things. Shelly was unable to get anything from the home, so you'll need to get them some clothes and essentials right away. We'll issue your first clothing allowance check tomorrow, and we have some things that you can borrow, like booster seats for your car."

"Those are out in my back seat," Shelly said. "I'll go grab them for you."

"Thanks," Val called after Shelly's retreating figure. When she heard the front door close, she turned to Paige. "Definitely didn't expect our next meeting to be under these circumstances. This is kind of surreal," she said, glancing over at the children. Ian was snuggled up close to Lily, and they both looked exhausted, even though it wasn't yet noon.

"I know," Paige replied. "I was actually planning on texting you tomorrow about lunch. Now we've got more important things to deal with." She gave Val a sympathetic smile. "Just focus on them, and you'll be surprised how quickly you fall into a rhythm. They already know you, so that's a huge bonus."

"I hope so. You're their case worker, then?"

"Yes. That means you can call if you need anything, and I'll come do home visits every month," Paige said. So much for their lunch date. Damn.

"Every month? How long do you think they'll be with me?" Val began twisting the hem of her T-shirt, and Paige put a comforting hand on her arm. Val's skin tingled at the touch.

"It's hard to say. I'll have to pursue relatives and try to find their birth father to see if anyone is willing to take them. Once their mom goes to court, we'll have a better idea of what we're looking at. In the meantime, yours is the best place for them to be. It's going to be fine— you'll see." Paige gave Val's arm a squeeze. "And I'll check in to make sure you're doing okay." Paige caught Val's eye, her smile filled with caring and warmth, and she slowly removed her hand. Val immediately missed the touch that had calmed her so quickly. What was it about this woman that affected her so much? She was like the antidote to her mental hamster wheel of worry. But it was more than that. Paige was becoming important to her.

Glancing again at her little story hour buddies turned foster children, Val saw that they had fallen asleep. A wave of protectiveness washed over her, so strong it nearly made her gasp. "Yes," she whispered. "Everything's going to be fine."

CHAPTER TEN

Val checked the time, feeling more and more anxious as eight o'clock approached. The first night in a new place was always hard, and she remembered how terrified she had been when she was first placed in a foster home.

She had taken the kids to McDonald's for dinner, then to Walmart to get them some pajamas, toothbrushes, an outfit for the next day, and at Lily's suggestion, Pull-Ups for Ian. She tried to make shopping fun for them, like they were all on an adventure together. Once they had taken a bath and put on their pajamas, Val downloaded a couple of her favorite children's books to her tablet, then sat between the kids on the couch and read to them. Ian had yet to speak, but he followed Val's every move with his big dark eyes. Lily, ever his protector, had barely left his side all day.

When she had finished reading, Val said, "I believe it's time for bed, kiddos."

"Why?" Lily said.

"Because you need your rest. We're going to see Miss Paige in the morning. When is your usual bedtime?"

"We don't have one," Lily replied. "We can stay up as long as we want." Val noticed the slight lift to Lily's chin, challenging her.

"Well, I, for one, am super tired, and I can't go to bed until I know you're safe and sound in your own bed. Let's go get Ian tucked in, okay?" Val knew that Lily had likely been Ian's caregiver more often than not, and she was going to have to tread lightly when she asserted her authority.

Lily appeared to be thinking it over, but then she suddenly stood up. "Come on, Ian. Time for bed." She took his hand and pulled, but Ian resisted, shaking his head. "Come *on*," she said again, pulling harder. This time, Ian started to fuss. "He doesn't have Pete. He always sleeps with Pete," Lily informed Val.

"Who's Pete?"

"His stuffed penguin. He left him at home."

Oh, hell, Val thought, as Ian looked at her expectantly. Mind scrambling, she remembered the toy frog Sasha had won for her out of one of those claw machines when they were in high school. She'd named it Coqui, like the little Puerto Rican tree frogs her abuelita had told her about, and it was on a shelf in her room.

"Ian, Pete couldn't come with you today, but he has a friend I'd like you to meet. Come on, I'll show you." Val held out her hand, and after a moment, Ian took it and wriggled off the couch. Val led him down the hall to her bedroom doorway, Lily following close behind. "Stay here, guys. I'll go see if he's awake." She quickly went in and grabbed the frog, putting it behind her back. Back in the hall, she squatted down in front of Ian. Holding out the frog, she said, "This is Coqui. See, he's just like the frog on my shirt. He's so happy you're here. He hasn't had a little boy to play with him in a very long time. Do you want to hold him?"

Ian stared at the frog for what seemed like an eternity to Val, but finally he nodded and took the frog, holding it to his chest. Val let out a relieved breath. "Let's go check out your room again. Coqui hasn't been in there before." The kids followed, and Val made a show of pulling down the covers and plumping the pillows on the guest bed. "Ian, show Coqui how comfy the bed is." She winked conspiratorially at Lily, who climbed in on the other side. Ian pulled himself up onto the bed, the frog held tightly in his hand. "Okay, now. Coqui has a song he likes me to sing every night. Do you think it'd be all right if I sang it in your room?" Both children nodded, Lily as intrigued as Ian now. Val began to sing "El Coquí," the Puerto Rican folk song from her childhood. A powerful vision of her abuelita singing to her brought a sharp sting of tears, and she felt her energy, almost as if she was giving Val the strength to be for these children what Abuelita had been for her—a safe haven.

By the time she'd finished singing, both children were cuddled under the covers, looking sleepy. "Okay, guys, I'll leave a night-light on in the bathroom, and this little lamp on in here." Val looked down at the children and smiled. "Sweet dreams. I'm really glad you're here."

As she turned to leave, Lily quietly said, "Good night, Miss Valerie."

Val turned around, touched. "Good night, honey. See you in the morning."

Val left their bedroom door ajar and got herself ready for bed. She was exhausted, but her mind wouldn't stop racing through the list of things she had to do tomorrow. She thought of Paige. If she was the kids' caseworker, then whatever might have been simmering between them would have to be put on the back burner. The thought made Val feel a twinge of regret. At least they'd see each other every so often, if only in a professional capacity. Val sighed. It was...whatever. She'd have her hands full with the kids anyway. The hamster wheel started spinning again, and she tried to relax by reading the novel she'd left on her nightstand. After only a few pages, Val couldn't keep her eyes open any longer.

❖

The dream was always the same. Val ran through a dark house, trying to find a place to hide, but he kept coming. She found a closet and closed the door, huddling in the corner beneath some coats. Her heart pounded so loud, she was sure he could hear. Footsteps walked by, then stopped. Suddenly, the door was flung open, and a hand grabbed her. She screamed.

Val sat up in bed, drenched in sweat as her heart raced and she got her bearings. Taking deep breaths, she realized that the screams were no longer coming from her dream. Jumping out of bed, she ran to the guest room. Lily was sitting up in bed, holding the covers over her head, half yelling, half sobbing. Ian lay beside her, unbelievably sound asleep. Val went to Lily and tried to calm her.

"Shh, Lily, it's okay. Shh." Val uncovered Lily's head and began to stroke her hair. The child flinched at her touch, crying and mumbling incoherently. "Did you have a bad dream, honey?" No response. Val tried to get Lily to lie back down, but as soon as she put her hands on her shoulders, Lily began to thrash and scream. Startled, and afraid

Lily would hurt herself or her brother, Val sat beside Lily and embraced her, holding her arms down. As the girl continued to struggle and cry, Val held on, whispering and shushing, rocking Lily in her arms as tears slid down her own cheeks. Eventually, the child stilled and went limp in her arms. Spent, Val laid her down and covered her back up, wiping the damp hair from her forehead. She went and grabbed the pillow and comforter from her own room, and settled herself on the floor. "I'm right here," she whispered. Sleep was a long time coming.

Chapter Eleven

Six weeks later

"Mom?"

"Hmm?" Paige responded absently as she flipped through a stack of bills.

"I said, can I ask a friend over for a playdate on Saturday?"

Paige looked up at her daughter. "I don't think we have anything going on. Who is your friend?"

"Her name's Lily. She's new, but I like her a lot."

Paige went back to her bills, only half listening as Emma chattered on.

"So can I, Mom?"

"Get her number, and I'll call her mom, okay?"

"I already did," Emma declared, holding out a ripped-off slip of paper. A phone number was scribbled on it in purple crayon.

Paige sighed, smiling. "When I'm done with these bills, I'll call."

"Yay!" Emma skipped out of the room.

A half hour later, Paige picked up the phone and made good on her promise.

"Hello?"

"Hi. This is Paige Wellington. My daughter Emma is in your daughter's class, and I'm calling to invite her for a playdate."

Paige heard quiet laughter on the other end of the line, then a familiar voice said, "Paige, this is Val. Lily just told me last night that she made a new friend named Emma."

"Val?" Paige said, smiling at the little surge of pleasure she always got when she heard Val's voice. "Well, that explains why this number looked familiar. How did I not know our girls were in the same class?"

"The kids just transferred two weeks ago. The school district didn't want to keep busing them across town to their last school. And you know what? She remembers meeting Emma at the library at that animal show months ago. Crazy, right?"

"Yeah," Paige said. "But there's a small problem. Since I'm Lily's caseworker, I can't really have her over to my house."

"Ooh, yeah, I can see how that might be a problem. It's okay."

"Hang on," Paige said before she could stop herself. "There's no reason why the girls couldn't accidentally on purpose meet up somewhere. How about the playground at the park?" Paige didn't want to miss the chance to hang out with Val some more. They'd never gotten the chance to have that lunch they'd been planning before Val's life had been turned upside down, but Paige had felt something between them. Despite her lack of experience in such matters, she was pretty sure Val had shown some interest. It sucked that the current circumstances kept her from pursuing anything, but if they met up, it would be for the kids. What could be the harm in that?

Val chuckled. "That could work. What time Saturday do you want to accidentally meet?"

Paige grinned. "How about eleven? I can bring along some sandwiches. Weather's supposed to be nice."

"It's a date," Val said. "A playdate, I mean. Lily will be so excited. I'll have to bring Ian, though."

Paige tried to ignore the tiny thrill she got at the word *date*. "Of course. See you then."

"See ya." Val hung up, and Paige touched her warm cheeks. The girls wouldn't be the only ones excited for Saturday.

❖

Val parked the car and walked with the kids to the playground. She caught sight of Paige, standing with her back to them as she watched Emma climb the ladder of a tall red slide. The weather was unusually warm for mid-October, and Paige was wearing black shorts that showed off her long shapely legs. When Lily called out to her friend, Paige turned, and the smile that lit up her face nearly made Val stop in her tracks. She'd seen plenty of women that one could offhandedly call beautiful, but Paige truly was. Her blond hair was pulled back in a ponytail, revealing dangling silver earrings and a long graceful neck. Her face radiated warmth and kindness, which made her far more attractive to Val than simple looks did.

Ian stood back with Val as Lily and Emma ran off, hand in hand, to the swings. He looked overwhelmed by the huge space and its large variety of playground equipment.

"Hey, buddy," Val said, squatting down to speak to him. "What would you like to play on first?" Ian stood motionless for a few moments, then pointed to the large sandbox area, complete with a hand-operated digger that he could sit on. "Okay, let's go." Val took Ian's hand and began walking to the sandbox, motioning with her head for Paige to follow.

Once Val got the boy settled in the sandbox, she took a seat next to Paige on the bench nearby.

"So, hi," she said, feeling shy all of a sudden.

"How are you?" Paige replied with a warm smile.

"Happy to see you," Val replied, then dropped her head in her hands, embarrassed. "Sorry. This is kind of awkward." She peeked through her fingers to see Paige's reaction.

"It's okay," Paige replied, her smile making the sun seem a little bit brighter.

She gazed at Paige and somehow found the courage to address the elephant in the room. "You should know that I was getting up the nerve to ask you out when Connie dropped the bombshell on me," she said, nodding toward Ian. "I mean, I don't even know for sure if you're into women or whatever, but I just really like being around you."

Paige put a hand on Val's arm, the heat searing her bare skin, then quickly withdrew it. "Yes, I'm into women or whatever, and I like being around you, too. But I was in line to receive the next foster care case, and totally unlucky that my case ended up involving you."

Val nodded, relieved that she hadn't made a complete fool of herself. Paige was into women, and it seemed like Paige was into her. She turned to watch Ian. "Not completely unlucky," she said, her affection for the little guy making her smile.

"How are the kids doing?"

"They're doing pretty well. Lily has been better at letting me be the parent, although she still struggles with it, especially at bedtime. I've moved them to separate beds, though—so far, so good."

"Have her nightmares subsided?" Paige asked.

"Not completely, but it's easier for me to calm her now. I don't have to sleep on the floor in their room anymore, thank God. My back was killing me."

"I know—had to do that a few times with Emma in the beginning, too. It's heartbreaking when they're so upset they can't even rest." Paige gestured toward the kids. "They look great, though. Both of them have gained a little weight."

"Yep. When I went to get this month's WIC checks, they weighed Ian, and he's gained five pounds. He's heading to the normal range on the growth chart, and he isn't anemic anymore. It's great to see some color in his cheeks finally." As Val talked, she kept making sidelong glances at Paige, because she just looked so damn good. It was all she could do not to slide closer, because she really wanted to feel Paige's warmth again. Instead, she tucked her hands under her thighs, just in case they decided to wander.

"How's the play therapy going?"

"Really well. Penny says Ian is becoming more comfortable expressing himself with play, even though he still won't speak. Lily told her that their mother yelled at them all the time to be quiet, and I've noticed that he gets upset if he hears loud voices. At least I can hear him whispering now with Lily when he doesn't think I'm watching."

"They've been through a lot of trauma," Paige said. "Once he feels more comfortable, I bet he'll start talking like crazy."

"I hope so. I feel like he has so much going on in that little head of his. He doesn't miss a thing. If I can get Lily to stop speaking for him, maybe he'll talk." Val watched Ian making hills of sand with a toy dump truck, his tongue sticking out a little in concentration as if he was doing very important work. Her heart swelled, but then she heard Connie's voice in her head yet again, warning her not to fall in love, because foster care was so often temporary. Too late, she thought.

"Well, you'll have lots of good things to report at the service plan review on Monday, if they ask," Paige said.

"Tell me how that's going to go again?"

"It's basically a meeting to see if the birth parent is following the service plan and doing what needs to be done to get the kids back. So it'll be the law guardian, the parenting coach, you, me, and my supervisor. Kayla, their mom, will be there by phone. Everyone will report on how things are going and make a recommendation for the kids."

Val was silent as her heart dropped into her stomach at the idea of the kids going back. She knew she was supposed to be supportive of birth families staying together, but that was way easier said than done.

"Hey," Paige said gently, patting Val's knee, which had begun bouncing up and down. "You're doing a great job with the kids, and I know how tough it is not to get attached."

Val looked at her in surprise, wondering how she had read her mind so easily.

"I know how it feels." Paige answered her unspoken question, reading her mind again. "I've been there, remember?" Paige gave Val's knee a squeeze, then removed her hand as the girls ran up to them.

"Mommy, Lily is going to be an angel for Halloween, just like me," Emma said excitedly.

Paige smiled warmly at them. "That's great, honey. Lily, what's your brother going to be?"

"A policeman, right, Mama? Um, I mean, Miss Valerie." Lily looked down at her feet, clearly uncomfortable.

Val covered her shock quickly. "That's right, Lil," she said, tapping the girl gently under her chin. "He's going to protect us while we're out trick-or-treating, aren't you, buddy?"

Ian had stopped playing and was listening to the conversation. He nodded, gave a little smile, and went back to digging holes. Lily visibly relaxed.

"Can we go over to the bumpy slide?" she asked, pointing to the far side of the playground.

"Yes, as long as you stay where we can see you, okay?" Val replied.

"Yay," Lily and Emma said together, then Lily gave Val a quick hug and ran off.

"Whoa," Val said, shaking her head.

"I take it she hasn't called you that before now."

"Nope. She shocked me."

"She looked scared to death there for a second, but you handled it beautifully."

"Thanks," Val said. *She called me Mama. And they say don't get attached. Yeah, right.*

❖

Val was already nervous about the service plan review, but her anxiety got decidedly worse when she saw the smug expression on the face of the bleached blonde in the suit, sitting right next to Paige at the conference table.

Oh, for fuck's sake. Why her? A few drinks and a weak moment of loneliness had landed Val in that woman's bed several months back. The sex had been good, but she'd broken her own cardinal rule to never stay until morning, sending a message of interest that wasn't really there. When she'd made it clear that she didn't do relationships, breaking things off had been extremely awkward. And now here she was once again, facing her past in the shape of—

"Lisa Webster, the law guardian for the children," Paige was saying as she made introductions.

Val had to bite her tongue to keep from groaning out loud. She refused to look at Lisa the Lawyer and focused instead on Paige, trying to calm down her insides. She sincerely hoped Paige had not seen the knowing smile on Lisa's face.

"So if we're ready, we can bring in the mom on a conference call." Paige dialed a number, and someone at the county jail answered. A few moments later, the birth mom was on the line.

"Good morning, Kayla. I'm Paige Wellington, caseworker for the foster care unit. We're meeting today for your first service plan review. With me are Lisa Webster, the law guardian for the children, Valerie Cruz, the foster parent, and Sandra Carrillo, my supervisor." There was silence on the line.

"Kayla, can you hear me?"

"Yeah," said a gruff voice.

"Great. We're going to take turns talking about any progress or planning that has been made for the children since they were placed. Please let me know if you have any questions, okay?"

"Yeah."

Paige proceeded to run the meeting, and the mom was quiet until Val was asked to give an update on the children. As she spoke about how they were doing, a strangled gasp and a snuffling noise came across the line. Val was pretty sure the woman had started to cry. She met Paige's eyes, unsure if she should continue. She swallowed the lump in her throat and quickly finished up her comments.

Paige concluded the meeting, letting Kayla know that once she went through sentencing, they would meet again to determine the next course of action. When the conference call ended, everyone in the room let out a collective sigh.

Lisa the Lawyer spoke up first, saying, "Have you had any luck locating family members, Paige?"

Val tensed, the question feeling like a punch in the gut.

Paige caught and held Val's gaze as she answered. "As far as we know, neither birth father has ever been in the picture. Kayla's mother is not a candidate due to past CPS history. We're waiting on information about an aunt who lives over in Rochester."

Val could feel herself calming as she focused on Paige. She could not and would not have an emotional reaction in front of these people, especially Lisa. The woman had a say in what happened to her kids, damn it. As the meeting adjourned, Val stayed in her seat while the others left. Lisa made a point of passing behind her seat and pausing for a moment.

"So nice to see you again, Valerie. I'll look forward to the next meeting."

Val simply nodded, and eventually the lawyer walked out, likely pissed off if the quick, sharp staccato of her heels in the hall was any indication.

"Everything okay?" Paige asked quietly.

She stood gathering papers, very aware that something had just transpired between Val and the law guardian. Val's lips were set in a grim line, and she stood stiffly, as if holding in some unpleasant feelings.

Val met her eyes, then looked away. "Sorry. I just didn't expect to run into her again."

"I take it you have a history?"

"A very brief history, yes. We were together a couple of times, and she wanted more. I didn't, and she wasn't too happy about it." Val seemed embarrassed as she fidgeted with her hands. "I probably should have been nicer to her. I just didn't want to encourage a reconnection."

"Are you going to be okay dealing with her?" Paige asked.

"What choice do I have? She's the law guardian," Val replied. "The way the courts work, she was probably assigned the case yesterday. I can request that the county give it to someone else."

"How would you explain that? Oh, they've had sex, so it's weird." Val sighed in frustration. "It's fine. I can be an adult about it."

Paige smiled. "Good to know."

Val didn't quite smother her grin. "So what do you think will happen at Kayla's sentencing?"

Paige set down her papers and said, "Well, my understanding is that she violated Leandra's Law by driving under the influence with the kids in the car. That, along with the other charges, could get her some jail time."

"What does that mean for the kids?" Val asked.

"If they go to a relative, she could petition to get them back once she's released."

"Seriously?"

"Yes. You know I have to explore all options with Kayla's family members, right?"

"I know. It's just…so many kids go to family homes that are only minimally better than the parents they've been taken from." Val brushed her hair back from her face and sighed.

"It's not a perfect system, Val. When Emma was in care with me, I almost lost her to some cousin who had popped up out of nowhere. She had never even met this person, but because she was a relative of the birth mom's, the county had to consider her. The situation got as far as the cousin getting unsupervised weekend visits. I remember what a wreck I was, how I'd inspect every inch of Emma when she came back to me. I don't know if you're religious or not, but I swear divine intervention kept her from going there."

"What happened?"

"The county found out that the cousin had a boyfriend living with her who had just gotten out of jail for drug charges. He'd only been out two months when he got busted for possession, and they found drugs and a handgun in the home. Emma never had to go back there again, but it messed with her. She was afraid to even go to daycare after that."

Val watched the emotions wash over Paige's face as she told the story, and she was struck not only by her deep connection to her daughter, but also by her willingness to share such a personal thing to help her cope with the challenge she was facing.

"But you had a happy ending. You got to keep Emma."

"Yes, thank God. Her adoption day was the best day of my life."

Val said a silent prayer that Lily and Ian would get their happy ending, too.

"So," Paige said, brightening, "do you have to go back to work?"

"Not for another hour or so."

"It's gorgeous outside, and there are some picnic tables out behind the building. Would you like to go and discuss the case some more?"

Val nodded with a smile.

Outside, Paige handed Val one of the water bottles she'd snagged from the break room on her way by, then took a sip from hers as they sat down. A few county employees occupied the other picnic tables, taking smoke breaks or an early lunch, and she felt several eyes on her and Val as they claimed their table. Paige suddenly felt stupid for suggesting Val come out here.

"What's wrong?" Val said.

"What? Oh, nothing," Paige said, waving her hand. "It's just not as private out here as I was hoping."

Val's eyes flashed as she grinned. "Do we need to be somewhere more private? To discuss the case, I mean?"

Paige's face flushed hot. "No. Yes. Ugh." Now she felt like the whole city's eyes were on her. She lowered her voice. "You're enjoying this, aren't you?"

Val laughed. "You're cute when you blush."

"Stop it," Paige said. "We're supposed to be having a professional conversation."

"By all means. Let's converse." Val's voice still held a hint of teasing, but she sat up straight and schooled her features into a more serious look.

Paige tried to muster some semblance of professional decorum and ignore the fact that she was embarrassingly aroused. "So I just wanted to make sure you are clear on the process I have to go through regarding the kids."

Val looked at the table. "I understand you need to look for relatives."

"But are you okay with that? I know the kids are special to you."

"I have to be okay with it, right? You and Connie beat it into our heads during MAPP class that foster care is usually temporary."

"Your brain might know that, but it's sometimes hard to convince your heart. I just want you to know that I get it, and I'm here to support you, too," Paige replied.

"Thanks, but I'm good," Val said. Paige could practically see the shutters fall into place as Val fought her emotions. "Whatever's best for the kids, right?"

"That's the idea," Paige said.

"Well, thanks," Val said, standing up quickly. "Guess I'd better head back to work. See you later."

Paige watched her walk away, feeling like utter shit that her job was at odds with Val's hopes. Would Val ever forgive her if she lost the kids?

CHAPTER TWELVE

Ian stared up at the fire engines, a cinnamon doughnut clutched in one hand, a cup of apple cider in the other. The local volunteer fire department was holding their annual Halloween pre-trick-or-treating hot dog roast, and several dozen families were there, eating and talking. Most of the kids were running around, comparing costumes, but Ian had immediately become fascinated with the ladder truck.

"That truck is pretty awesome, huh, buddy?" Val said. "You'd better eat your doughnut, though, so we can go trick-or-treating." Ian nodded and took a huge bite.

Shaking her head with a smile, Val scanned the group nearby and saw Lily, still chatting with a couple of classmates as she finished her hot dog. Many folks were starting to head over toward the elementary school, as that neighborhood was a popular Halloween destination.

"Lil, you about ready to go?"

Lily nodded and headed her way, then with a grin, she ran right past Val. Turning, Val met the laughing eyes of Paige.

"Somebody's excited," Paige said, as she watched Lily and Emma exclaiming over each other's angel costumes.

You got that right, Val thought, taking in Paige's appearance. She was dressed as a football player, complete with helmet, shoulder pads, and tight pants. Val's gaze kept traveling back to those pants. With a jolt, she realized she was ogling Paige. *Act like a creep much? Jeez.*

Mercifully, Paige was talking to Ian, telling him how handsome and brave he looked in his policeman costume. He smiled, his mouth covered with cinnamon sugar. Looking up again at Val, Paige took off the helmet, and her hair cascaded down to her shoulders.

"Ugh, this thing is making my head itch. What, no costume for you?" she said.

"I never even thought about it," Val said, pretending to fix something on Ian's costume that didn't need fixing. "I haven't dressed up for Halloween in forever."

"Wish I had known. I could have at least brought you a witch's hat or something. Looks like the girls are ready to go. What do you say, Ian? Let's go get some candy."

Ian grabbed Val's hand and started to pull, making Paige laugh. Why did she have to be so damn sexy? Val thought, wondering why she felt a connection with Paige that she hadn't felt with anyone else in years, and why her bad luck was making sure she couldn't do anything about it.

"Did you get to go trick-or-treating when you were a kid?" Val asked, needing to move her mind to safer ground.

"I did, although I don't remember it feeling like this," Paige replied.

"What do you mean?"

"Everybody here seems to be having fun just being together. Halloween always felt like a game of one-upmanship in my neighborhood. It was all about who had the best costume, or the best decorations, or gave out the best candy. Don't get me wrong—I was all about finding who gave out the best candy." Paige chuckled, then sobered again. "I think I stopped wanting to go when I was about nine. So many of the other girls had turned it into a judging contest, and I was over it. What about you?"

"Our neighborhood was barely safe during the day, let alone at night. The Boys and Girls Club used to have a little parade and Halloween party in the afternoon, so we could get some candy and enjoy ourselves but be home before dark. Abuelita used to make our costumes. One year, my brother and I went as a burro. I was the backside and had to stay bent over. That was the worst."

Paige burst out laughing. "You were the ass end of an ass?"

Val feigned outrage. "I prefer to say burro butt."

"How about donkey derriere?" Paige said, still giggling.

"Okay, this topic has totally outlived its usefulness," Val said, trying to suppress a grin. How had Paige lived the childhood she had yet still be so much fun? Why no one had snapped up this incredible woman was beyond her. Her curiosity took over.

"So, have you always been a single parent to Emma?" Once the words left Val's mouth, she wanted to cram them back in. Paige had an odd look on her face, confirming to Val that she had been a complete idiot for asking.

"Well, yes, I have. Why do you ask?"

Crap. "I don't know. Just wondered why someone as great as you isn't with someone." *Oh my God. Please, Earth, swallow me now.*

Making Val's mortification complete, Paige laughed out loud. "Great, huh?" she said.

"What, you don't think you're great?" Val was feeling a little defensive now.

"I don't know, but my last girlfriend never used that term. She was more likely to say I was too emotional, needy, annoying…but never *great.*" Paige's expression grew much more serious, even a little sad, and Val felt like a fool for saying anything.

"I'm sorry, but hey, if she was too stupid to see how great you really are, then screw her, right?" Val was rewarded with a stunning smile that lit up Paige's whole face, even in the deepening shadows of dusk.

"Thanks for saying that, Val," she said, touching Val's arm. "She was a major reason why I have been alone for the last eight years." Paige kicked the toe of her sneaker through the fallen leaves on the sidewalk, as they watched the kids skip up to the next house. "It's just been Emma and me, no complications, and I guess I've always been content with that."

"I get that," Val replied, nodding her head slowly. Suddenly, Paige turned and fixed Val with a questioning look.

"So how about you? Why don't you have someone telling you how great you are?"

"Hey, for the sake of our self-esteem here, we need better adjectives than great. How about fabulous? Outstanding? No, wait… *incredible* works, don't you think?"

Paige was laughing again, and Val realized how much she enjoyed making that happen. Plus, she was pretty sure her deflection had worked, until Paige swatted her lightly on the shoulder.

"You didn't answer my question, Valerie."

Val sighed. "It's always been easier going solo. Like you said, no complications." She was saved from further revelations when the kids ran up to them, breathless.

"Mommy, can we cross over to that side of the street now?" Emma asked.

Paige smiled. "Yep. Everybody hold hands and look for cars." The kids immediately complied. "Okay, all clear. Let's cross together."

With Ian's cold little fingers clutching hers, Val wished she was holding Paige's hand instead.

CHAPTER THIRTEEN

Three weeks passed before Paige had the chance to see Val again. Another home visit had been scheduled for today, and when Val answered her knock on the door, Paige was amazed at the visceral reaction her body had whenever she laid eyes on Valerie. Even standing there in jeans and a hoodie, the woman was stunning.

"Hey there. Come on in." Val's smile was warm. "The kids just got home from school. Have a seat while I get them."

Paige settled on the couch while Val rounded up her charges. "Come on and say hi to Miss Paige," Val was saying as she reentered the room, followed by Ian and a grumpy-looking Lily.

"Hi, guys," Paige said. "How are you doing?" Ian gave her a thumbs-up, but Lily just sulked, not meeting her eyes.

"Lily, Miss Paige is talking to you." Val exchanged glances with Paige when Lily still didn't engage. "What's wrong, kiddo?"

Lily's face crumbled as tears spilled down her cheeks. "I...I don't wanna say in front of..." Lily cast her eyes in Ian's direction.

Val nodded. "Ian, you can go back to your room to play now, okay, buddy?" He gave her a quick smile and scampered off down the hall.

Val sat on the couch, gently pulling Lily to stand before her. "What happened, Lil?"

Lily looked over at Paige, then back at Val. Before Paige could offer to leave the room, Val said, "It's okay to tell us, honey. Maybe Miss Paige can help, too."

Lily took a deep shaky breath. "I got into a fight. On the bus." Her bottom lip quivered as fresh tears fell.

"A fight? Are you hurt?"

"No. It was just a yelling fight. Jimmy Valerino is a big jerk. He made fun of Ian." Paige had to smother a smile as Lily stood, arms crossed in indignation, ever the determined protector of her little brother.

"What did he say?" Val asked.

"He called Ian a freak and said he must be retarded because he doesn't speak." Although Val was keeping her expression carefully neutral, Paige could see the muscles bunching in her jaw.

"Did Ian hear him?" Lily shook her head.

"Good," Val said. "What did you say to this Jimmy?"

"I told him Ian wasn't a freak, that retarded isn't a nice word to call someone, and that he was the big jerk-face for making fun of a little boy."

Val grinned, then quickly schooled her features.

"Well, I'm proud of you for sticking up for your brother. Do you think you handled the problem well?"

More tears. "No," Lily said in a tiny voice.

"How come?"

"Because I called Jimmy names, too."

"Like jerk-face?"

Lily nodded. "And dummy and meanie."

"Ah," Val said. "So you were pretty mad, huh?"

"Yeah."

"But people shouldn't call others names when they're mad?"

Lily shook her head. "That's what Mama always did when she got mad at us. I didn't like that. She hurt our feelings."

Val held out her arms, and Lily fell into the hug. As she rubbed Lily's back, she said, "You are a smart and caring little girl, and you're right. Name-calling hurts, and it isn't okay." After comforting the child for a moment, Val held her away at arm's length. "If Jimmy says something again, what could you do?"

Lily thought for a moment. "I could tell him it isn't right to make fun of people, and maybe he should try being nice."

Val grinned. "Excellent idea. Thanks for telling me what happened. Feel better now?"

Lily nodded and smiled. "Can I go play now?"

"Absolutely."

Paige was impressed. Instead of getting upset like many parents would, Val had problem-solved with Lily and helped her process some very big emotions. "You handled that perfectly, you know."

Val sat back with a groan. "So you couldn't tell that I wanted to find Jimmy what's-his-name and beat the snot out of him?"

Paige laughed. "Nope, not at all." Then she pointed a scolding finger at Val. "And you won't be doing any such thing, right?"

"Nah, my fighting days are over. Glad you were here, though. Your levelheadedness rubs off on me."

"Good," Paige replied. "You said your fighting days are over. Did you get into a lot of fights when you were a kid?"

"Plenty. I've learned to rein in my temper, but when I was a kid, I ran on pure emotion. A lot of the time, though, I was sticking up for younger kids. I always felt like I had to protect them."

"Like Lily?"

"Yeah, like Lily. She reminds me of myself when I was young. She challenges me—it's still hard for her to trust me with Ian." Val sighed. "Part of me wants to know what those kids went through, but I know if I knew all the details, I'd be beyond angry."

Paige nodded. "I think in some ways it's better not to know, since we can't change what happened. Foster parenting is about taking the kids where they're at and trying to move them forward. Still, knowing about the kids' past can sometimes help us understand them better, even if the knowledge is heartbreaking."

"You used to work for child protective, right?" Val said. Paige nodded. "You know all the awful situations these kids deal with, then. I'm sure we've both heard some horror stories. It's no wonder that mental health issues are skyrocketing. How do you deal with it all, day after day?"

"I've asked myself that very same question, more than a few times over the years. I think I have to focus on how amazing and resilient kids are, and when they are with me, I try to give them my best. I don't ever want to be just another adult they can't count on."

"Wow," Val said. The depth of emotion Paige saw in those gorgeous brown eyes was impossible to look away from. Val held her gaze for another long moment. "You're kind of amazing yourself."

Paige felt her cheeks flame. "No, I'm not. Children just need us to look out for them."

"Yeah, but look how many adults don't. I mean, you genuinely care about the kids. They're not just a job to you."

"I could say the same about you, Val. I've seen you in action, remember?"

Val dropped her gaze to the floor, her fingers fidgeting with the hem of her shirt. "I know how it feels to not matter, to be an afterthought. I couldn't do that to another child."

Paige reached out and lightly touched Val's knee. "I know how it feels, too. Maybe that's why we care so much, because we've been there."

"I don't know. I've known lots of people who had terrible childhoods and turned out to be just as bad to their own kids. Don't you ever wonder why some people don't seem to learn from their experiences?"

Paige could see that the conversation was starting to get to Val. Her face was set in a frown, her eyes telegraphing the pain of her past. Needing to lighten the mood, she said, "Let's just agree that not everyone can be as awesome as we are, okay?" She smiled and saw Val's face relax as she smiled back.

"Deal."

Paige picked up her binder from the coffee table. "Now that we've covered that, I'm supposed to be going through home visit protocol with you. Like, have you documented all of the kids' medical or counseling visits for the month?"

"Yep."

"Have they been doing okay at school?"

"Until today's bus incident, yes."

"Do you have any questions or concerns?"

"Just one. I had a voicemail from the law guardian." Val grimaced. "Do I have to call her back?"

Paige laughed. "Thought you could be an adult about all that. Just call the woman."

Val let out an exaggerated sigh. "Yeah, yeah. Whatever."

Paige didn't respond for several moments, imagining Lisa and Val together.

"Why so quiet?" Val's question pulled her back to the here and now.

Paige tried to deflect. "Oh, no reason."

"Uh-huh. You got a weird look on your face when I mentioned Lisa," Val said.

"No, I didn't."

"Yep, you did. You have questions, I can tell."

"Why would I have questions? Your personal life is your business," Paige replied, alarmed at where this conversation was going.

"I think you're wondering why I got with Lisa, or why I didn't stay with Lisa."

Paige was beyond uncomfortable. "Val, please."

"I want to tell you about it. Maybe if I do, I won't feel so weird around her." Val took a deep breath and let it out slowly. "On the last anniversary of Abuelita's death, I was having a particularly rough time. I needed to get out of the house, so I went down to Pony's. I was shooting tequila, just to forget. Lisa started talking to me, and the next thing I knew, I was in her bed. The next morning, she suggested we get together again, sober. We did, but she was way more interested in me than I was in her. Plus, I felt like an emotional train wreck and had no business leading anyone on. So I let her down as gently as I could. She got mad and said I'd just used her. It wasn't like that, but she wouldn't believe me. That service plan review meeting was the first time I'd seen her since."

"You didn't need to tell me all that, Val," Paige said after a moment.

"I know, but I'm not proud of it, and it's important to me that you know I don't go around picking up strange women all the time. And Lisa is definitely not my type."

"Val…"

"You're such a good person, Paige. I just don't want you to have a bad impression of me."

Val's earnestness was so adorable, Paige just wanted to wrap her up in a hug. Instead, she said, "Thank you for your honesty, but that story doesn't change my opinion of you, which happens to be very positive. If anything, the way you handled Lisa shows integrity. So now that Lisa is off your chest, literally and figuratively, can we move on?"

Val looked at her, wide-eyed, then burst out laughing.

Chapter Fourteen

The parking lot was packed when Val, Sasha, and Jen arrived at the bar, and they ended up having to park three blocks down the street. Priscilla's Holiday Musical Revue at Pony's always drew a huge crowd, and Val was looking forward to her first night out since getting the kids. At the last foster parent support group, Ellen had graciously offered to babysit, and she'd brought along a plate of her famous brownies. Lily and Ian liked her instantly.

As they neared the door of the bar, Val felt herself smiling. She loved this event—part drag show, part coffee house, part musical theater, but always a great time. She normally wasn't a fan of squeezing into small spaces with tons of loud, sweaty people, but she made an exception for Priscilla's.

"Babe, wait till you see this show," Sasha was telling Jen, as they stood in line to get in.

"Yeah," Val agreed, "last year they had this drag king a cappella group that sounded just like Pentatonix. They were unbelievable."

"Can't wait," Jen said, giving Sasha's arm a two-handed squeeze.

When they finally got inside, it took a while to find a spot, but Val finally found some standing room near a pillar to the left of the stage while Sasha and Jen went to the bar.

When Sasha returned, drinks in hand, she barely fit in the area Val had tried to keep open for them. "Jen went to the bathroom. Hope she can find her way back over. Damn, this is the biggest crowd I've ever seen here."

"I know. Every year we tell ourselves we're going to get here early enough to get a seat," Val replied, enviously eying the people sitting comfortably at several round tables set up on the dance floor. "Why do we never seem to pull that off?"

Sasha shrugged, searching the crowd for Jen. After several minutes, she caught sight of her and waved her over.

"Holy crap. That was an adventure," Jen said, scooting in under Sasha's arm and taking her drink.

Just then, the lights dimmed, and a cheer went up from the crowd. A garishly dressed emcee took the stage, and the spectacle began.

Val kept her back to the pillar, which helped a little to keep people from bumping into her. She had already taken note of all possible exits, and every few minutes, she scanned the audience, her instincts on high alert for trouble. Sasha and Jen were in front of her, arms entwined, as the performer onstage sang "Santa Baby." Val watched them, noticing their little touches of affection, how they looked at each other with such emotion. She was startled by a sharp twinge in her chest, and she looked away, confused.

As a reincarnation of the Village People took the stage, Val tapped Sasha on the shoulder.

"Hold my spot."

Wading through the sea of bodies, Val felt like people were watching her, but she avoided meeting anyone's eyes. She made it to the line for the bathroom and waited until, finally, she closed herself into a stall. Taking a deep breath, she willed her heart rate to slow down. Her anxiety was up tonight—not unusual in large crowds—but Val was feeling something else. She thought about her reaction to the closeness between Sasha and Jen.

Am I jealous? No…I'm so happy for Sasha. She deserves a good relationship. So what's my problem then?

Val put the thought aside as she washed her hands and exited the bathroom. As she began to squeeze through the crowd, a flash of shimmery color caught her eye. A woman was walking just ahead of her, and her holly-green dress stood out in the crowd of people dressed predominantly in black, white, and denim. Val admired the woman, from her blond hair swept up off her elegant neck in a French twist, to the deep dip in the dress that exposed her slender back, to the very shapely bottom that moved enticingly, right down to the lovely calves made more defined by a pair of three-inch heels. Val watched as the woman made her way to a front-row table occupied by four others and sat, her back still to Val.

It had been a long time since she'd been out with a beautiful woman. That was it. *Maybe I'm just feeling a little lonely.*

❖

Paige was having a terrific time. When Joe and his husband had invited her and a couple more of their coworkers out tonight, she had hesitated. She hadn't been out to the bar for years, and it brought back some not-so-happy memories of her last girlfriend. Joe had insisted that she'd have a blast, though, so she'd dressed up and come along. The show had been great so far, and Paige let herself relax and enjoy the bar's festive atmosphere.

A twenty-minute intermission was announced, and Joe got up to refresh everyone's drinks. His husband, Charlie, scooched his chair closer to Paige.

"So what do you think, honey? Glad you came out with us tonight?"

"Yes, I am, actually," Paige replied with a smile. "Being a single mom doesn't allow for too many nights like this."

"Well, I'm glad you could come, then." Gesturing toward their other two tablemates with his chin, Charlie whispered, "What's their story?"

Paige looked at Summer and Kristie, two young junior caseworkers in her department. They had been only inches apart all night and seemingly oblivious to everything else around them. Summer whispered something in Kristie's ear, making her giggle.

"I think it's safe to say they're an item."

"What about you?" Charlie asked. "Forgive the clichéd line, but what's a beautiful woman like you doing alone tonight?"

Paige's cheeks heated, from both pleasure at the compliment and embarrassment at the sad state of her social life. She tried to blow it off.

"You know, single mom thing again. Don't have time for drama or to get to know someone new."

Charlie snorted. "Uh-huh. Let me guess—you've been burned."

"Something like that." Paige fiddled with her wineglass, not meeting Charlie's eyes.

"Oh, honey, you can't imagine how many awful experiences I had before I met Joe. But he was worth the wait."

"Who was worth the wait?" Joe asked, appearing with drinks in hand.

"You, handsome," Charlie said, laughing. "I was just telling our lovely Paige here that I went through lots of duds before I found true love." He grasped Paige's hands in his own. "Don't let some woman, who clearly was an idiot for not seeing how terrific you are, keep you from finding Ms. Right."

"After all this time, I honestly wouldn't know where to begin," Paige protested. "Being single is just easier."

"Bull honky," Joe declared. "Anything worth doing takes effort. I bet there are plenty of nice women out there if you'd take a chance."

"I've even noticed several women tonight checking you out," Charlie put in.

"Oh, come on." Paige laughed. "You're exaggerating."

"I am not." Charlie put his hand to his chest, affronted. "In fact, that delicious-looking woman behind you in those fabulous boots has been eyeing you for quite a while."

Paige turned around and scanned the crowd. She saw the woman, in knee-high black boots, tight black pants, and a gauzy, see-through white blouse over a low-cut red tank top. When her eyes focused on the face, Paige gasped. The delicious-looking woman was Val.

❖

Val was having fun people watching from the relative safety of her pillar, but her gaze continually scanned back to the woman in the green dress. She hadn't even gotten a glimpse of her face yet, but every other part of her was stunning. The short, bald man she was talking to suddenly nodded in her direction, and the woman turned around.

Oh my God. Paige. Val felt like she couldn't breathe until Paige smiled and nodded her head in acknowledgment. *She's stunning.*

All the people milling around kept getting in the way of Val's line of sight, and although her feet remained rooted to their spot, Paige's smile beckoned. Finally, she moved, slowly making her way around tables and chairs and people until she stood behind Paige's seat. Paige rose, her smile widening.

"Hi, Val."

"Paige, hi. You look…incredible."

"Thanks." A blush rose on Paige's lovely cheeks, making her even more beautiful. "You look pretty incredible yourself."

Val smiled, and they just gazed at each other like shy schoolkids.

"Haven't I met you before?" A man's voice interrupted the moment, and Val broke eye contact with Paige in time to see the man who'd drawn Paige's attention to her swat the larger man on the arm.

"Oh, sorry," Paige said. "Joe, Charlie, meet Valerie Cruz. You met at the foster care picnic, remember, Joe?"

"Right, right. You're a new foster parent."

"Yes," Val said, summoning her social etiquette. "Good to see you again, Joe." She shook his hand, then extended hers to the man with him.

"I'm Charlie, Joe's better half," he said. "So nice to meet you." He grabbed Joe's arm. "Look, babe, there's some people we need to go talk to." As he led the bewildered-looking Joe away, he smiled at Val. "Take my seat, honey."

Val sat down as Paige chuckled. "Charlie's a trip, isn't he?"

"Yeah. They seem like nice guys."

"Oh, they're the best. So," Paige said, fingering the silver pendant that rested on her chest, "you came to see the show?" She cringed inwardly. *Duh.*

Val grinned. "Yep. My friend Sasha and I always try to make it every year. She's over there somewhere," she gestured at the crowd, "probably making out with her girlfriend. They do that a lot."

"Joe insisted I come to the show, since I'd never seen it before," Paige replied. "The evening hasn't disappointed so far." *In more ways than one.*

The lights flickered, indicating the end of intermission. Folks from the surrounding tables reclaimed their seats, and Val scooted her chair closer to Paige to make room. The next act took the stage, and they settled in to watch. Paige was almost painfully aware of Val, how their knees nearly touched, how she could feel the heat from Val's arm draped casually over the back of her chair. She hadn't had that feeling in a very long time.

Val laughed aloud at the comic onstage, and Paige turned to study her profile. Her dark hair framed her face in long waves, softening her high cheekbones and long straight nose. Full lips parted in a smile, creating a tiny dimple in Val's cheek. Paige's eyes traveled down Val's throat to the swell of her breasts not covered by the red top, and she bit her lip as a rush of arousal came over her.

"God, this guy's a riot," Val said, turning to look at Paige. Busted, her eyes shot up to meet Val's amused gaze. Her cheeks had to be bright red, judging from the heat burning them. Paige hoped the lights were sufficiently dim to hide her embarrassment.

Val touched Paige's far shoulder. "Are you having a good time?"

Paige nodded. "Yes."

"Good," Val replied, leaving her fingers lightly resting on Paige's bare arm.

Paige tried to process all the thoughts flying through her head. Was Val flirting? Circumstances prevented anything romantic from happening, and she thought they'd come to terms with that. They were becoming friends, and even that challenged Paige's professional boundaries a bit. But Paige hadn't enjoyed being around another person so much in maybe forever, and this, right now, felt amazing. Willing herself to just be in the moment for once, she leaned ever so slightly into Val's touch.

❖

"There you are." Val turned around at Sasha's words. "Thought you'd up and left us."

"Nope, just got lucky to find a seat."

"And who is this lovely lady?" Sasha was smiling at Paige.

"Sasha, this is Paige Wellington, the caseworker for the kids. Paige, this is Sasha Thomas, my best friend."

"Pleasure to meet you," Sasha said, shaking Paige's hand. She quirked an eyebrow at Val, questioning.

"We just happened to run into each other. Weird, huh?" Val fidgeted with her shirt sleeve. "Where's Jen?"

"She decided to brave the bathroom line again. That was a great show, right?"

"There's definitely a lot of talented people in this town," Paige said. "Can't believe I'd never heard of this event before."

"You're a first-timer? A Priscilla's virgin? Oh, I gotta buy you a drink."

Paige laughed. "No, thanks, Sasha. I drove, so I'm sticking to water."

"Next time, then."

The women moved aside as bar employees began removing the tables to clear the dance floor. Fifteen minutes later, the DJ turned up the music, and a dance party ensued.

Jen came over to them then, and after introductions, she pulled Sasha onto the dance floor. Before long, their moves were leaving little to the imagination.

"See what I mean?" Val asked as they watched.

"Um, yeah. No public shyness there," Paige replied.

"Well, what do you say we make the most of our kid-free night out and dance?"

"Oh, I couldn't—I haven't danced in forever," Paige said, shaking her head.

"Come on. It's just like riding a bike." She took Paige's hand and led her into the crowd of dancers.

"I'm not very good at this," Paige complained, awkwardly trying to find her groove. Val was dancing like a pro, moving effortlessly to the music.

"Don't try so hard. Just feel the rhythm." She took Paige's hands in hers. "Just let go. You look amazing."

After a couple more fast songs, the DJ switched gears. Paige stood for a moment, watching as couple after couple embraced in a slow dance, then turned to leave the floor. Val's hand on her arm stopped her.

"Not yet. Dance with me?"

Despite the alarm bells clanging in Paige's head, Val's beauty was magnetic, her smile impossible to resist. Paige slowly took Val's hand and allowed herself to be drawn into the dance. Her heels brought her to the perfect height, and as Val touched her cheek to Paige's, everything else seemed to disappear. Paige was mesmerized by Val's warm hand on her back, gently stroking her bare skin, her breath soft in her ear. Paige was so aroused she nearly whimpered. *God, it's been so long.*

Val pulled back slightly and looked into her eyes. The intensity between them was staggering, and Paige felt something shift as Val leaned closer. *She's going to kiss me.*

And the song ended. As the music changed to an up-tempo beat, Val looked at Paige, almost in surprise, blinked, and took a step back.

"Wow. Okay, I need a drink." Val moved away, then turned back around. "Stay right here. Please."

Paige nodded, and as she watched Val weave her way through the crowd, she let her breath out in a whoosh. What just happened?

Paige's thoughts were interrupted by a loud, familiar voice, saying, "You two were looking awfully cozy there."

Paige turned and met the unexpected face of Lisa Webster. "What are you talking about?"

"Don't you think you're blurring the line just a bit?"

Paige's stomach clenched. "I don't see how this is any of your business, Lisa. I'm not doing anything wrong."

Lisa put up her hands in surrender. "Okay, okay. I don't mean to put my nose where it doesn't belong. Just be careful, that's all."

"Of what?" Paige asked, although she really didn't want to hear the answer.

"Professional boundaries aside, I just don't think Valerie Cruz is someone you should get too invested in. I mean, she's gorgeous and charming, but take it from me—she doesn't do relationships. I just don't want to see you get hurt."

Paige felt like she'd been punched in the gut. Her mind replayed the last hour—the touches, the closeness. Val had nearly kissed her, and she had wanted her to, badly. Lisa's words brought the reality of her situation back into focus and made all of her warning bells start clanging, nearly obliterating what she had just felt dancing in Val's arms. She scanned the room and caught sight of Val, leaning on the bar and talking to another woman. *Oh, God, what am I doing? I barely know her. I should never have let things get this far.*

Needing some air, Paige nodded at Lisa and headed for the door as fast as she could.

❖

Val was having the best night she'd had in…she couldn't remember how long. Music had always been a good way for her to deal with her anxiety, and dancing was like medicine for her stress. Still waiting for her drink, she turned around and leaned against the bar just in time to see the stricken look on Paige's face before she bolted for the door. Lisa the Lawyer caught her eye, then looked away.

Val rushed across the room. "What did you say to her?"

Lisa shrugged. "I might have just cautioned her not to let things get too serious with you. Plus, she's working on your case. You get the conflict of interest, don't you?"

"How is this your business? You had no right." Val was so angry her clenched fists were shaking. Before she could give in to her strong desire to slap Lisa's face, she shoved past her and ran out the door. She scanned the parking lot and the street, then saw headlights come on to her left. She recognized Paige's vehicle and ran over.

"Wait," Val yelled, knocking on the driver's side window. Paige looked at her through the glass, then slowly lowered the window.

"Paige, please, you don't have to go. Whatever Lisa said to upset you…"

"It's fine. I'm just tired and want to get home to my daughter."

Val couldn't get Paige to meet her eyes, and her anxiety spiked. "Are we okay?"

Paige sighed. "Listen, I'm sorry. I stepped a bit too far outside my professional boundaries, and Lisa just reminded me of that. I had a really good time tonight, but I've got to go. Have fun with your friends, okay? Good night, Val."

Val felt helpless as Paige closed her window and slowly drove away. She smacked her palm down on the nearest car. "Shit."

CHAPTER FIFTEEN

Paige sat in the break room, absently staring at her untouched mug of vanilla chai. She could not for the life of her get motivated this morning. Saturday night's events had taken up residence in her brain, traveling on a continuous loop of uneasiness and disappointment, and sleep had been elusive. She looked up as Connie breezed in, all chipper and smiling, then dropped her attention back to her mug.

"Good morning, sunshine," Connie said, then stopped in her tracks. "Ooh, maybe not." She poured a cup of coffee, then dropped into the chair opposite Paige. "Okay, spill it."

"Spill what?"

"The reason why you look like you just lost your best friend."

"I'm just tired, that's all," Paige deflected, not looking at Connie.

"That's what I thought when you interrupted my babysitting fairly early Saturday night, but now I'm thinking there's more to the story than sleep deprivation." Connie sat back in her chair, crossed her arms, and waited.

"Why can I never hide anything from you? You're like a bloodhound." Paige couldn't help but smile at the determined look on her colleague's face.

"Damn right. Now, what's got you looking so sad?"

"Guess I just got my hopes up about somebody and found out I shouldn't have."

"Hmm...anyone I know?" Connie arched an eyebrow inquiringly, a knowing smile on her face. "Our lovely Valerie, perhaps?"

"Ugh, how do you do that?"

"Do what?" Connie was the picture of innocence.

"Figure things out before anyone else does."

"I've been around a long time, honey, and reading people is my special gift. So, it's Val, isn't it?"

Paige nodded, then filled Connie in on what had transpired at the bar. By the time she finished, Connie's eyes were flashing with anger.

"Maybe Lisa's intentions were good, though I doubt it. At any rate, she shouldn't have meddled."

"Val told me that she and Lisa hooked up a while back. Lisa wanted to take things further, but Val didn't."

"Let me get this straight—Lisa has a tiny bit of history with Val and apparently felt obligated to remind you of your professional obligations. You and Val were just having a good time and aren't even seeing each other, yet you got upset enough to leave. That about sum it up?" Connie said.

"Well, when you put it that way. Oh my God, I feel like such an ass."

"Because you have feelings for Val. If you didn't, Lisa wouldn't have scared you away."

"What? No, I…I mean, we're just friends. I can't have feelings for her. Lisa was right about the professional boundaries thing, wasn't she?"

"To a certain extent," Connie replied, "but those boundaries won't be there forever. Do you care about Val?"

Paige sighed. "I'm starting to, but Lisa hit on the exact reason why I haven't dated in years. My last relationship was pretty much one-sided, and it ended badly. I didn't want to believe what she was saying about Val, but part of me just got scared, I guess." Paige scrubbed her hands down her face and sighed. "I guess I just got ahead of myself. I don't even know Val that well."

"I'm certainly not privy to the details of her love life, and Val would be mortified if she knew we were even discussing this. She does have a hell of a story, but that's hers to tell. I will say that Val is as loyal and honest as they come. If there's information to be had, you'd best get it from her."

Paige nodded. "Thanks, Connie."

"Any time, sweetie." Connie patted her hand and left the room.

Now she just had to get up the nerve to talk to Val. *Who probably hates me. Well done.*

❖

"Look what I got at school!" Lily waved a sparkly pink card in Val's face as she helped Ian with his coat at the daycare center.

"What is it?"

"It's for a birthday party, and it's at Chuck E. Cheese's." Lily was nearly exploding with excitement. "Can I go, please?"

"Whose party is it?" Val asked, scooping up Ian's backpack and herding them toward the parking lot.

"Emma's, and it's gonna be so fun. I've never been to Chuck E. Cheese's. I really, really wanna go. Please?"

Emma's birthday. That meant Paige would be there. They hadn't spoken since Paige ran off from the bar that night two weeks earlier, and Val wanted to avoid what was sure to be an awkward encounter. But she couldn't disappoint Lily over her own ego. "Okay, kiddo. You can go."

Lily let out a squeal and hugged Val tightly. "Thank you." Then just as quickly, her face fell. "I have to get her a present, though. I don't have any money."

"I'll help you out with that. What do you think Emma would like?"

Lily just stared at her. "You'll give me money?"

"Well, of course, silly. You're not old enough to make your own money yet." Val opened the car door and buckled Ian in his seat. When she turned around, Lily was just standing next to the car, tears streaming down her face. "What's the matter, Lil?"

"My…my mom never let me go to birthday parties. She said she wasn't gonna waste her money on someone else's brat."

"Oh, honey," Val said, her heart twisting, "you don't need to worry about that. Emma's your good friend, and I'll make sure you get to help her celebrate her birthday, okay?"

"Okay," Lily replied, looking like she wasn't at all sure she could trust this good news.

As Val drove home, an old memory resurfaced.

She'd been so excited. She had her best outfit on and had brushed her hair half a dozen times. She grabbed the gift she had carefully made by hand with scraps from Abuelita's sewing bag—a little doll for her best friend Maria's eighth birthday.

"Mama, it's time to go to the party," she'd called, running down the hall from her room. The sight before her made her stop dead. A pot of water was boiling over on the stove, the unopened box of mac and cheese on the counter. Enrique was sitting in his high chair, tears drying on his sleeping face. The contents of his filthy diaper had leaked onto his leg. She turned off the burner and put the pot in the sink, then turned to look for her mom. She saw her in the living room, half sprawled on the couch, asleep.

When she got closer, her heart sank. The strap was still around Mama's arm, just above the needle. She wouldn't be waking up anytime soon. Tears of anger ran down her face as she put down the birthday gift and went to take care of her brother. She'd never made it to Maria's party, and yet another piece of her childhood was destroyed.

Val blinked rapidly, then glanced in the rearview mirror. Ian was asleep, his sweet face flushed. Lily was reading her library book. She glanced up and caught Val's eye in the mirror. Her sweet smile made Val's heart ache. *Yes, little one. You will go to that party.*

❖

"Hold out your hand for the stamp, Ian," Val instructed as they gained entry into Chuck E. Cheese's. Lily was bouncing on her toes, looking at all the lights and games. Taking the kids by the hand, Val walked toward the area in the back of the restaurant that was marked with party balloons. A blur of pink came from the right, tackling Lily in a hug.

Emma was dressed from head to toe in sparkly princess pink, complete with a birthday crown. "Come on, Lily. Let's go get your tokens."

Val nodded to her to go on and watched the girls run off to... Paige. There she was, looking simultaneously adorable and sexy in a ponytail and purple hoodie, handing out little plastic cups of tokens. She was fully in mom mode, greeting and directing the kids, chatting with the other parents, and arranging the birthday gifts on a small table.

Val brought Ian over. When Paige saw them, her smile faltered and her cheeks flushed, but she recovered so quickly that no one seemed to notice, except Val.

"Hello, Paige." Val caught and held her gaze, smiling.

"Hi. Thanks for coming." Paige broke eye contact and squatted down to greet Ian. "Hey, buddy, glad you're here. Want to play some games?" Ian nodded, wide-eyed, and Paige handed him his cup of tokens. He immediately began tugging on Val's hand.

Well played, Val thought, glancing back at Paige as Ian pulled her away. Conversation avoided, for now.

Thirty minutes later, Ian's tokens were gone and he had redeemed his handful of tickets for a small red bouncy ball, a plastic snake, and a purple bracelet for his sister. She took him over to the jungle gym area and let him loose, then sat at a nearby table. Scanning the crowd, she saw Lily with Emma and two other girls playing Skee-Ball. Looking the other way, she found Paige, who was putting a pink napkin beside each paper plate on the long party table.

❖

Paige sensed the connection before she looked up and met Val's eyes. Neither one looked away, and Paige felt her belly tighten as she remembered how it had felt to dance with her. Across the room, Val's hand moved to her throat, then up to smooth back her hair. Her lips parted as if she wanted to speak, then just as quickly, she closed her mouth with a slight shake of her head and looked away. Paige felt like she'd been slapped. *I've hurt her.*

The next hour was a flurry of activity as the kids had their pizza and cake, and Emma opened her presents. The party was a good diversion from her feelings, but Paige was still conscious of Val's presence. They had to talk.

As the other parents began gathering their children to leave, Paige approached Val.

"Hey, do you think you could stay for a few more minutes? I could use the help, if you wouldn't mind." She gestured to the leftover cake and piles of presents she had to take to the car.

"Uh, sure." Val put down the kids' coats and waited. Twenty minutes later, the kids and presents were loaded up, and they were standing outside at Paige's car.

"Thanks for your help, Val. Always helps to have another pair of hands at these things."

"No problem. You all set?"

"Actually, I was hoping we could find a time to talk." There, she'd said it. Paige held her breath, waiting for Val's response.

Val's dark eyes studied Paige. "What about?"

Paige looked down, turning her car keys over and over in her hand. "I want to explain why I left the bar that night."

"Does it matter?"

Paige looked at Val and recognized the same wary distance in her eyes that she'd seen when they first met. "Yes, it matters, a lot actually."

"You don't owe me any explanations, Paige. Maybe it's best if we just forget it."

"But I—"

"I need to get the kids home. I'll see you next week, okay? And thanks for inviting Lily and Ian today." Val offered a small smile. "Bye."

"Bye." Paige didn't move as she watched Val get into her car and drive away. So much needed to be said, but apparently Val wasn't going to go there with her. Maybe Lisa was right, damn her. Just keep it professional. Paige nodded to herself and got in the car, willing herself not to cry.

"Mommy?" Emma said.

"Hmm?"

"Did you and Miss Val have a fight?"

Startled, Paige glanced in the rearview mirror at her daughter. "No, honey. Why?"

"You just looked really sad when you were talking to her."

"We weren't fighting, just having a grown-up talk."

"That's good. Lily and I think you guys should be friends like we are, because we all have a lot in common, right?"

"Yep." Paige needed to divert her astute little girl to a new topic. "Did you have fun at your party?"

That worked. Emma chattered happily all the way home, giving Paige a blessed reprieve from thoughts of Val.

CHAPTER SIXTEEN

Christmas shopping was kind of crazy, Val decided. She hadn't had anyone but Sasha to buy for in years, so she'd avoided the crowds, packed parking lots, and retail marketing overload, until now. Having two young children who believed in Santa Claus changed things drastically.

She'd taken the day off to do her shopping, but judging from the line she was standing in, so had everyone else in town. As she stood waiting and people watching, a little old woman shuffled by. Val did a double take and gasped. *Abuelita.* The woman was small, her face deeply lined beneath her head scarf, and she wore a worn flowered house coat and heavy stockings under her thin winter coat. Val stared, her heart pounding. She knew it wasn't her grandmother, but holy Christ, the resemblance was incredible. Val's mind was suddenly flooded with memories.

"Come with me," she had said. Abuelita took Val's five-year-old hand and brought her into her bedroom, to the little table that held her shrine to the Virgin Mary. On the edge of the table were what looked like several little lumps of wood.

"Look closely, my granddaughter. What do you see?"

Val picked up a piece of wood and studied it, then laughed in delight. "It's a tiny burro, Abuelita." She looked at the others—people in robes, other animals, an angel, and a baby. "Where did they come from?"

"My papa, he made them for me long ago. It is the nativity, the birth of Jesus. This, Valerie, this is Navidad. No toys or presents, but this. It is love that makes us happy, not the things. Remember."

And Val had remembered, during the years that her mother gave them a used toy from Goodwill, or shot up their Christmas money, or told them that Santa wasn't coming because they'd been bad. Christmas had been sitting with Abuelita and feeling her love.

Val looked in her cart, at the soccer ball and toy truck, the doll and art set, the new clothes and books, and she stepped out of line. Pushing her cart back to the seasonal section of the store, she searched the holiday decorations until she found what she was looking for. The little white ceramic nativity set was perfect. She would set it up in the kids' bedroom, and tell them all about the first Christmas...and what was truly important.

❖

Today would be Val's first time going to court, and she was nervous. The kids' mom had been sentenced to three years in state prison, so today's permanency hearing was going to be critical. Paige had already told her that the biological fathers were not being considered as guardians, as one was in jail and the other had signed away his rights years before. But there was the matter of another relative that was still up in the air.

Val's stomach was in knots. Just this morning, Lily had told Val she loved her as she headed off to school, and Ian's sweet hugs made her day. She wanted these kids, and the uncertainty was eating her up.

"Where are you headed?" the deputy asked as Val put her keys and wallet in the bin at the security checkpoint.

"Family court." Val walked through the scanner, retrieved her items, and headed up the stairs of the old courthouse.

Paige was in the hallway outside the courtroom, talking to an older man in a suit. Val checked in with another deputy at the desk, then walked toward them.

Paige saw her and waved her over with a smile.

"Hi, Val. This is Jim McCrea, our attorney. Jim, meet Valerie Cruz, the foster parent in the case we were discussing."

"Ms. Cruz," he said, shaking her hand. Just then, the courtroom door opened, and the bailiff called them in.

The butterflies in Val's stomach flew around faster when she saw the bio mom, Kayla, sitting at a table wearing the county jail's orange and white striped jumpsuit. She turned around as Val was taking a seat and stared at her. Val could see the exact moment that recognition dawned, when Kayla's expression changed from disinterest to something so venomous that Val felt the chill. She looked away, shaken, wishing the floor would swallow her up. Anxiety was joined by irritation when she looked to her right and saw Lisa the Lawyer. Val's hands and teeth clenched in tandem—she had to close her eyes and will herself to breathe.

"All rise," the bailiff intoned. "The Honorable Judge Roy Foster presiding."

❖

Paige hadn't prepped Val ahead of time about today's hearing, and the look of trepidation on Val's face made Paige want to kick herself. She tried to focus as Jim McCrea outlined the case for the judge.

"Your Honor, Ms. Smith has been sentenced to three years on her DUI charge and violation of Leandra's Law, due to prior convictions for drug possession and prostitution. Due to the length of her sentence, custody of the minor children will need to be transferred. Ms. Smith informed the county that her aunt, Mrs. Sheryl Watkins of Rochester, New York, could be a potential placement for the children. We received word just this morning that Mrs. Watkins is willing to assume guardianship."

Paige heard an audible gasp behind her and turned. A succession of emotions, from shock to despair, showed on Val's face, and Paige felt a stab of guilt. She had told Val that she was required to seek out any known relatives, who would have rights of custody until and unless the children were in foster care for a year. They had only been with Val four months—she was going to lose the kids, and Paige felt responsible.

"Ms. Wellington," Judge Foster said, pulling Paige's attention back where it belonged, "what is the county's plan?"

"Your Honor, we will be conducting a background check and home study on Mrs. Watkins. If all is in order, transfer of the children will take place in approximately two to three weeks, and the county will close the case."

"Very well. Ms. Webster, do you have anything further?"

"Yes, Judge. As the children are unfamiliar with Mrs. Watkins, I am asking that visitation begin immediately."

Paige glanced back at Val and watched helplessly as she wiped away tear after tear. She looked heartbroken, and Paige knew exactly how she felt. Her own eyes began to burn, and she looked away.

"Ms. Smith, upon the county's approval, you will hereby relinquish custody of your children to Mrs. Watkins. Do you understand these terms?"

"Yes, sir," Kayla croaked out, head hanging.

"All right, then. This hearing is adjourned."

CHAPTER SEVENTEEN

Val walked quickly out of the courtroom, and Paige followed, desperate to know how Val was doing emotionally. She waited until they were outside before calling out.

"Val, wait."

Val stopped but didn't turn. Paige caught up and put her hand on Val's arm. "Are you okay?"

"Why didn't you tell me? I thought I could handle this, but…" Val stifled a sob with her hand.

"I'm sorry." *I never wanted to hurt you. Can you ever forgive me?*

"Visitation? They don't even know this woman. What about Christmas? Will they be with me?"

"I'm sure we could arrange that."

Val wiped her eyes with her sleeve. "This sucks."

"I know," Paige replied. "Will you be all right? I have to get back for a meeting, but…"

"I'm fine." Val looked anything but.

Paige squeezed her arm. "I'll call you later, okay?" She turned to go.

"Paige?"

"Yes?"

"How do I tell them?" Val's entire body telegraphed such pain, Paige nearly embraced her right in the middle of the sidewalk. "They're going to think I'm giving them up."

"I'll help, okay? We'll explain everything so they understand." Paige gave Val what she hoped was a reassuring smile.

Val nodded. "Okay." Paige pressed an arm to her roiling stomach as she watched Val slowly walk up the block to her car. She was sick over the whole damn situation, and she figured Val was feeling ten times worse.

And she'd thought this job would be easier to take than child protective. *That would be a big fat negative.*

❖

When Paige stepped off the elevator, she nearly ran into Connie.

"Hey, there. How did court go?"

Paige shook her head. "Val didn't take it well. I'm a little worried about her, actually."

Connie sighed. "Val is a passionate person. Whatever she feels, she feels deeply. Maybe I'll go check in on her after work."

"Would you? I don't know if she really wants to talk about it with me. I mean, it's my fault this happened," Paige said miserably.

"You've got to snap out of that mindset right now, Paige. You are doing your job. All we can do is our due diligence to make sure the children will be okay. You'll never please everybody, so quit blaming yourself. Got it?"

Paige smiled despite herself. "Yes, ma'am."

"Good. There's homemade cookies in the break room. Go eat one—you'll feel better."

"Thanks, Connie."

"You got it, kiddo."

Paige grabbed a cookie as ordered and went to her desk. She had plenty to do, but she couldn't get the image of Val's sad eyes out of her mind. With a sigh, she picked up the phone to call Sheryl Watkins about visitation.

"Mrs. Watkins? This is Paige Wellington from the foster care unit—we spoke this morning…Yes, the hearing is over, and I'll need to come out soon to conduct your home study. The law guardian for the children would like visitations to begin as soon as you are approved… No, I would transport them to you…Okay, you two discuss it, and I'll talk to you Monday?…Great, thanks. Good-bye."

Paige hung up the phone and put her head in her hands as a tear escaped down her cheek. She remembered how gut-wrenching it had been to send Emma off to visitations with strangers. She knew Val loved Lily and Ian and vowed to support her as much as she could. If Val would let her.

❖

Val jumped at the knock on her door. Her nerves had been shot all day, and she'd even snapped at Ian for forgetting his mittens at school. Now she felt even more terrible, if that was possible. When she opened the door, she was surprised to see her visitor.

"Connie. What are you doing here?"

"Great to see you, too, kiddo. Mind if I come in?"

"Of course not. Sorry." Val stepped aside, and Connie swept in, bringing a wave of cold air with her. The kids were on the couch watching TV, and they looked up to see who was here.

"Hi, kids," Connie said as she removed her coat. "What are you watching?"

"*The Adventures of Puss in Boots*," Lily announced.

"That's one crazy cat," Connie said, and the kids giggled.

Val took Connie's coat and motioned toward the kitchen. "Let's go sit in there. Want some tea?"

"I'd love some. It's freezing outside."

Val microwaved two mugs of water and set an assortment of tea bags on the table, along with sugar and honey. "So, what's up?" she said as she sat.

"I heard court was a little rough this morning," Connie said.

"Paige told you. Yeah, I was upset. Please don't say *I told you so*, because I really can't hear that right now." Val glanced over at the kids, but they seemed engrossed in their show. "I'm not telling them until after Christmas, okay? It's only a week away—Paige can wait that long before scheduling visitation, can't she?"

"Absolutely. Background checks and a home study need to be done first. Val," Connie said, reaching for her hand, "tell me how you're feeling about all this."

"I'm feeling like getting into foster parenting was stupid," Val replied, her voice low. "I didn't think about how I'd feel if they...you know," she said, glancing again at the kids. She pulled her hand away and stirred her tea a little too aggressively.

"You've been terrific with these kids, so it was not a stupid choice. Think of how far they've come because of you. That little lady didn't make things easy at first," Connie said, nodding in Lily's direction, "but you handled her like a pro."

"That's because she reminds me of myself. Our stories are so similar, it's scary."

"Then you were exactly what she needed."

Val swiped at her eyes as Lily came into the kitchen, and she tried to muster a smile. "Is your show over?"

"Yep. Can we get juice boxes?" Lily asked. Then she looked harder at Val, tilting her head. "Why are you crying?"

"Oh, we were just talking about something sad. It's okay," Val deflected. "How about you guys go play in your room now, so we can have our grown-up time to talk."

"Okay," Lily replied. She turned to leave, then came back and gave Val a hug. "Emma always gives me a hug when I'm sad, to make me feel better." Then off she went to the fridge to get juice boxes. "Come on, Ian. Let's go play."

Val barely held it together until the kids were out of earshot, but then her tears flowed freely. "How the hell am I going to tell them that they have to go live with strangers?"

"You just have to be honest. You tell them that their mom has to go to jail for a while because she made some bad decisions. You reassure them that they'll be okay, and that the people they're going to live with are part of their family. It won't be easy, Val, but you know how resilient kids are. They'll get through it."

"Yeah, but will I?" That sense of trepidation she'd always felt when she moved to a new place came rushing back, and Val felt like she was going to be sick. She stared into her tea.

"Yes, because you'll always know you gave them your best, and that it made them stronger." Connie tapped her finger firmly on the table. "Valerie, look at me." After a moment, Val complied and Connie continued, "You have had a huge impact on these children, and they on you. But your job is to help them through this, to be strong for them. You don't get to fall apart right now."

Val sat back in her chair and took a deep breath. "I know, Connie. I know."

Chapter Eighteen

Val trudged through the next day at work like a zombie. She'd barely slept the night before as every what-if imaginable ran through her worried mind. She'd put the kids to bed with two stories and extra hugs and kisses, trying not to let on that a big change was coming for them. When she was alone, though, the reality of the situation was eating her up inside.

Val and the kids had only been home for a few minutes when her phone beeped.

Have you guys eaten yet? read the text from Sasha.

Nope. Why? Val replied.

Bringing pizza. Be there in twenty.

Soon, Sasha and Jen came in bearing hot pizza and some cookies for the kids. Val gave them each a huge hug.

"I love you guys. I can't believe you drove all the way down here."

"It's only an hour. Besides, you never call me at work, so when you did, I figured you were due for some emergency pizza therapy."

Val laughed. "You are so right."

"Hey there, kiddos," Sasha said, giving Lily a hug and Ian an exploding fist bump. The kids had been around Sasha a couple of times before, and they loved her. The thought made Val want to cry. Lately, everything did.

They attacked the food until everyone was stuffed, then Jen took the kids to their room to play Uno so Val and Sasha could talk.

"So," Sasha said, plopping down on the couch, "fill me in."

Val sat on the other end of the couch, tucking her legs up underneath her. "I don't even know where to begin."

"Tell me about court."

Val related everything that had happened, including the fact that visitation would start in just a few days, right after Christmas. "I'm running out of time to figure out how to tell them. It's tearing me up, Sash."

"Man, this sucks. I don't know if it's better to be a little kid or an older one when they move you, but either way, all you can do is tell them the truth."

"I know. It's just that I'm worried about their reaction. Ian has finally started talking, even if it's just a few words here and there, and Lily has been so happy. She loves school and even has a best friend." Val felt a pang in her chest when she thought of Emma, which of course led to thoughts of Paige. "I'm afraid that this move will set them back."

"I know these guys are very special to you, Val. Maybe being a foster parent is like dating. The first breakup always seems to hurt the worst, right?"

Val snorted. "Maybe. Connie kept telling us in MAPP class that foster care was usually temporary and not to let ourselves think long term, but it is so hard when you really have a bond with the kids. I'm not gonna lie, Sasha—I love those two, and I want to protect them from the kinds of things you and I went through."

"You've always been very protective of kids, Val, and you're great with them. But in this situation, you've got to let go, or you'll drive yourself crazy. I guess you have to trust that the county is doing what's best."

"Yeah, well, trust and I haven't had the best relationship, and you know damn well the county doesn't always make the right call."

Sasha nodded, her usual smile gone. "I know that's true. But God, Val, what choice do you have?"

"None. I get that the goal is to keep families together, but why don't they realize that blood means nothing if there's no relationship there? I mean, this Sheryl woman is just as much a stranger to them as some random person on the street. But the kids haven't been here long enough to give me the right to petition for custody. I can't do a damn thing about any of this." Val felt her eyes burn with tears, and she dropped her head into her hands.

"Do you remember Mrs. Daley?" Sasha asked quietly.

Val looked up. "Yeah. Why?"

"We were only with her for five months before we moved to the farm, and I never saw her again. Did you?"

"No."

"But you know what? I still think about how kind she was, how she used to tell us that we could do and be anything in this life if we just believed in ourselves. In five months, she had a lifelong impact. You get me?"

Val couldn't hold back her tears. Moments later, she felt Sasha's arm around her shoulders. She tried to take a deep breath, but to her embarrassment, it came out as a sob.

"Listen to me, chica. What you've done for Lily and Ian has made a huge difference. You matter to them, and I bet you always will."

Val allowed herself to be held while she cried, but after a bit she pulled herself together. "I don't know why I thought this was a good idea, being a foster parent. Having the kids here, especially Lily, has brought up a lot of stuff that I thought I'd already dealt with."

"Yeah, I get it. For me, it's been my relationship with Jen. Before her, I think I was just duct taped together. I had to let her love me before I really started to heal," Sasha said. "I know it's not the same as what you're going through, but maybe we both just needed something big to happen to get us unstuck."

"If this is what healing feels like, I think I'd rather be stuck in my safe little solitary world."

"Solitary may be safe, but taking chances is what makes life worth living, my friend." Sasha stood up from the couch. "I'm going to go check on Jen and the kids."

Val watched Sasha walk away, her words reverberating in her head. She wondered if she would ever again be brave enough to take a chance. Then her mind brought her an image of laughing blue eyes and a gentle smile. Paige.

CHAPTER NINETEEN

Christmas Eve dawned sunny and cold. Val sat sipping her coffee, thinking through her plans. Soon she would wake the kids up, take them out to breakfast, then begin a day full of surprises. The next few days would be bittersweet, but she was determined to be upbeat and positive for Lily and Ian.

Val showered and dressed, then went into the kids' room. Lily was buried under the covers, the comforter over her head. Val pulled it back and smiled when Lily groaned, squinting against the light.

"Morning, sunshine. Time to get up. Got a big day ahead."

"We do?" Lily said, sitting up and rubbing her eyes.

"Yep. It's Christmas Eve."

Lily bounded out of bed at that, making Val laugh. She sat on the edge of Ian's bed. "Time to get up, buddy." He climbed into her lap, his warm, sleepy body snuggling in for a hug. Val felt tears threaten, but she fought them back.

"Mornin'," he mumbled, hopping down.

Val sent the kids off to use the bathroom and brush their teeth while she picked out warm clothes for them to wear. Half an hour later, they were in the car on the way to Denny's.

After a breakfast of chocolate chip pancakes, Val put the kids in the car, then retrieved a large shopping bag from the trunk. Getting behind the wheel, she passed the bag to Lily.

"Why don't you check out what's in there," she said as she started the car. The Christmas station was on the radio, and the Carpenters' version of "Christmas Song" filled the car. Lily pulled out a pink, squishy garment while Ian grabbed a large blue plastic disk.

"Um, what is it?" Lily asked. Then comprehension dawned. "Ian, that's a sled." Lily held up the garment. "And these are snow pants."

"That's right," Val said. "Figured they'd come in handy since we're going sledding."

Lily squealed, and Ian's chocolate-chippy grin spread ear to ear. Val drove to the large sledding hill in the park. At just after ten, the parking lot was mostly empty. The kids would have the hill to themselves for a little while. Val helped them bundle up in their snow pants, mittens, and hats, then let them go. She watched as Lily helped Ian trudge up the hill and get on his sled, and then gave him a push.

Val used her phone to take picture after picture of Ian's wide-eyed excitement and Lily's flush-faced grins. They were making memories, and Val's heart was full. After an hour of fun, the kids were sweaty and tired from climbing the hill.

"Did you have fun?" Val asked as they headed for the car. Ian nodded vigorously.

"That was awesome," Lily said. "I want to go again soon. Can we bring Emma?"

Swallowing hard, Val forced a smile. "Maybe, kiddo." Just like that, she was hit with her impending loss. She was going to lose the kids, and once they were gone, Paige probably would be, too. Life was just reminding her that getting close to people wasn't worth the heartache. That was the well-worn mantra she'd lived by for years, wasn't it? But as she looked at Lily and Ian, she realized how much had changed. Every single minute with the kids, and with Paige, had been worth it.

Back at home, Val had the kids take a warm shower, then they all had a mug of hot cocoa with marshmallows. Afterward, they plopped on the couch to watch *Rudolph the Red-Nosed Reindeer*, her favorite Christmas cartoon. As the show began, Lily laid her head on Val's shoulder with a sigh.

"This is the best day ever," she said.

Val put an arm around her and hugged her close. "Yes, it is," she whispered, placing a kiss on the top of Lily's head.

God, please help me get through this.

❖

Though trying valiantly to stay awake, Lily and Ian could hardly keep their eyes open. Val had taken them out again at dinnertime for hot dogs at Heid's, then to Lights on the Lake. The kids had oohed and aahed over all the light sculptures, and Ian had talked more than she'd ever heard him, pointing out all the things he was seeing. Back at home, they had stayed up playing Uno and watching Christmas shows. Val had shown them NORAD's Santa Tracker on her laptop, which had sparked a spirited discussion about how Santa managed to bring presents to the whole world in one night.

"All right, kiddos, time for bed. Santa won't come until you're sleeping."

"Do you really think Santa will find us? He didn't come last year because we moved, and now we're in another place again." Lily's worried eyes shone with unshed tears, and Ian stared at the floor, his bottom lip quivering.

Val pulled them close. "I absolutely know he's coming. A little elf friend of mine told me so."

"You know an elf?" Ian said, eyes wide.

"Yep, since I was a kid. He only lets me see him, though, once a year at Christmastime." Val ruffled his hair, then kissed the top of his head. "You need to get to sleep now, young man. You, too, Lil."

Val tucked the kids in, switched on their night-light, and quietly walked to the door. Just before she closed it, Lily murmured, "'Night, Mama."

Ouch. "Good night, little one. Sweet dreams."

Val went to her room and pulled their already wrapped Christmas gifts from the closet. She waited until she was sure the kids were asleep, then placed the packages beneath the little tree they'd set up in the living room. She straightened and stood looking at the half dozen ornaments the kids had made in school, hung front and center on the tree. Val's heart ached, and the strain of keeping up the excitement for the kids' sake had taken its toll. A wave of pain washed over her as she slipped into bed, and she cried herself to sleep.

Chapter Twenty

The week after Christmas had been a busy one for Paige so far. She'd made phone calls, answered emails, gone on home visits, and gotten two new cases. She managed to postpone until Thursday afternoon the one contact she really didn't want to make, but she couldn't put it off any longer. She took a deep breath and let it out slowly, then placed the call.

"Hello?"

"Hi, Val…it's Paige."

"Oh, hi. How are you?"

Not much better than you're about to be. "Good. How was Christmas with the kids?"

"Great." Paige could hear the smile in Val's voice as she answered. "They were so excited." Just as quickly, she heard Val's smile disappear. "I'm so glad I could give them that," she said quietly.

"Me, too." Paige cleared her throat, hesitating. *Just do your job.* "Listen, Val, I have to arrange the first visit with Sheryl Watkins. I was thinking Tuesday. Would that be okay?"

"I haven't told them yet." Val's voice suddenly sounded very small.

Oh, honey. "Do you want me to be there when you do?" Paige asked.

"I don't know. I mean, have you ever done that before for anyone else?"

You're not just anyone else. "Well, no, but I know it's going to be a tough conversation, and I can be there for moral support." Val was silent, and Paige could imagine the internal battle taking place on the other end of the line.

Finally, Val replied, "I think I would like you to be there." She sounded so vulnerable, Paige wanted to run to her right then. A flicker of hope warmed Paige's heart. *She isn't pushing me away.*

"Okay. I could come over tomorrow afternoon or Monday."

"Maybe Monday, so they don't have too much time to think about it. Hey, you met her, right?" Val asked.

"Sheryl? Yes, I did her home study."

"Can you tell me about her?"

Paige completely understood Val's need to know. "Well, she's in her early fifties and seemed very nice. The house was clean, and she has a cat. She told me how she used to see Kayla a lot when she was young, but there had been a falling out between her and Kayla's parents. She'd had no idea that Kayla's life had spiraled out of control, or even that she had children. But she seemed willing to help."

"Is she married?"

"Yes, but her husband was at work, so I didn't get the chance to meet him." Val was silent for so long, Paige thought the call had dropped. "Val?"

"I'm here."

"Listen, I know this is hard, but it's important to make the transition as smooth as possible for the children. I have every reason to think that they'll be fine. Okay?"

"Yeah," Val said, her voice gruff. "Guess I'll see you Monday, then."

"Yes. I'll be there by three thirty. Have a good night, Val."

"I'll try. Thanks, Paige."

"No problem. Bye." Paige held her ear to the phone long after Val ended the call, feeling miserable. The proximity of her coworkers seemed to close in on her as she willed herself not to cry. As difficult as her job was sometimes, Paige knew without a doubt that she'd never struggled this much. Paige could no longer deny why this case felt so personal.

❖

Val's stomach felt like she'd swallowed a beehive, and it was all she could do not to throw up as she headed home from work. Linda had thankfully sensed her mood and left her alone all day, rather than bombarding her with the usual chatter. The kids would be getting off the bus just a few minutes before Paige arrived, and then they'd have to do it. She still had no idea how to tell Lily and Ian that they had to leave.

Val parked in the driveway and had just gotten her key in the front door when Paige pulled in behind her. She stepped out of her car, looking stunning and sophisticated in a long gray wool coat accented by a burgundy scarf and gloves. Her golden hair was loose, a slight breeze moving it against her cheeks. She looked up at Val, and the compassion in her eyes nearly made Val crumble right there on her front step.

"Hey," Paige said, raising her gloved hand in a wave as she approached. "You okay?"

"Not even a little bit," Val replied with a shaky smile. "Come on in."

They removed their coats and sat at the kitchen table. Paige was quiet, which was exactly what Val needed to get herself together. Finally, Val looked at her and sighed. "I'm not gonna lie, Paige. I have no idea how I'm going to do this. Do other foster parents have such a hard time when kids leave?"

"Sometimes, depending on how long the kids were with them and how strong a bond they developed. Maybe it's harder for you because you've been on the other side of it."

"Yeah. I've definitely been remembering stuff I haven't thought about in a long time." Val fidgeted with her eagle pendant, the cool silver grounding her. "My grandmother used to tell me and my brother how strong we were, how she believed our lives would turn out okay. Guess she was right about me. I really hope my brother is doing okay, too. Wish I knew."

"If he's anything like you, I'm sure he's fine," Paige replied. Val looked at Paige's lovely face and saw genuine kindness and concern, and she didn't know what to do with that. She generally didn't trust such platitudes from others, no matter how well meant. She usually felt that people were simply trivializing her concerns or had their own agenda. But something about Paige made her believe she truly cared, and that was enough to make all her red flags stand up and wave.

Outside, the brakes of the school bus squealed, signaling that the kids had arrived home. Val went to the door to greet them, and she felt the hot sting of tears as she watched Lily take Ian's mittened hand and walk him across the road. Once safely across, they broke into a run, all rosy-cheeked youthful exuberance, and nearly tackled Val with hugs.

"Hey, guys. How was your day?" Val asked, somehow summoning cheerfulness. Ian gave her a grin and a thumbs-up. Lily launched into her daily chatter about life in third grade as she removed her coat and boots.

"We had a sub today, and the boys were bad. We all had to miss ten minutes of recess," she said indignantly. "Oh, and I got an A on my math test, and Sadie's still out with the flu." Lily walked into the kitchen and stopped dead in her tracks at the sight of Paige.

"Hi, Lily. Hi, Ian," she said with a smile.

"Hi. Where's Emma?" Lily asked.

"She's at her Brownie meeting. She goes to Mrs. Wallace's room after school."

"Oh, yeah."

"Miss Paige is here to talk to us. Why don't you go put your backpacks in your room while I get you a snack?" Val watched as they scampered down the hall, then she abruptly turned and went to get some animal crackers, banging the cupboard door a little too hard in the process.

"Val, just breathe," Paige said behind her. "I'll do all the talking, okay?"

Paige sipped from her bottle of water as the kids ate their snack, going over in her mind what she would say. When they were done, she glanced at Val, who was standing behind Ian's chair, then smiled at the kids.

"Okay, guys, I came over today because I've got some news." Ian fiddled with the straw in his juice box, but Lily stared at her, waiting, and Paige smiled. "You have a family member who would like to meet you."

"A family member?" Lily said, frowning.

"Yep. Her name is Sheryl, and she's your mom's aunt, so that makes her your great-aunt."

"We don't know her," Lily said. "Why does she want to meet us?"

"Well, you know your mom got into some trouble, right?" At this, Ian's gaze snapped up. "She won't be able to come home for a while, so Aunt Sheryl wants to make sure you have family around to be there for you."

"Oh." Lily eyes traveled to Val, then Ian, then back to Paige. "When do we have to meet her?"

"I can pick you up early from school tomorrow, and we'll go to her house," Paige replied. "She's very excited to meet you."

"Where does she live?"

"In a place called Victor, outside of Rochester. It's about an hour and a half from here."

"That's far," Lily said. "We can't go that far on a school night, right, Mama?" Lily looked at Val, and Paige watched as Val gripped the back of Ian's chair so hard her knuckles turned white, giving away the tremendous effort it took for her to muster an encouraging smile.

"It's okay, kiddo. You'll be home in time for bed."

Lily thought about it for a few moments, then shrugged. "Okay." Ian looked at his sister, then nodded.

"Go on back to your room and do your homework while I talk some more with Miss Paige, okay?" Val said.

"C'mon, Ian," Lily said, and off they went.

Val sat down heavily in the chair Ian had vacated. "That went better than I expected," she said. "Thank you."

"You're welcome. That Lily is a smart one, huh?" Paige said.

"Yes. That's exactly what I'm afraid of. She's going to figure out what's going on, and I don't know how she'll react."

"Guess we'll find out," Paige replied. She reached out and put a hand on Val's arm. "You did great, by the way."

"It's going to get a lot harder, and soon. I remember when I left my first foster home to go to another one. They had to drag me to the car, kicking and screaming. Lily's a lot like I was—what if she reacts that way?" Val looked up at Paige, and tears tracked slowly down her cheek.

"We'll just have to do our best to prepare her. That's all we can do." Paige ran her thumb up and down the soft cotton of Val's shirtsleeve, then gave her arm a squeeze and reluctantly removed her hand. The emotion on Val's face was so raw that Paige wanted to gather her in her arms and not let go. She needed to leave before she crossed that line.

Clearing her throat, she stood up and grabbed her purse off the counter. She pulled out a folded paper and a pen.

"I need you to sign this transport form. I'll bring it to school when I pick up the kids tomorrow. The visit will be four hours, so I should have them back between seven and eight."

"Okay," Val said, picking up the pen. She scribbled her signature and gave the paper back. "Are you going to stay with them the whole time?"

"Just the first hour or so, until they settle in. Val, listen. I know you're going to worry, but it'll be okay."

"That's what you keep telling me." Val softened her words with a small smile.

"I've got to go pick up Emma. See you later." Paige put on her coat and walked to the door. Val opened it and stood there, her shadowed eyes revealing her exhaustion. "Good night, Val."

"'Night."

As Paige drove home, she thought about the numerous situations she'd been in with other foster parents, when it was no problem for her to keep her professional distance. For the umpteenth time, she contemplated what it was about Valerie Cruz that affected her so deeply. She was attracted to her, of course, but it was more than that. Paige yearned to know everything about her, to soothe her pain, to make her laugh, to show her how special she was. She wondered if she'd ever get the chance.

Chapter Twenty-one

The next visit was to be an overnight, and all day Val was painfully aware that the kids wouldn't be there after school. At lunchtime, she was surprised to receive a phone call from Connie.

"Hey there, kiddo. Mind if I stop over after work for a bit?"

"Um..." Val hesitated. She was not in the mood to be social.

"There's chocolate involved," Connie teased.

Val chuckled. Maybe she could use a visit of the Connie variety. "Okay. What time?"

"How's four o'clock sound?"

"Good. Guess I'll see you later, then," Val replied.

"Ta-ta for now," Connie chirped cheerfully.

At precisely four, Val's doorbell rang. She opened the door to a smiling Connie, bearing an unmistakable box from the Chocolate Pizza Factory. She took the box and groaned as Connie removed her coat.

"If you bring these on all your visits, you're invited weekly," Val said, gazing at the confectionery masterpiece.

"Ha. I just happened to be near their store the other day and remembered the first time you and I ever tried one," Connie said.

"Oh, yeah. You came out to the farm to see Sasha and me, and Leigh had given it to us as an early graduation gift. We ate it all in one day."

"And got a little sick, if I recall."

"Totally worth it," Val said with a grin.

"Well, break that thing open. We'll have a bite and chat," Connie said.

Val got them each a generous piece of chocolate pizza and a bottle of water, then joined Connie at the table.

Connie savored her first bite of chocolate, toffee, and almonds, then got down to business. "So how are you doing, Val?"

"Right this second, or in general?"

Connie gave her a look, and Val smiled. "I'm all right."

"How are the kids handling their visits?"

Val shrugged. "They seem to be okay. Lily came home last time and told me that they'd gotten Happy Meals, watched a movie, and played with Sheryl's cat. She didn't act upset or anything. Neither did Ian, although I don't know how they'll handle staying overnight. Ian likes our little bedtime routine."

Connie just looked at Val and sipped her water, and Val could feel her tension growing under the scrutiny. She ran a hand under her hair to rub the back of her neck.

"You're stressed and upset," Connie said matter-of-factly.

Val rolled her eyes. "And you know this how?"

"You always rub your neck when you're stressed and upset," Connie replied. "So tell me, how are you really doing?"

Val knew she couldn't hide from Connie's apparent mind reading powers, so she didn't bother trying. "To be honest, things just suck right now." Connie nodded but didn't reply, another habit that drove Val crazy, since it was usually followed by Val spilling her guts. "I know you told me not to get attached, but damn, Connie, it was impossible."

"Yes, it can be difficult," Connie agreed. She looked at Val with a little tilt to her head, like she was trying to figure something out. "I was just telling Paige earlier how important a good night's rest is for one's mental health."

Val perked up at the mention of Paige's name. "Um, okay, random statement."

"Not random at all. I told her and I'll tell you, too, because neither one of you looks like you've slept in days."

Paige wasn't sleeping either? "What did she say?"

"That she had a lot on her mind," Connie replied. "She's worried about you."

The tiny surge of happiness Val felt wrestled with her deep-seated defensiveness. "What for? I'm sure she's got plenty of better things to do than worry about me."

Connie had a way of raising an eyebrow at a person and making them feel like they didn't have a freaking clue. "Uh-huh," she said. "So anyway, back to you. You aren't sleeping, are you?"

"Not well," Val said. She appreciated the concern in Connie's eyes, but at the same time, it made her look away. She rolled her water bottle between her hands for a few moments as the feelings surfaced. "I've been having nightmares again."

"Oh, honey," Connie said. "Same as before?" Val nodded. "Were you having them before you got the kids?"

"Hardly at all, actually," Val said. "I don't get it. I really thought all that crap was behind me."

"I'm not surprised at all. I was worried that foster parenting might trigger some things for you," Connie said.

"Then why'd you encourage me to do it?" Val said, her voice tinged with anger.

"Because I also know how strong you are, and what you have to offer far outweighs any bad memories you might have."

Val softened at Connie's words. "Sorry."

"You've done a great job with those kids, and they're better for it. Maybe you bonded so strongly because of the parallels between their story and your own," Connie said.

Val nodded. "It's unbelievable how much Lily is like me. Our stories really are similar, except for the part where the brother and sister get to stay together." Tears pooled, and Val finally let them go.

"And hopefully, the part where the kids are stuck in the system until they're eighteen."

"I know, Connie," Val said, wiping her eyes. "It just sucks."

"You did mention that," Connie said sweetly, and Val smiled in spite of herself.

"Well, I'm going to get out of here and leave you to your evening. Got any plans?" Connie asked, rising from the table.

"Sasha's supposed to come down later. Jen's at a training, so we thought we'd hang out and binge watch *Game of Thrones* or something."

"Excellent. So listen, one more thing." Connie put on her coat, then laid her hand on Val's shoulder. "Remember Dr. Susan Brown?"

"My old therapist?"

"She's younger than me," Connie teased, "and she happens to still be in practice. Her office is on Seneca Street."

"I'm not a kid anymore, Connie. I don't have to go talk to anyone," Val said.

"Oh my God, there's an age limit for therapy? There's at least twenty adult therapists in this town alone. I don't think they got the memo," Connie said in a stage whisper.

"Stop," Val said, laughing.

"It's just a thought, Val. Now I've got to get home. Peter and I are going to the casino to play late-night bingo later, and this old lady needs a nap first."

"Have fun. And Connie, thanks for coming over to check on me," Val said.

"You're welcome, sweetheart," Connie responded with one of her rib-bruising hugs.

"Bye," Val called, as Connie walked to her car. "You two kids behave yourselves tonight. I've heard stories about those crazy bingo players."

"I have no intention of behaving myself. Life's too short," Connie replied, with a toss of her fiery hair. She drove off in her bright blue Mini Cooper, leaving Val shaking her head and grinning.

❖

After four episodes, Val and Sasha decided that there were only so many hours of *Game of Thrones* a person could tolerate in one sitting. Val turned off the TV, stood up, and went to the kitchen. She felt restless and off-kilter without the kids. She kept wanting to peek in on them, except they weren't there. Their nighttime routine had become such a pleasant way to end her days that she didn't know what to do with herself now.

"Need anything?" she asked.

"Nah, I'm good," Sasha replied. "I'm still full from dinner."

"So, Connie stopped by today," Val said, opening her third bottle of the Mike's Hard Lemonade Sasha had brought and plopping back down on the couch. "Checking up on me."

"Let me guess—her freaky sixth sense told her you were upset."

"You're dead-on, woman. Talking to her helped, though." Val sipped her drink. "She suggested I go back to the therapist I used to see in high school."

"Oh, yeah? Why?"

"I've been having nightmares again, like, a lot."

"Oh, man, that bites. You used to seriously scare the hell out of me when you'd wake up screaming. Are they bad like that?"

"Yeah. I had one the first night the kids were here, and they've been happening ever since."

Sasha whistled. "I'm sorry. Do you remember them?"

"Kind of," Val replied. "There's one where someone's chasing me through a house, and they find me hiding in a closet. Sometimes it's someone holding me down so I can't move. I always wake up right before...well, before something happens to me."

"Are they memories? I mean, did that stuff actually happen?" Sasha asked.

"I think maybe. Dr. Brown, the therapist, was starting to go there with me, but I quit going to see her. She was freaking me out. I mean, if my mind doesn't want to remember stuff, there must be a reason."

"Or maybe your dreams are trying to tell you something," Sasha said. "Maybe if you figured them out, they'd stop."

"I don't know, but I'm so tired. Maybe this stuff will help me sleep tonight," Val said, holding up her bottle.

"Temporary fix. Maybe you should give the therapy thing another try," Sasha said.

"Maybe."

"What time are the kids supposed to be back?"

"By noon," Val replied, yawning.

"That's in ten hours. Better get some sleep."

"You want to crash in Lily's bed?" Val asked.

"Actually, I really like this couch. All I need is a blanket."

Val retrieved a fleece stadium blanket from her closet and brought it to Sasha. "Here you go. I put a new toothbrush on the bathroom sink for you."

"Thanks, chica."

"Thank you for keeping me company tonight, Sash. I really appreciate it."

Sasha stood and gave Val a hug. "How many times have you been there when I've needed you? I'm happy to return the favor." Sasha held Val at arm's length. "You're probably the strongest person I know, and I love you. Now go get some sleep."

Val wiped her eyes. "Why'd you have to go and get all sappy on me? Love you, too. G'night." Val went to her room and dropped into bed. Cuddling under the covers, she thought about how blessed she was to have Sasha and Connie in her life. Then Paige came to mind, the image of her gentle smile soothing Val's frayed edges. Concentrating on that vision, she prayed for a few hours of sweet, dreamless oblivion.

Chapter Twenty-two

Paige looked in the rearview mirror at the children in the back seat. Ian had fallen asleep, surprisingly, as it was only ten in the morning. Lily was quiet, just staring out the window. Paige was annoyed at Sheryl Watkins, who had asked when the kids were moving in, loudly enough for Lily to hear. She knew Val hadn't explained to them yet that they'd be moving to Sheryl's home, and she was afraid the cat was prematurely out of the bag.

"You okay back there, Lily?"

The girl simply nodded, her gaze never wavering from the scenery speeding by outside. *Not good. So not good.*

An hour later, Paige pulled up to Val's house but had to park at the curb. A dark green Jeep was in the driveway behind Val's car. Paige was forty-five minutes earlier than she'd expected to be—what if Val was entertaining someone? A hot rush of jealousy hit Paige, taking her by surprise. *Jump to conclusions much? Good God, get a grip.*

As Paige was getting the kids out of the car, the front door opened and someone emerged. She let out a sigh of relief when she recognized Val's best friend she'd met once in the club. She was tall and fit, with close-cropped hair, and a dazzling smile spread across her face when she saw the kids.

"Sasha!" Lily took off running and tackled the woman.

"Hey, Lily Pad, how are the frogs jumping?"

"You know I don't have any frogs, goofball," Lily replied, grinning.

Paige walked up to the door with a sleepy Ian, who was clutching Coqui.

"But Ian does. Hey, little man." Sasha squatted down and gave the boy a gentle hug. Paige looked up to see Val in the doorway, watching the scene with a sad smile on her face. Sasha stood up and smiled at Paige, offering her hand.

"Hi. You're Paige, right?"

Paige shook Sasha's hand. "I am. Good to see you again."

"You, too." Sasha turned to Val. "Call me tomorrow, chica, or sooner if you need to."

"Okay," Val said. "Bye, and thanks again." Then she bent to the kids, who had climbed the front steps, and encircled them both in a hug. "Hi, guys. Missed you." Lily clung to her, and Val looked at Paige, a question in her eyes.

Paige nodded toward the house. "Let me just pull into the driveway. I'll be right in."

When she entered the house, Val was helping Ian out of his jacket. His cheeks were flushed, and he was dragging. "You feeling okay, buddy?" Ian didn't respond. Val put her hand on his forehead, then looked up at Paige. "He feels hot."

"Do you have a thermometer?" Paige said.

"No, I never bought one. I'm going to have to go down to the drug-store." She rubbed the back of her neck. "Lily, we need to go back out."

"Val, you stay with the kids. I'll go. Be right back."

Val's shoulders sagged in relief. "Thank you."

"No worries. See if you can get him to drink some water." Paige went back out to her car and drove the two miles to the store. She picked up a digital thermometer, some children's ibuprofen, and a large bottle of orange Gatorade. Emma always drank that when she was sick.

Back at the house, Val had Ian on the couch, propped up on pillows with a blanket tucked around him. Lily was standing nearby, her face a mask of worry. Paige put her purchases down in the kitchen, removed the thermometer's packaging, and brought it to Val. Ian moaned when she put it in his ear.

"Holy—" Val bit back the cuss word. "It's 103.2."

"Oh, poor little guy," Paige replied. "Might be the flu." She went into the kitchen and measured out some ibuprofen. "Here, give him this. I think Urgent Care is open until five, if you want to take him. I can hang out here with Lily until you get back."

"Paige, I'm pretty sure that's way outside your job description."

"I'm off the clock. Right now, I'll just be a friend who wants to help out. Emma is at a Brownies sleepover, and I don't need to pick her up until four." Paige touched Val's shoulder. "It's fine. Go."

"I owe you big-time," Val said, as she bundled Ian up in the blanket.

"Where are you going, Mama?" Lily said.

"I need to take your brother to the doctor. He's not feeling so good."

"I want to go with you," she whined.

"No, honey. You need to stay here with Miss Paige."

"But I want to be with you," Lily insisted, her voice getting louder.

"I bet you're hungry, Lily. How about I make us some lunch?" Paige looked at Val, who nodded her approval.

Lily looked back and forth between them, then relented. "I guess. Can I have peanut butter and Fluff?" Lily said.

"Sure. Why don't you get everything we need, and I'll be right back." Paige nudged Val out the door before Lily could change her mind. Outside, Val got Ian buckled in his seat and closed the car door.

"How did this fever come on so fast? Didn't anyone notice he was sick at the visit?" Val said.

"Sheryl didn't mention anything. Ian was quiet when I picked them up, but that's not unusual. I did think it was strange that he was so tired at this time of day—he slept all the way back. If it's the flu, it would make sense."

Val blew out a breath. "Okay, well, thanks again for…being a friend."

She looked so vulnerable that Paige couldn't stop herself from hugging Val. She held her closely enough to smell the warm coconut scent of her hair, and long enough to feel Val tense, then relax. A muffled spate of coughing came from the back seat, and Val jumped.

"Go," Paige said. "Be careful, and I'll see you soon."

Val held her eyes for a moment, a parade of emotions crossing her face, then nodded and got in the car.

Paige watched her drive away, her feelings in a jumble. She told herself it was not unusual to do what she was doing, that she offered to stay because Val didn't have anyone else in town to help her. A professional courtesy, that was all. And for a second there, she almost believed it.

❖

"Where's Emma?" Lily asked when she'd finished her sandwich.

"She's with her Brownie troop. They had their first sleepover last night," Paige replied.

"That sounds fun." Lily was quiet for several moments, then said, "Can I tell you something?"

"Of course, sweetie," Paige replied.

Lily hesitated, then blurted, "Aunt Sheryl says she wants us to live with her."

Shit, shit, shit. Paige did not want to have this conversation without Val here.

"Um, that's nice."

"I thought about it, and I want to live here with Mama. Then I can join Brownies with Emma, right?"

Aw, hell. "Well, honey, I think your mom wants you to be with family, and the judge agrees."

"What's a judge?"

"He's someone who helps decide where kids like you and your brother will live if they can't be with their parents," Paige replied, growing more nervous by the second.

Lily cocked her head to the side, as if in deep thought. After a moment, she said, "Family is people who love you, right?"

"Yes, that's right."

"Then we already are with family, so I'll just tell the judge that I want to live here."

Lily's determined little face made Paige's heart sink. "Well, I guess we can talk more about it later, because we need to clean up our lunch plates." *Weak deflection, Wellington.* Thankfully, Lily let the topic drop and helped tidy up.

"Can I go watch TV now?" Lily said.

"Sure." Paige sat at the kitchen table, her mind racing. How in the hell was she going to convince Lily, and how would Val handle it if she couldn't? The last thing any of them needed was a traumatic good-bye.

Chapter Twenty-three

Paige was having a hell of a time getting her head into work mode Monday morning. She stared at her calendar, wishing that her entire afternoon would not have to be spent in court. She had a ton to do at her desk. *And none of it is going away if you don't start.* Deciding that she needed just one more excuse to ignore her paperwork for a while longer, she picked up the phone and called Val.

"Hello?"

"Hey, Val, it's Paige. Just calling to check in on Ian. Did the Tamiflu work?"

"Yeah. His fever's down below a hundred, and he actually wanted to get up and play this morning."

Val's voice sounded gravelly and exhausted. "That's good news. Hey, are you okay? You're not getting sick, too, are you?"

"Nah, just tired. Haven't been sleeping well."

Val didn't offer more, and Paige didn't press. Of course Val wasn't sleeping. This whole situation with the kids was hitting her hard. Worrying about Val—hell, just thinking about Val—was what kept Paige up at night. "Will Ian go back to school tomorrow?"

"Hopefully."

"Okay, well, let me know if you need anything," Paige said.

"Will do. Thanks."

"Bye," Paige said, but Val had already disconnected.

Val hadn't just sounded tired. Her voice seemed flat, dull, defeated. And she couldn't do a damn thing to take away her pain. Knowing this train of thought would likely derail her whole day, Paige tried to shake the concern about Val from her head by attacking her email. The fifth one down made her stomach drop—it was from Sheryl Watkins. She hesitated, then clicked to open it.

> *Ms. Wellington,*
> *My husband is going on a business trip next week, and I thought that would be the perfect time to get the children moved in and settled. I'd like them on Monday. Please confirm that this is doable.*
> *Sheryl Watkins*

Paige sighed. This was exactly the outcome that she hoped for in all her cases. She should be happy, but instead, her chest felt heavy with discontent. Connie's voice rang out in laughter down the hall, and Paige jumped up to intercept her.

"Morning, Connie," she greeted.

"Paige, hi. You have to come to the break room. Joe brought Krispy Kremes." Paige smiled and followed Connie to where Joe was laying out three boxes of the doughnuts and a stack of napkins.

"Joe, I'd marry you if I didn't think Charlie would kick my ass," Connie gushed, eying the doughnuts with pastry lust.

Joe laughed. "Doughnuts do not make a marriage, sweetheart."

Connie rolled her eyes. "Don't I know it. Still, I'd give it a go."

"Tell you what. Whenever you need a Krispy Kreme fix, just let me know. No commitment required."

"You're on, big guy." Joe laughed again, high-fived Connie's upraised hand, and left.

"You two are a riot, you know," Paige said, grinning.

"Well, somebody's got to be the comic relief around here. So, what's eating at you this morning?" Connie selected a chocolate glazed and sat down at the table.

"How do you know something's eating at me?" Paige said. Connie just leveled her with a look that said, *Girl, please.* Paige rolled her eyes and sat down. "Right. It's your superpower."

"So?" Connie said through a mouthful of doughnut.

"I received an email from Sheryl Watkins. She wants Lily and Ian to move in on Monday."

Connie nodded. "Have they had their overnight visit?"

"Yes, this past weekend. When I brought them back, I ended up staying at Val's for a while." At Connie's raised eyebrow, she hurried to explain. "Ian had spiked a high fever, so I stayed with Lily while Val took him to Urgent Care. Poor little man had the flu."

"Oh, no. Nasty strain of it this year," Connie said.

"So I've heard. He's better now, but anyway, Lily told me something that's got me concerned. She said Mrs. Watkins told the kids she wanted them to come live with her."

"And?"

"Lily has made up her mind that she wants to stay with Val. I explained that her mother wanted them to be with family, and she said, *Family is people who love you, so I'll tell the judge I want to stay here.*"

"Hmm," Connie replied, her brow furrowed. "She's a smart one, that Lily. Did you tell Val?"

Paige felt her face flush with embarrassment. "No. She was so caught up in caring for Ian, I didn't want to lay that on her, too."

Connie nodded. "This may be a tough transition."

"Val's already upset about losing the kids. If it's a difficult separation, I'm worried about how she'll react."

"Unfortunately, this falls under the lousy category of our job, but my experience tells me that they'll adjust. You have to be careful that you don't get too emotionally involved, Paige."

That fucking ship had sailed. "I know. It's just—"

"Hard. I get it. Listen, honey, I know you care about Val. As cold as this may sound, you just have to do your job. I'll make sure Val's okay." Connie's kind eyes softened the words.

Paige fought the sudden sting of tears. "Right. Okay. I've got court all afternoon, so I'll talk to Val tomorrow."

"Good plan." Connie stood and threw away her napkin. As she headed to the door, she turned. "Listen, kiddo—I won't say this gets easier, but you will get better at dealing with it."

Paige shrugged. "Huh. Wish I had your confidence."

"You've got a big heart, which is a blessing and a curse in this business. The trick is to try and keep everything in perspective," Connie said.

"I'll work on it," Paige replied.

"I know." Connie left and shut the door behind her.

Paige sat alone, staring at the table. For a second, she seriously considered putting herself into a Krispy Kreme coma, but thankfully, the impulse to stuff her face with sugar passed. With a shake of her head, Paige stood. *Come on, Wellington. You've got work to do.*

❖

There was no answer when Paige called Val's cell the next morning. Figuring she'd gone back to work, she dialed the library and was transferred to her number.

"Children's section, Linda speaking. May I help you?"

"Hi, Linda. This is Paige Wellington from the county foster care unit. May I speak to Valerie?"

"Oh, sorry. Val isn't working today. Is there something I can help you with?"

"No, thanks. I need to speak with her. I tried her cell but she didn't answer," Paige said.

"Actually," Linda said, her voice dropping conspiratorially, "she texted me early this morning and said she was calling in sick. She's never done that once since I've known her."

"I see. Thank you. I'll try her cell again in a little bit."

Paige did try twice more, with no luck. By lunchtime, she was worried. "Janet, I'm going out for lunch, if anyone is looking for me," she called to the receptionist as she left the office. She drove over to Val's house, her stomach in knots.

Val's car was in the driveway. Paige knocked on the front door once, then again. No answer. She knocked a third time, long and loud. Finally, she heard the lock click. The door opened slowly, and Paige gasped.

Val looked like a ghost. Her normally glossy hair hung lifelessly, and her skin was gray. She stood unsteadily in old sweats and a T-shirt, her arms crossed as she shivered. She could barely open her eyes, and Paige could feel the heat pouring off her as she grasped her upper arm.

"Oh my God, Val. You don't look so good."

"Must be why I feel like roadkill," Val rasped.

Paige sprang into action. She got Val to the couch, where it appeared she'd already been lying. Looking around, she spotted the thermometer on the kitchen counter.

"Here, let me take your temperature," Paige said. She read the screen, eyes widening in shock. "Val, you have a very high fever. It says 104.5. I need to get you to the emergency room."

"No," Val protested weakly, "just need to rest. Gotta be here for the kids." Just those few words had her gasping for breath.

Paige hesitated, then nodded. "Okay, plan B. We need to get your fever down." She went to the kitchen and rummaged around until she found some dish towels. Then she opened the freezer and pulled out the ice tray. She ran the towels under cold water, squeezed out the excess, and hurried over to Val. "Val, I need to lift up your shirt. Actually, taking it off would be better. Can you sit up?"

Val moaned but managed to push herself up a couple of inches. Paige grasped her T-shirt from the back and slipped it up over her head, alarmed at how hot Val's skin felt. She took one of the cold towels and laid it across Val's back, then eased her back down. She covered her chest with another towel and folded a third over Val's forehead.

"Cold," Val murmured, her eyes closed.

"I know, honey, but we've got to lower your temperature. Do you have a hammer?"

Val opened one eye. "Gonna put me out of my misery?"

Paige laughed. "No, I'm going to make some ice chips for you to suck on."

"Oh. Toolbox is in the laundry room cupboard."

Val retrieved the tool, put the ice cubes in a plastic bag, and gave them a few good whacks. She brought the pieces to Val.

"Here, open up." Val parted her dry lips and Paige slipped the ice onto her tongue.

"Mmm." After a moment, Val opened her mouth for another piece, like a baby bird waiting to be fed. Paige smiled and complied, giving Val a few more.

Paige touched the towel where it lay already warm on Val's belly. "I need to change the towels. Hang on, okay?" She got them cold again and reapplied them to Val's skin. Val murmured something, too low for Paige to hear. She leaned close. "What was that?"

"This isn't the way I pictured you getting me naked."

Paige felt her cheeks flame as she looked at Val in surprise. Val's eyes were still closed, but the ghost of a smile played on her parched lips. *It's the fever. She's delusional.* Still, Paige couldn't resist putting her hand gently on Val's cheek.

"Just rest." She pulled out her phone, went to the kitchen, and called Connie.

"Hello?"

"Connie, it's Paige. Val's really sick and I'm trying to get her fever down. I need to stay, because the kids—"

"Whoa, slow down. You're at Val's place?"

"Yes. She didn't answer her phone so I went to check on her. She has a really high fever and shortness of breath."

"Okay. Where are the kids?"

"Still at school. That's why I'm calling. Could you pick them up, and Emma, too? They get out at three." Paige took a deep breath, trying to slow her racing heart.

"I can do that. Am I on the approved pickup list?" Connie asked calmly.

"I'll call and give permission for you to get them. I need to stay with Val. She doesn't have anyone else to help her." Paige's voice broke, and she tried to cover it by clearing her throat.

"Relax, Paige. Everything will be fine. I'll let folks know you'll be out the rest of the day. Just focus on Val."

Paige let out a sigh of relief. "Yes, ma'am."

"I'll call you once I've gotten the kids. I can bring them to my place for tonight if necessary," Connie said. "You all right?"

"Yes. Val just looked so awful. She could barely walk." Paige shivered at the memory. "I'm just worried about her."

"She's lucky you have that big heart and thought to check on her. You're a good woman, Paige."

"Thanks, Connie." Paige's eyes filled at the kind words.

"Talk to you later, kiddo."

Paige called the school to arrange for Connie to pick up the kids, then went back to check on Val. She appeared to be sleeping. Paige touched her arm, the skin clammy but not as hot. Val shifted a little but didn't awaken as she gently took her temperature: 102.8. Thank God.

Paige looked around for a blanket. She checked the living room and laundry area, to no avail. Feeling slightly uncomfortable, but also curious, she entered Val's bedroom and turned on the light. Standing in

Val's private space, Paige immediately felt like an intruder, yet the faint lingering scent of coconut drew her in. The room was simply decorated in beiges and browns, the only furniture a rumpled bed, a small dresser, a bookshelf, and an upholstered chair.

Paige approached the bookshelf, where several items caught her eye. On top, a bud vase held an artificial red rose and a small Puerto Rican flag on a wooden stick. A white knitted lace doily lay beneath a wooden statue of the Virgin Mary and a small glass containing a blue votive candle. The shelves below were crammed with books of all types.

Paige turned to the dresser. On its surface were two picture frames, one holding a picture of Val and her friend Sasha, and the other a worn, faded photo of a dark-haired girl and a tiny old woman. Next to the pictures lay the eagle necklace that Val always wore. On impulse, Paige picked it up and ran a finger over the intricate details. The silver felt warm, as if it had its own energy. *Strength.* Val was strong and she'd get through all this. Feeling an inexplicable sense of peace, Paige set down the necklace and looked to her left. Neatly folded on the back of the chair was a fleece blanket.

Out in the living room, Paige was relieved to see that Val's skin had lost a little of its previous pallor, but she still looked tired. And vulnerable. And beautiful.

She went to the couch and lightly touched Val's arm. Val inhaled sharply and opened her eyes. It seemed to take a moment for her to focus on Paige, but when she did, she smiled.

"Hey you," Paige said.

"Hey," Val whispered.

"How you feeling?"

"Like a train hit me."

Paige laughed. "I'm sure. Your fever's down some, but I need to get some ibuprofen into you. Think you could swallow a couple of pills?"

Val nodded. Paige gave her the meds, then removed the damp towels and tucked the blanket around her shoulders. Val settled back with a sigh and closed her eyes. A moment later, her eyes flew open and she sat up, the blanket falling from her bare chest.

"The kids?" she said, her voice panicked.

Paige gently pressed Val back down and covered her again. "With Connie right now. If you want, I can bring Lily and Ian back home and stay here with them tonight. Emma can stay at Connie's."

"You'd do that?"

"Of course."

"That would be good. Thank you." As Val looked at Paige, her dark eyes filled with tears.

"Hey, what's wrong?" Paige leaned closer, gently stroking Val's arm.

"You took care of me," Val said, her voice breaking.

"Well, yeah, silly. I couldn't just leave you like that. You could barely move."

"I know, but if you hadn't checked on me, the kids would've come home and I..." Val's tears spilled down her cheeks.

"It's okay. They're fine, you'll be fine. Everything worked out." Paige smiled, then, unable to stop herself, she reached to brush a strand of hair from Val's forehead.

Val captured her hand in hers and held it. "Just...thank you."

Paige stilled. The emotion passing between them was so palpable, she dared not move lest it disappear.

"You're welcome." Paige held her gaze for several moments, her own eyes growing moist. Swallowing hard, she lowered their joined hands to the blanket and gently removed hers. "Rest now, sweetie."

"Okay." Val's eyelids had grown heavy.

Paige stood looking at her for several more moments, her heart full. Val had needed her, and she'd been there. Paige realized in that moment that she wanted to be there for so much more.

CHAPTER TWENTY-FOUR

Paige had made an epic attempt on Tuesday to postpone the inevitable, but Sheryl Watkins had insisted on her timeline for the move. Val was still home recuperating, but Paige couldn't put off the news any longer. Late on Wednesday morning, she drove to Val's house, feeling like an elephant had taken up residence on her chest.

She knocked on Val's door and was pleasantly surprised that it opened quickly. Val looked a million times better. Her hair shone, soft and clean looking, and her gorgeous skin was returning to its usual glow. She was dressed simply in a pair of jeans and a long-sleeved Syracuse University T-shirt, but she managed to make even that look amazing. Paige's heart skipped a beat when Val smiled in greeting.

"Hey there. What brings you by?" Val said, motioning Paige inside.

"Just wanted to check on the patient, make sure she's drinking her fluids and eating chicken soup and stuff."

Val laughed. "The patient is following all prescribed protocols."

"Good." Paige took the offered seat on the couch. "You look a lot better."

"Thanks. I'm still tired, but I couldn't stand it any longer. I had to get up and clean. I even opened up all the windows and sprayed Lysol on everything I'd ever touched. Sorry, it's still kind of cold in here."

"It's fine." Paige sat quietly, biting her lip. She felt Val's eyes on her, but couldn't meet her gaze. After a few moments, Val sat beside her.

"This isn't just a social call, is it?" Val stated quietly.

Oh, for God's sake, Paige, just spit it out. She took a deep breath and forced herself to look at Val. "I have a confirmed moving date for the kids."

Val's eyes widened for a brief moment, then her shoulders slumped as a look of resignation settled on her face. "I knew it. When?"

"Monday."

"Damn, that's not much time." Val stood abruptly. Paige heard her go to the kitchen and open the fridge. "Would you like something to drink?"

"Whiskey, neat?" Paige replied sardonically.

Val snorted. "I was thinking more along the lines of bottled water."

"Since it is only eleven a.m. on a work day, I'll go with that."

When Val was seated once again, Paige said, "There's more."

Val raised an eyebrow and sipped her water.

"That day when you took Ian to the doctor, Lily told me that Sheryl spilled the beans about them living with her." Val flinched but didn't speak. "Lily also told me that she wanted to stay here. She thinks if she tells that to the judge, it will happen."

"That's so not good." Val rubbed the back of her neck, hard.

"I'm sorry I didn't tell you sooner, but with Ian sick and then you…"

Val waved her off. "I get it. It's not like I didn't know this was coming, but if Lily really feels that way, it's going to be difficult. Does Ian know?"

"I don't think so, but I can't be sure." Paige blew out a frustrated breath. "For the record, I'm not any happier about this than you are, but I don't have a choice."

"I know. You have to do your job, and everyone's intentions are good. It's just that, when you're the foster kid, none of that matters."

Paige watched Val's expression change, could actually see the mask of indifference slip into place.

"I'm sorry, Val. Do you want me to tell them?"

Val shook her head firmly. "No. I've got this. I'll do my best to prepare them." She stood and shoved her hands in her pockets. "Thanks for letting me know. I've got some things to do, so…"

Paige felt the dismissal like a slap. She stood quickly. "Yeah, I've got to get back to work. Call me if you need anything."

Val simply nodded, then walked over and opened the front door.

❖

Val was torn. Should she tell the kids now and give them time to get used to the idea, or should she wait until the weekend so they didn't have too much time to dwell on it? Neither option was ideal, as she knew only too well. As she sat ruminating, her mind wandered back in time.

"Girls, I need to talk to you. I'm afraid I have some bad news," the foster mother had said.

Val was ten when she'd been placed with Mrs. Croft along with Mary, who was two years younger. They had liked it there, and Val had finally begun to feel comfortable, but everything had changed that night. Mrs. Croft's mother was ill and needed to come live with her. She'd told the girls that she had to give up foster parenting and that they would be moving on in just two days' time. Val had never forgotten the look on Mary's face.

"But we've been here a long time," Mary had said, her lip trembling. "Aren't we going to stay together?"

"That's not up to me. You'll go with whoever can take you," had been the reply.

Val remembered storming off to the room she shared with Mary, the girl she would ultimately never see again. On that day, she had learned that nothing good ever lasted. On that day, the shutters that had hovered uncertainly around her heart had slammed shut.

Val rested her head on the back of the couch, willing herself to breathe deeply. The memory had spiked her anxiety but had also made up her mind. She would tell Lily and Ian tonight.

❖

Val took her time washing the dinner dishes, letting the warm water soothe her while she steeled herself for the conversation to come. Finally, she called the kids to the living room.

"Come here, both of you." Val sat on the couch and gathered the kids to her, one on either side. "I'd like to tell you a story. Did you know that I was also a foster child?"

The children shook their heads, looking at her with the same rapt attention they used to give her at story hour. God, it seemed like forever ago.

"When I was just a little older than you, Lily, I was also taken from my mom, for much the same reason you guys were."

"She crashed a car?" Ian whispered.

"No, buddy, but she used drugs and made bad decisions that kept her from being a good mom." He nodded.

"See, I didn't have any family members who could take me. My grandmother had died, so I went to a foster home."

"Just like us," Lily chimed in.

"Right. But because I didn't have family, I got moved around a lot, from home to home. I lived with seven different foster families up until I graduated from high school," Val said.

"Why didn't you just stay at one?" Lily asked, frowning.

"There were lots of reasons, too many to explain. But see, with you guys, it's different. The foster care people, like Miss Paige, have a rule they have to follow. They have to try and keep families together. For you, Aunt Sheryl is family."

A frown, followed by a flash of understanding and a stubborn lift of her chin told Val the exact moment Lily figured out what she was getting at.

"I already told Miss Paige that we want to stay here with you. Family is people who love you. She said so. You love us, right?"

God, please get me through this. "Yes, honey, I do, but I don't get to choose. I have to do what the judge says, and so do you."

"No. Emma's here, and school, and...and...everything! I don't want to go." Lily pulled away and stood up, tears streaming down her face.

Ian had pressed himself close to Val's side, and she could feel his little body trembling. If she looked at him now, it would be her undoing. She pressed on.

"Aunt Sheryl can give you guys a good home, and you'll make new friends. It'll be fine there."

Lily shook her head vehemently. "I'm gonna tell the judge no." She stood there, arms crossed and eyes flashing.

No more explanations. Just let them feel. "I know this hurts, honey. You're angry and sad. So am I, and that's okay." She hugged Ian tightly with one arm and held out the other to Lily as her own tears began to fall. Lily crumbled, allowing herself to be held. The three of them cried until no more tears would come.

❖

"Ms. Cruz, this is Mrs. Ryan at Park Street Elementary. I got your message, and I'm so sorry to hear that Lily is leaving us."

"I know, I am, too. How's she doing?"

"Well, we've had some tears, but her friends have been trying to cheer her up. She's doing okay, considering. So Friday will be her last day?"

"Yes."

"Well, we'll be sure to give her a proper send-off," Mrs. Ryan said.

"Thank you. Lily has really enjoyed being in your class."

"And we've loved having her. I appreciate you letting me know what's going on."

"No problem. Thanks again."

Val hung up with the teacher. She was worried about the kids. She'd already spoken to Ian's kindergarten teacher, who reported that he hadn't smiled or spoken a word all day. He'd come so far, and she was afraid this move would undo months of progress. And there wasn't a damn thing she could do about it.

"You okay, Val?" Linda asked, for the hundredth time. Val had filled her in, and Linda had been overly attentive. She was sweet, but she was driving Val crazy.

"Yep. I'm going to run up to the book depository and see if we have any returns. Be right back." Val was doing everything she could to stay busy, leaving the bulk of customer interactions to Linda. She didn't think she could conjure up a cheerful smile if she was Dumbledore himself.

It was a slow and tiring journey to three o'clock, but Val was out the door like a shot once it arrived. She had plans to do something special with the kids tonight, and she wanted to make it fun. She got home with fifteen minutes to spare before the school bus arrived. Grabbing the bag of craft items she'd purchased on her lunch hour, she went inside.

Val quickly changed her clothes, then laid out the craft project on the kitchen counter. Donning her coat, she went back outside to wait for the bus, letting the cold winter breeze clear her head. Moments later, she heard the familiar rumble coming down the street.

Val's heart constricted as she watched the kids get off the bus. Lily held tightly to Ian's hand, leading him across the street and slowly up the driveway. Gone was their usual after-school exuberance, and their grave expressions mirrored her own emotions. Val smiled broadly, determined not to let them all wallow in sadness. Time was short—she would make it count.

"Hi, guys," she greeted, giving them each a hug. "Go on in. I've got some cookies waiting for you."

The kids perked up at that and made quick work of shedding their outerwear and backpacks. When they were both seated at the table with peanut butter cookies and some milk, Val asked about their days.

Ian just shrugged and focused on his cookie. Lily frowned.

"I told Emma I was leaving. She cried."

"Aw, I bet she did. You're a good friend." Val saw Lily starting to tear up. "Hey, would you like to make her a gift?"

"A gift?" Lily sniffled.

"Yep. Check this out." Val showed the kids what she had purchased. "You could make a card, or a picture, or whatever you want."

Lily fingered the colorful papers, sparkly stickers, and new set of markers. "Can I make it now?"

"Absolutely. How about you, buddy?" Ian came over to investigate, wearing a milk mustache and peanut butter cookie crumbs. Val chuckled. "Let's clean up your face first, little man, then I'll help you make something, too."

❖

When Paige picked up Emma from the after-school program, her daughter had a scowl the size of Texas on her face. Opting to tread lightly, Paige said, "Hi, baby. How was your day?" That was it. The dam burst, the heavens fell, and her child dissolved into a blubbering mess in the back seat.

When Emma had stopped wailing long enough to speak, she said, "Lily's moving. A judge is m-making her leave." She said the last word in a drawn-out moan.

"Oh, honey, I'm sorry." Paige figured she'd better not cop to having known all along. *I'm a terrible mother. Should have seen this coming.*

"She's my best friend. She can't leave," Emma cried. Suddenly, her little tear-stained face brightened. "Mommy, you can fix it! You know the judge. You can tell him Lily wants to stay."

Oh, my achin' ass. "Honey, I can't. The judge won't keep Lily and Ian in foster care if they have a place to go. That's the rule."

"Well it's a stupid rule," Emma shot back, angry now. "They're happy here. Nobody ever listens to kids."

The child's kinda not wrong. "I'm sorry you're upset, honey. Want to go get a hot chocolate and talk about it?"

"No." Emma sat in the back seat, arms crossed, scowl firmly back in place. She didn't say another word all the way home.

Later, after they'd eaten a quick dinner in near silence, Paige had an idea. "You know, I could make sure I get Lily's new address so you can keep in touch. You could be pen pals."

"What's a pen pal?" Emma asked, intrigued.

"It's when two people who live away from each other send letters or cards back and forth. Back before cell phones and Skype, it's how friends communicated sometimes."

"Oh," Emma said, brightening. "So we could keep sharing our drawings, and I could tell her about school and everything?"

"Yep."

"That would be awesome," Emma said, smiling broadly.

Paige had another thought. "Emma, would you like to give Lily a going away gift?"

Emma jumped up, eyes wide. "Could I?"

"Uh-huh. Grab your coat. Let's go see what we can find."

CHAPTER TWENTY-FIVE

Val filled the weekend with as much fun as she could, both to keep the kids busy and to make memories. They went to the bouncy house place at the mall, saw a movie, and went sledding on the big hill behind the high school. She took tons of pictures and had prints made of the best ones. They all had a wonderful time together, but that time was fleeting. By Sunday afternoon, the weight of their impending good-bye lay heavily on their hearts.

Paige was scheduled to pick up the kids at nine in the morning, so all their packing needed to be done by bedtime. Val had washed all of their clothes and laid out clean outfits for tomorrow. Lily's new purple suitcase lay open on her bed next to Ian's red one. Val was helping them pack their clothes, along with the toys and books they'd accumulated in their time with her. The energy it took to stay positive for the kids was taking its toll on Val.

Lily laid Emma's gifts of a mermaid stationery set and a stuffed unicorn on top and zipped her suitcase closed. Ian grunted as he tried to force his soccer ball into his.

"Hang on there, Ian. Gotta move some stuff around." Val helped him rearrange until everything fit. When he was done, the only thing remaining was Coqui. Ian picked him up, then looked at Val, uncertain.

"Coqui's yours now, buddy. Will you take good care of him for me?"

Ian nodded, and his bottom lip started to quiver. Lily sat on her bed, her head hanging.

"I've got something for you both. Wait here, okay?" Val went to her room and retrieved a bag from her closet. Inside were her parting gifts for the kids. She stood in her room for a moment, taking deep breaths and willing herself not to cry.

"Come out here to the living room," she called, and she sat the kids down on the couch. From the bag she drew two wooden boxes and handed one to each child.

"Ooh, what is it?" Lily asked, tracing her fingers over the flowers carved into the lid. Ian's box was carved with sailboats, and he turned it round and round in his hands.

"They're keepsake boxes. Here, lift this latch and look inside." Val said.

Val had very carefully chosen the treasures inside each box, and she watched as they discovered each new thing.

"See those stones?" she said. Lily pulled out three colorful polished rocks, each inscribed with a word. "Can you read them?"

"*Special, brave, kind,*" Lily read.

"Yes. Ian's say the same, because I want you both to remember that you are special, brave, and kind. Now take out that little pouch there." The children each lifted a small drawstring pouch from their boxes. "Open it."

Inside the pouches were silver eagle pendants, each strung on a sturdy leather cord. Ian's eyes widened. "Like your bird," he said.

"Yep." Val touched her own necklace. "My grandma gave me this when I was little, to always remind me that I am strong. Now you can remember, too."

The last item in each box was a miniature photo album. The cover photo was their school picture, and inside were photos of each child's special moments from their time together.

Lily flipped through hers excitedly. "There's when we went sledding, and there's us at Halloween. Look, Ian, yours has a picture of you feeding the giraffe at the animal park." Ian's face lit up as he smiled.

The final page of each album was a selfie of the three of them that Val had taken at Christmas. Underneath she had written the words *You Are Loved.*

"You can take these with you, and whenever you find a new treasure, you can add it to your box," Val told them. If the looks on their faces were any indication, the children loved their gifts, and Val felt a warm satisfaction that she was sending them off in a positive way.

They made mini pizzas for supper, played games, and the kids had a bath. Before they knew it, it was bedtime.

"Mama," Ian said as he climbed into bed, "who's gonna sing the coqui song to me?"

Val's chest ached as she looked at his worried little face. Digging deep, she managed a smile. "We've been practicing it every night, so I think you know how it goes." She had taught them the Spanish words, and Lily especially had picked it up quickly. "From now on, you can sing it together at bedtime. Wanna try?"

Lily climbed onto Ian's bed, and Val knelt on the floor at its side. Ian held Coqui, and they sang. It was one of the most bittersweet moments of Val's life.

❖

Paige's head was ready to explode, and it wasn't even nine in the morning. She'd spent a restless night worrying about how the move would go for Val and the kids, then contemplating why she was so emotionally invested. She'd been in plenty of difficult situations where emotions ran high, but so far she'd been able to maintain her professional distance. Until this one.

Maybe it was because Emma and Lily had bonded that she felt more personally affected by this case. *Sure, let's go with that.* Paige scrubbed her hands across her face, took a deep breath, and knocked on Val's front door.

It opened immediately, and Paige's gaze flew to Val's face, uncertain what kind of welcome to expect. Val stood tall, resolute. A ghost of a smile touched her full lips, but her dark expressive eyes telegraphed sadness.

"Hey," Val said. "Come on in. They're ready."

Paige entered and saw Lily and Ian sitting on the couch, each holding the handle of the suitcase at their feet. "Good morning," she said, smiling at them. Lily looked serious but calm, and Paige quirked an eyebrow at Val.

"We've talked it out. They understand," Val said in reply to her unspoken question. "Everything's going to be fine, right, guys?"

"Uh-huh," Lily mumbled. Ian shrugged.

"I bet Miss Paige needs to get going, so let's get your coats on," Val said, a little too brightly.

The children stood and wheeled their suitcases over to the door. Ian looked up at Val, then dropped his handle and threw his arms around her waist.

"Don't wanna go," he mumbled into her shirt.

Val squeezed her eyes shut and bit her lip for a moment as she stroked his hair. "I know, baby," she said, her voice thick. "But remember, you're going on a whole new adventure, okay?"

Lily stood by, tears streaming down her cheeks. Val beckoned to her, and the three hugged tightly.

Paige had to turn away before she lost it. She felt like the enemy, and though she knew Val didn't blame her, the guilt burned like acid in her chest. She wiped her eyes, then turned and picked up the suitcases.

"I'll just take these out to the car," she said. Moments later, Val and the children followed, hand in hand. When they got to the car, Val squatted down in front of Ian and took his face gently in her hands.

"Be a good boy, okay?"

"'K." Val kissed him on the forehead, then straightened and put her hands on Lily's shoulders.

"You be good, too, Lil." Lily shrugged one shoulder and looked away. Val dipped her head to catch Lily's eyes. "You've got this, kiddo." She tapped Lily's new pendant with her finger. "Remember."

Val opened the car door and buckled Ian in his seat while Paige let Lily in on the other side. She came back around to the driver's side and paused.

"You okay?"

Val stepped back and shoved her hands in her pockets, her expression wooden. "I'm good."

"I'm sorry," Paige said.

"It's...whatever. Drive safe." She took another step back dismissively and looked away.

"Okay, then. Take care, Val."

Val waved to the kids as Paige backed out of the driveway. Heading down the street, with the kids sniffling in the back seat, Paige felt like gum on the bottom of the universal shoe.

CHAPTER TWENTY-SIX

Having children, no matter how briefly, had changed things. Sliding back into her old routine hadn't been easy for Val. When she made her lunch in the morning, she found herself thinking about which kind of jelly Ian preferred on his PB&J. She glanced at the door every time a school bus rumbled by, and on more than one occasion, she'd realized she was humming the coqui song in her head. Lily and Ian entered her thoughts frequently, and not knowing how they were doing was tough.

Unfortunately, though the kids were gone, Val's nightmares had stuck around, continuing to rob her of much-needed sleep. Old memories had even begun surfacing in her waking hours, making it hard to focus. It was getting to be a problem. As much as she didn't want to, maybe she really did need to give therapy another shot. Couldn't hurt, right?

❖

Two weeks later, Val entered the lobby of Susan Brown's building for her first therapy appointment in eleven years. To say she was nervous was an understatement, as her sweaty palms and churning stomach could confirm. She got on the elevator, took out her phone, and started a game of Candy Crush to distract herself.

After checking in with the receptionist in Susan's office and filling out some paperwork, Val took a seat to wait, which had never been her strong suit. Knee bouncing, Val glanced at the magazines on the table beside her. Front and center, a headline jumped out at her: *What Are Your Dreams Trying to Tell You?*

Really, Universe? Is this your idea of a not-so-subtle hint? Val smiled to herself, thinking about Connie's there-are-no-coincidences life view. Val reached for the magazine.

"Valerie." Val looked up at the sound of the warm, instantly familiar voice. Susan smiled in welcome. "It's good to see you. Come on in."

Val followed Susan to her office. The space was warm and inviting but did little to settle Val's nerves. She took a seat on one of the comfortable dove-gray armchairs. Hung on the wall opposite her was a painting, the very same seascape that Val had stared at dozens of times during her high school sessions with Susan. She flushed hot as her heart tried to beat out of her chest.

"Val. Look at me," Susan commanded gently. Val made eye contact but immediately looked away. She felt like this woman could see right through her to the ugliest parts of her soul.

"Sorry. I'm just nervous."

"I know."

Val instantly remembered why she had liked Susan. Her voice was low and calming, and her eyes conveyed acceptance and compassion.

"I imagine a lot has happened in your life since high school. Tell me what you've been up to since we saw each other last."

Okay, safe topic. Breathe. Val told Susan about college and her work as a children's librarian.

"That's wonderful. You've done very well for yourself," Susan said, "which leads us to what brought you in to see me."

"I recently became a foster parent."

"Wow, that's a big deal."

"Yeah, well, I started having nightmares again, like before. A lot of them. I don't even want to go to bed at night."

Susan nodded. "That doesn't surprise me at all."

"It doesn't?"

"You entered the system again, even if as a foster parent this time. I can see how that could be a pretty powerful trigger for memories."

"I have remembered a lot of things I haven't thought about in years," Val said, "but why the nightmares?"

"My guess is there are some significant parts of your history that you haven't fully acknowledged or come to terms with. The dreams are letting you know that you've got some unfinished business."

Val nodded. She knew there was truth to what Susan said, and ignoring it wouldn't make it go away this time.

"That's why I'm here, Doc."

❖

"Em, you got another letter today," Paige said as she sorted through the mail.

Emma jumped up from the puzzle she was doing on the floor. "Ooh, lemme see." She tore open the envelope and ran off to her room with the contents.

Paige shook her head, smiling. "Crazy kid." Emma and Lily had really gotten into the whole pen pal idea. Thankfully Sheryl Watkins was helping out on the other end. A few minutes later, Emma came back in the room, far more subdued.

"How's Lily?" Paige asked.

"She's sad. There's a girl in her class being mean to her, and her aunt's cat died. She wants to come back home."

Paige sighed and opened her arms as Emma's eyes filled with tears.

"Come here, baby." She hugged Emma and stroked her hair. "I know you feel bad for Lily, but that's her home now. Things will get better."

Emma pulled away. "You don't know that, Mommy. I don't understand why they can't just let Lily live where she's happy. She told them she doesn't want to stay there, but they're making her."

Paige didn't like the sound of that. If Lily wasn't adjusting to the move, that would make things difficult for the family moving forward. She was due to follow up with them this week anyway—sounded like she'd better call sooner than later.

"I know it doesn't seem fair, Em. All you can do is keep being a good friend."

As Paige lay in bed that night, she couldn't stop thinking about her own words…and Val. They'd had no contact since the day she took the kids, though Paige had thought of her several times. They'd had a connection, but she'd let Val push her away. Paige's stomach hurt as she thought of Val now, picturing her beautiful face awash with tears.

"I am such an asshole." Paige needed to reach out to Val. Maybe she wouldn't want to have anything more to do with her, but Paige needed to take that chance.

Chapter Twenty-seven

Val was shelving books in the teen fiction section when Linda sought her out. "Val, there's a call for you."

Back at the circulation desk, Val picked up the line. "Hello, this is Valerie. May I help you?"

"Val, hi. It's Paige."

Val's heart skipped a beat. "Paige…hi."

"How are you?"

Exhausted and going through the motions, that's how. "Okay, you?"

"I'm fine. Hey, I was wondering if you'd like to grab lunch or coffee sometime this week and, you know, talk."

Part of Val was excited that Paige wanted to see her, but her cynical side didn't see the point. Paige's voice interrupted the internal battle.

"Val, are you there?"

"Yeah, sorry. I guess we could do coffee."

"Great. That's great." Paige sounded nervous. "How about tomorrow after work? I don't have to pick up Emma until five thirty."

"Okay. Where?"

"Is Cuppa Josie's okay with you?"

"That's fine. Guess I'll see you then," Val replied.

"Yes, you will. Bye, Val."

"Huh," Val said, apparently aloud, because Linda asked if everything was all right.

"Yeah, just an unexpected call. I'm going to be in the office for a bit—I have to finish the flyers for next month's book club."

Once Val was in the office, she closed the door and sat on the edge of her desk. Why did hearing from Paige have her in such a twist? Now that the kids were gone, Paige no longer had any reason to contact her, but she had. Val had already convinced herself that the feelings they shared for each other were just collateral damage from the foster care process, just another loss she'd have to get over. But Paige was reaching out. What did that even mean?

Half an hour later, Val sat staring at the untouched flyer on her computer, daydreaming about the lovely woman with the golden hair and kind eyes.

❖

Sipping her macchiato, Paige watched the door of the busy coffee shop. She knew Val was supposed to get off work fifteen minutes ago, but she'd yet to arrive. Paige's hands were sweaty on her cup as she imagined all the ways this meeting could go wrong. Was Val pissed at her for not reaching out before now? Did she still have the walls up that made Paige feel cast aside? Maybe she'd just be a no-show, leaving Paige with even more questions. Paige pulled out her phone as a distraction to try to keep the what-ifs from running away with her mind. She busied herself scrolling through and deleting emails.

"Hi."

Paige looked up to see Val.

"Hi. I didn't see you come in," Paige replied, feeling even more nervous.

Val smiled. "You were pretty engrossed in your phone. I'm going to go order—be right back."

As Val stood in line at the counter, Paige had the opportunity to really look, and Val looked incredible. Her hair was pulled back in a loose ponytail that lay over her right shoulder. The tangerine blouse she wore complemented her glowing skin, and tan dress pants fit all her curves to perfection. A man joined the queue behind Val and rather blatantly checked her out. Paige was instantly irritated at the guy, until she realized she'd been doing the exact same thing, albeit not as creepily. Val didn't seem to be aware of the ogling, thankfully, and a few minutes later, she returned to the table with her drink.

"So…how's it going?" Val asked, taking a seat.

"Good, good. How have you been?"

"Oh, you, know…living the dream," Val replied sardonically, rolling her eyes.

"Listen, Val, I'm sorry I didn't check in with you sooner. The last time we saw each other was difficult, with the kids and—"

"It's fine. It's not your job to check up on me. Anyway, I'm good," Val said, with a slight lift of her chin that almost dared Paige to disagree with that statement.

"Oh, okay. That's good to hear. I was kind of worried," Paige said, clearly seeing the wall go up in Val's eyes.

"What for? Do you worry about other foster parents, too?"

Paige felt her face flush hot. *Ouch.* "It's not because you're a foster parent. You know you mean more to me than that." She looked away.

"Sorry," Val said, her tone softer. "I appreciate your concern, but I told you, I'm fine."

"Emma and Lily are pen pals now," Paige blurted, watching Val's face.

"Cool." Val shrugged and looked away, then reached back to rub her neck. Paige knew she'd hit a nerve.

Did she have any freaking idea how stubborn she was? "Val, you can't just pretend the whole experience with the kids didn't affect you."

Val looked up, eyes flashing. "Oh, I can't? Suddenly you get to tell me how to feel? You have no idea what you're talking about."

"Maybe I understand more than you think. I get loss. I get abandonment. Growing up—"

"Now you want to compare childhood miseries? I think I win."

Paige was stung by Val's words, but she also knew Val was using her pain to push her away.

"I don't want to compare. I just want to understand."

"Why?"

"Because I care about you, okay?"

Val blinked at her for a moment, then looked away. "You don't need to waste your time caring about me. I'm fine. I'm always fine."

"I don't believe that, and I don't think you do, either."

"I'm not going to do this here," Val said, her tone measured and low.

"I agree. Let's go out to my car, where we can talk in private," Paige said, standing.

"We don't need to—"

"Ugh, Val, just come *on*." Paige walked out of the coffee shop and toward her car, hoping like hell that Val was following. She unlocked her car and slid into the driver's seat, refusing to look. Nearly a minute went by before the passenger door opened and Val got in.

Paige looked over at her. "Thank you."

"Can I tell you something?" Val said.

Paige nodded, taking in Val's flushed face and shining eyes.

"You're pretty sexy when you get all bossy like that."

"And you're sexy as hell when you're mad," Paige shot back, then bit her lip, shocked that she'd actually said that out loud.

"At least we can agree on something," Val said, smiling. "Look, Paige, I'm not good at the whole *let's talk about our feelings* thing. I've spent a lot of years keeping to myself, and I know it's maybe not the healthiest way to go through life, but it's worked for me."

"I get it, Val, and I'm not trying to make you uncomfortable. If we're being honest here, there's just something about you that makes me want to know more."

Val reached over and gently pulled a strand of Paige's hair through her fingers. "There's something about you that makes me want to tell you," she said quietly. She looked into Paige's eyes, and Paige felt the intensity shoot straight to her groin.

"Come home with me," Paige said. Val's eyebrows shot up, and Paige's cheeks flamed. "I mean, I have to go get Emma, but then I can make us some dinner and we can continue our conversation."

"Okay."

"Really?"

"Lead the way," Val replied, opening her door. "I'm parked just over there. Give me a minute, and I'll follow you."

Paige drove to the elementary school, checking her rearview mirror every ten seconds. *The most beautiful woman I've ever seen thinks I'm sexy. How is this even happening?*

Val waited while she went in to collect Emma, then they continued on their way.

"Em, Miss Val is going to come have dinner with us tonight. She's following right behind us."

Emma craned her head around to look, then waved out the back window. "Cool. Can we have hot dogs?"

Paige smiled. "I think I need to do better than that for a guest. How about pasta?"

"With meatballs?"

"Sure."

"Yay! I bet Miss Val will like that." Emma chattered on all the way home, while Paige relived the moment when Val touched her hair and set her body on fire.

❖

"That was the best meal I've had in forever," Val said, sitting back in her chair with a sigh.

Paige laughed. "Spaghetti and meatballs? You've got to broaden your horizons."

"I don't really cook for just me. I haven't even turned the oven on since…" She shot a look at Emma, who was happily slurping up the last of her spaghetti.

"I know," Paige said. "Emma, go on and get cleaned up, and then do your homework."

"Aw, do I have to? I wanna hang out with you guys."

"Miss Val and I have some grown-up stuff to talk about. You can do your homework, and then watch TV in my room. Deal?"

"I guess," Emma said and headed off to the bathroom.

"I'll take care of the dishes later," Paige said, moving toward the living room. "Come, sit."

"Yes, ma'am," Val replied, giving a two-finger salute.

"What? I'm being bossy again?"

"Nah, I'm just playing." Val sat on the couch, and Paige took the chair adjacent to her.

"So," Paige said, smiling.

"So," Val echoed. "Apparently you're interested in my sordid past, although I can't imagine why."

"Well, you're interesting, and a little mysterious. That intrigues me," Paige replied, surprised at her own boldness.

"Wow. Most people think I'm just boring and unapproachable."

"A persona you've cultivated, I'm thinking," Paige replied.

Val looked at her in surprise. "Are you usually so direct?"

"Actually, no. Sorry if that was rude. Maybe I've been hanging around Connie too much," Paige replied, chagrined.

"You're not wrong. My therapist would call it a defense mechanism."

"Ah, so that's the million-dollar question—what are you defending against?"

Val shifted in her seat and didn't respond.

Paige groaned inwardly. *You're pushing too hard, idiot. What makes you think she'll open up to you?*

An agonizing minute passed, then two. Paige forced herself to be still and wait.

"Nearly everyone I've let past my defenses has hurt me," Val said, quietly, "with the exception of Sasha and Connie. Putting myself out there generally isn't worth the risk, and trusting people is just…hard."

Val had her arms wrapped tightly across her belly, and a frown creased her brow as she stared at some distant point on the floor. Her vulnerability made Paige's heart ache.

"Can I ask a question?" Paige said. Val looked at her and nodded. "How old were you when you went into foster care?"

"Nine."

Paige thought about Emma, who would be nine in the summer. So young. "Do you remember what happened?"

Val laid her head on the back of the couch and gazed at the ceiling for a moment before speaking.

"My mother did drugs. Sometimes she would take care of us, play with us, and sometimes she'd be passed out with a needle in her arm. We never knew which mom we'd see. Abuelita, my grandmother, tried to convince her to get help, but she never did. I loved Abuelita—she was so good to us. But she had severe complications from diabetes and could barely walk. There was no way she could help, even though she wanted to so badly."

Val's hand went to her throat, where her eagle pendant lay, and she rubbed it between her fingers.

"I started missing a lot of school. One day, the counselor called me in and asked me why, and I broke down and told her. The next day, CPS showed up and took us. We went together to a temporary foster home at first while the county looked for relatives. My father was in prison, but they found Enrique's father out West somewhere. Enrique went to live there, but they didn't want me. I haven't seen him since." Val hadn't moved, but tears were slowly rolling down her cheeks.

"I'm so sorry, Val. That must have been awful for you." Paige wiped away a tear of her own.

"I wanted to go with Abuelita, but they wouldn't let her take me because she was so sick. I think that's what killed her. She died of heart failure not long after."

"Oh my God, Val. What about your mom?"

"She never got clean. They told me she died of a heroin overdose a year or two later."

Val's voice had changed. She was talking in a flat, detached tone, and her face had taken on the same wooden cast Paige had seen the day she took Lily and Ian away. Paige slid from her chair to sit beside her.

"Val," she said, touching her arm.

Val flinched. "Don't."

Paige jerked her hand back. "I'm sorry. I...I just feel so bad that you had to go through all that."

"I don't need your pity. I don't deserve it," Val said, almost in a whisper.

"What do you mean?"

For the first time since she'd begun talking, Val looked Paige in the eye. "All of it was my fault. If I hadn't told, I wouldn't have lost my little brother, or caused the stress that killed Abuelita, or made my mother just give up. I'm to blame for all of it."

Paige watched in shock as Val curled in on herself and began to sob.

❖

Val felt like she'd been hit by a train. Her muscles ached, her eyes burned, and her head was pounding beyond belief. On top of all that, she was mortified. She'd lost control and fallen apart in front of Paige. Sweet, kind Paige, who'd sat beside her, silently handing her tissues. When she'd finally cried herself out, Paige got her a bottle of water and some homemade peanut butter cookies, then went to put Emma to bed. Now she was back, sitting in the chair, and Val could feel her eyes watching.

What do you say when you've made an ass of yourself? Val

wanted to be anywhere but here, and she couldn't stand the pity in Paige's silence.

"Look, Paige," she said, but the words came out as a strangled croak. Clearing her throat, she tried again. "I appreciate dinner and everything, but this…"

"Was more than you bargained for?" Paige supplied. She was looking at Val with concern. "I'm sorry that I asked such personal questions. I didn't mean to trigger all those memories." Paige's eyes were full of remorse.

"Not your fault. I went there, broke my own rules. That's why I don't get close to people, Paige. I'm damaged goods. You'd be much better off staying away from me." Val stood up. "I should go."

Paige stood and went to Val, putting her hands on her shoulders. "Forgive me for disagreeing, but the last thing I want to do is stay away from you." She took a half step closer, and Val's breath hitched as she looked into Paige's eyes. She saw compassion, but there was something more. Paige's hand cupped her cheek and Val closed her eyes. She wanted to sink into Paige's touch, surrender to her feelings. She felt Paige's hand slip beneath her hair, caress her neck gently. When she opened her eyes, the raw need on Paige's face took her breath away.

"Please don't push me away," Paige whispered, her eyes moist.

Val's resolve shattered. She wrapped an arm around Paige's waist and pulled her close. Paige's cheeks were flushed, her full lips parted invitingly. Val dipped her head and kissed her, and it was like every emotion she'd ever felt converged on that single point of contact. Paige moaned and deepened the kiss, threading her fingers through Val's hair. Val pulled Paige's hips flush with her own, trying to feel all of her. She was incredibly aroused, but this kiss was more intense than anything she'd ever experienced, like her black-and-white life had just exploded into a kaleidoscope of color.

"Oh my God," Paige murmured when they came up for air.

Val's eyes traveled from Paige's swollen lips to the gorgeous eyes that seemed to see into her soul. She could handle wanting Paige, and she did, desperately. But in that moment she realized how much she needed her, and she was suddenly terrified.

"Paige, you are incredible, but I…I'm all fucked up. You deserve everything, and I can't give you that. I'm just going to hurt you." Her voice broke on a sob. "I have to go."

"If you need to go, I understand," Paige said. "But know this—when I look at you, I don't see damaged goods. I see a strong, amazing woman who has more resilience in her little finger than most people will ever have. I see someone with a beautiful, giving heart who has no idea how wonderful she is. And"—she reached up and touched Val's face—"I see the woman that I want in my life."

Tears spilled from Val's eyes. "Paige, I…"

Paige placed a finger on Val's lips. "Shh. Go, take the time you need. I'll give you your space, but I'm not going anywhere. When you're ready, come back to me." She went to the door and held it open. "Take care of yourself, Val."

Val looked at Paige, her lovely face strong and determined despite the tears coursing down her cheeks. "You are the kindest, most amazing person I've ever met." She grasped Paige's hand and brought it to her lips. "Thank you."

It took everything she had to walk out the door. As she drove away, she glanced back in her rearview mirror to see Paige, still standing on her front step, her hand over her heart.

CHAPTER TWENTY-EIGHT

Four months later

"We haven't seen you in forever, chica. We're coming down on Saturday and you're going out with us. That's an order," Sasha said.

"We should be FaceTiming so you could see me sticking my tongue out at you," Val replied, laughing. "Besides, I'm a civilian, so you can't order me around."

"Whatever. We're rescuing you from your hermit-like existence. You can thank us later."

"Fine. When should I expect to see your bossy-assed face?" Val said.

"Probably around five. Dress nice—we're taking you out to dinner."

"Sash, that is so not necessary."

"Hey, everybody's gotta eat. No arguments, woman, because you know I can kick your ass."

"Okay, okay. I'll see you Saturday. Bye, Sasha."

"Later."

Val ended the call and sat back in her chair, smiling. Seeing Sasha and Jen would be great. The last few weeks had been exhausting and difficult, to say the least. She desperately needed a little fun.

Linda popped her head into the office. "Story hour folks are starting to trickle in."

"Be right there." Val still got the tiniest twinge of sadness every time she did story hour, since it reminded her of Lily and Ian. She'd been doing a lot better, though, thanks to Susan Brown and her weekly therapy sessions. Val was feeling lighter than she had in a long time. With a smile, she went out to greet her audience.

❖

"Paige!" She turned and saw Joe flagging her down from across the hall.

"Hey, Joe. What's up?"

"Listen, Charlie and I are going out Saturday. A really good band is playing at Pony's. Wanna come? We can celebrate surviving another Central New York winter."

Paige laughed. "Hmm, maybe. I'd have to find a sitter." Paige hadn't been out since she'd left Val in the Pony's parking lot months ago. She was due for a little fun.

"Well, get busy finding one, sister," Joe said with a wink.

"Yes, I'll babysit," Connie said a moment later when Paige passed her in the hall.

"How do you freaking *do* that?" Paige said, shaking her head.

"I could say I'm all-powerful and all-knowing, but if that were true, would I be working here?" Connie said. "I just overheard you two when I walked by. I agree with Joe—you deserve a night out."

"Thanks, Connie. You're the best."

"Yes, I know," she replied, with a dramatic toss of the head.

Paige laughed. The last few months had been beyond stressful, but things were looking up.

❖

Val gave Sasha a giant hug when she walked in the door Saturday afternoon.

"How are you guys?" she asked as they settled around the kitchen table.

"Great," Sasha and Jen said in unison.

Val laughed. "Do you finish each other's sentences, too?"

"Actually, now that you mention it…" Sasha said.

"We do," Jen finished.

"You two are like sunshine and rainbows," Val said, rolling her eyes.

"That was a compliment, right?" Jen said. She looked at Sasha. "Was that a compliment?"

"I think so." Sasha grinned and winked at Val. "I'm glad to see you followed my wardrobe directive," she said, looking Val up and down. "You look hot."

"Um, I wasn't going for hot, but thanks." She had opted for the only dress she owned, an above-the-knee black flare dress that she had bought in college. She'd accessorized with a simple silver belt and her black boots, and she'd replaced her eagle necklace with a black velvet and marcasite choker.

"I don't know what you were going for, but stunning is what you accomplished," Jen said.

"Yeah, I think it's all right to take her out in public," Sasha teased. "I made six o'clock reservations at Rosalie's, so we'd better get going."

Once they were seated at the restaurant, sipping their first glasses of wine, Sasha raised hers for a toast. "Here's to best friends." They clinked glasses. "Wouldn't want to celebrate with anyone else."

"What are we celebrating?" Val asked.

Jen and Sasha smiled at each other, then set their right hands side by side on the table. They wore matching silver infinity bands on their ring fingers.

Val felt a rush of excitement for her friends as she realized what she was seeing. "You're engaged?"

"Yep," Sasha said, beaming. "Jen's finally realized that she can't live without me."

"I think it's the other way around," Jen said, nudging Sasha with her elbow.

"Oh my God, you guys, that's fantastic," Val said, giving both of their hands a squeeze. "When's the wedding?"

"August," Jen said, "so clear your calendar."

"Val, you'll stand up with me?" Sasha asked, a hopeful look in her eyes.

"Wouldn't miss it." She gave what she hoped was a genuine smile as she tried to ignore the stab of envy she felt in her chest.

❖

As she entered Pony's, Paige caught sight of Joe and made her way over.

"There's our lovely Paige," Charlie said, kissing her cheek.

"Hi, Charlie," she said, giving him a hug, then hugging Joe. "Thanks for saving me a seat."

"Those are the perks when you're friends with the chronically early Joe Massey," Charlie said.

"And you'd rather be late and stand all night? Please," Joe retorted.

"He's right. I have very delicate feet," Charlie stage-whispered.

Paige laughed. "You guys are exactly what I need tonight."

"Good, honey. Can I get you a drink?"

An hour later, Paige was on her third glass of wine and feeling more relaxed than she had in weeks. The band was due to start at nine thirty, so she excused herself to go to the bathroom. When she was at the sink washing her hands, a familiar face appeared in the mirror.

"Hey, there. Sasha, right?" she said, turning.

"Oh, hey. How are you?" Sasha said.

"Good. Is Val here with you?"

"Yeah. She's at the bar."

"Great. Maybe I'll stop and say hi. Enjoy the show."

"You, too."

Paige exited the restroom, feeling a little jittery in her stomach. She hadn't seen or heard from Val in a long time, and she had no clue if Val would even want to speak to her. She'd promised to give her space, but still, what harm would it do to just say hello?

Paige walked toward the bar area, looking for Val. When she saw her, her heart skipped a beat. She was laughing, with her arm around a blond woman, and she looked incredible. Her dress fit her like a glove, and her gorgeous hair fell loosely to her bare shoulders. Paige took a tentative step toward her, then stopped as if she'd hit a wall. Val had just pulled the woman closer to whisper in her ear, then she kissed her cheek.

She has a girlfriend now? So much for not wanting to be close to anyone. Guess she just didn't want to be close to me.

Paige watched Val for a moment longer, feeling suddenly cold, then she went back to her seat. Her fun night had just taken a major nosedive.

❖

"Jeez, took you long enough," Val said when Sasha returned from the bathroom.

"Long line," Sasha replied, "and never enough stalls."

"Right after you left, some creepy drunk woman kept trying to hit on me," Jen said. "Val here did a noble deed and took over as my girlfriend in your absence."

"I only kissed her on the cheek, I swear," Val said in mock surrender.

Sasha playfully swatted her on the shoulder. "Whatever. Thanks for being my wingman, though. Where's the creepy chick?"

"If I tell you, do you promise no drama?" Jen said.

"Yeah, as long as she stays away from you," Sasha said, pulling her in for a kiss.

Jen pointed out a disheveled-looking woman at the end of the bar, who happened to be looking back and forth between Sasha and Val in what appeared to be drunken confusion.

Val laughed. "She must think you're a total player, Jen."

"She can think whatever she wants—from over there."

"Hey, Val, did that caseworker woman find you? We met in the bathroom and she asked me if you were here," Sasha said.

"You mean Paige?" Val said, instantly looking around. She had kept her relationship with Paige to herself, not even telling Sasha.

"Yeah, that's the one. She said she was going to come over and say hi."

"No, haven't seen her." Then a cold realization hit—if Paige had been looking for her, she'd likely seen her hanging all over Jen.

"Oh, no," she mumbled. Val started scanning the crowd. Eventually she saw Paige at a table, talking to that guy she worked with. Swallowing her nerves, she took leave of her friends and made her way over.

Joe stopped talking in midsentence when Val walked up, causing Paige to turn around. Val saw a flush on her cheeks and the beginnings of her gorgeous smile, then just as quickly it faded.

"Hi, Paige. How are you?"

"I'm fine. You?"

"Okay." The overly polite surface pleasantries almost hurt. "Sasha said you were looking for me?"

"Yes, and I found you. You were kind of...busy."

"I was helping Jen fend off some unwanted advances from a drunk," Val said, needing to explain.

"Jen?"

"Yeah, Sasha's girlfriend. Well, fiancée now."

"Oh," Paige said, flushing a brighter red. "I thought..."

"That I was with her? No, Paige. I'm not with anyone." She looked directly into Paige's eyes, her meaning clear. "I've been working very hard on me."

Paige searched Val's face, as if hoping to see a difference, an openness. After a moment, she gave a start. "Oh, I'm sorry. Joe, Charlie, you remember Val?"

"We most certainly do," Charlie said. "Forgive me if I'm overstepping, honey, but you look fabulous."

Val felt the heat rise from her throat to her cheeks. "Thank you." Her eyes flew quickly back to Paige, whose expression said she agreed wholeheartedly with Charlie's words.

"It's really good to see you," Paige said. Val's reply was interrupted by the distorted yelp of an electric guitar being tuned. The band had taken the stage. "I'm sorry, we don't have another chair."

"No problem," Val replied. "I'll just stand right here, if that's okay." Paige nodded, smiling up at her, and Val felt, in that moment, that all was right with the world.

The band began their set, and Val's vantage point allowed her to notice all the finer details of the woman in front of her. As Paige's head bobbed gently to the music, Val's eyes caressed her golden hair, swept up in a flawless twist, and the smooth skin of her exposed neck that her fingertips itched to touch. How was it possible that this woman affected her like no one else ever had?

Val rested her hands on the back of Paige's chair, her fingers close enough to feel her body heat. Paige was wearing an emerald-green silk blouse, open at the neck, and the swell of her breasts drew Val's gaze again and again. Once, she looked up to find Charlie smiling at her. He winked, and though she was embarrassed for being busted, she just smiled and threw her hands in the air, as if to say, *Can you blame me?*

❖

Joe was right. The band was excellent, and Paige was enjoying the music, but she was enjoying the close proximity of Val even more. She had been shocked at the surge of jealousy she'd felt after seeing Val and Jen at the bar, as well as the relief when she'd learned she'd misread the situation. The months they'd gone without seeing each other had done nothing to dampen her attraction to Val, and she was hoping the feeling was mutual.

As the band played, Paige became aware of Val's hands at her back, the occasional tiny brushes of her fingertips. She'd always thought people were exaggerating when they said they could feel another's eyes on them...until tonight. That they couldn't see each other's faces only seemed to sharpen her senses, and by the end of the sixth song, Paige was incredibly aroused.

She turned in her chair to find Val smiling down at her, her eyes dark with desire. Paige stood, but Val didn't step back. They remained mere inches apart without touching, but the electricity between them hummed.

"I need to go to the ladies' room," Paige said, a little breathlessly.

"Good idea," Val replied and stepped aside for Paige to lead the way.

The line was short, and it wasn't long before Val and Paige were inside the restroom. Paige entered a stall while Val waited outside, and she could hear the other patrons leave. When she opened the stall door, Val backed her inside and refastened the door. The cold metal wall shocked her hot skin as Val pushed her gently up against it.

"What are you doing?" Paige whispered, her palms flat against the surface behind her.

"Making up for lost time," Val replied. She ran her hands down Paige's arms, then back up to cup her face. "You are so beautiful," she said, before leaning in to kiss Paige's forehead. She nuzzled her lips along Paige's jaw, then sucked gently on her earlobe.

"You're driving me crazy," Paige breathed.

"I'm just getting started." Val brought her mouth to Paige's, nibbling on her bottom lip before requesting access with her tongue. Paige gave it, sucking Val into her mouth and starting a frenzied dance of tongues and lips. Paige found Val's waist with her hands and slid them slowly up, brushing the sides of her breasts before burying them in Val's soft hair. Val moaned, and Paige caressed her neck, only vaguely registering that the restroom door had opened.

After a moment, someone said, "Get a room, ladies. We've gotta pee!" Other voices giggled, and Paige pulled away from Val, her face on fire.

Val grinned, wiped a hand across her swollen lips, and opened the stall door. "Sorry about that."

Paige followed, thoroughly embarrassed, and the other women clapped. "Oh my God," she said, covering her face with her hand. Val grabbed her other hand and pulled her out of the restroom.

"I may die of mortification." Paige groaned.

"No, you won't, but that kiss…let's do it again," Val said, pulling Paige close.

Paige put her hand on Val's chest. "Stop it. Not here."

"Then where?"

"Did you drive?"

"No, Sasha and Jen brought me," Val said. "We're celebrating their engagement."

"Oh, wow. I don't want to interrupt…"

"No, it's okay. I'll go explain."

"I have my car, but I'm still a little buzzed," Paige said.

"I only had a beer. I can drive us to my place. Is that okay?" Val suddenly looked shy and uncertain, which Paige found endearing and incredible sexy.

"I'll have to get home at some point—Connie's babysitting Emma."

Val reached into her bra and pulled out her phone. "It's only ten thirty."

That was one lucky electronic device. "Let me just tell Joe and Charlie that I'm leaving," Paige said.

"I'll find Sasha and Jen and meet you at the door in five."

Paige made her way back to the guys. "I'm going to head out," she said. "Thanks for inviting me tonight."

"Leaving already?" Joe said.

"Why would she want to hang around with a couple of old men

when she has a much hotter prospect?" Charlie said. He winked at Paige. "Get out of here, before you and Val set off the sprinklers."

Paige couldn't stop herself from grinning. "Good night, boys. Enjoy the rest of the show."

She walked as quickly as she could to the entrance to find Val waiting.

"Ready to get out of here?" Val said.

"Absolutely." Paige gave Val her car keys and walked ahead of her out the door. She felt Val's touch at the small of her back and trembled at the contact. Once in the parking lot, Val took her hand. Their fingers entwined in a perfect fit, and Paige could hardly believe all that had transpired in such a short time.

In the car, Val again grabbed Paige's hand and placed it on her leg. Her dress had ridden halfway up her thigh, bringing Paige's fingers in contact with her smooth, warm skin. Almost instantly, she began to caress Val's leg, making her moan.

Even while her body was practically combusting, a niggling red flag appeared in Paige's mind, and her fingers stilled. "Val, what are we doing?"

"Um, is that a trick question?"

"Ugh, I know *what* we're doing, but we haven't had any contact in months. Shouldn't we at least play a little catch-up?" Paige said. She knew she was right to say it, but she held her breath, waiting for Val's reaction.

"You're right." Val continued driving until she came to a safe spot to pull over. She put the car in park and turned to Paige, taking her hand. "Remember you told me to come back to you when I was ready?" Paige nodded. "I was afraid to reach out, thinking maybe you had changed your mind, moved on. But when I saw you tonight, I knew I couldn't wait any longer."

"I know," Paige replied. "When I saw you with Jen and thought you were together, it hurt like hell. Nothing has changed for me, but I don't want to mess this up. What if we rush in and later regret it? I don't know if I could handle that. You're too important to me."

Val sighed. "You've got me so worked up, I can't believe I'm saying this, but would you rather go somewhere and talk?"

"I don't feel like being out in public, but..."

"Tell you what. We can go to my house, and I promise I'll sit on the other end of the couch. I'll even take a cold shower first if that would help," Val said, smiling.

Paige was so grateful that Val didn't seem angry, especially since she had just brought their libidos to a screeching halt. "Okay."

"Okay." Val pulled back onto the road and drove silently to her place, leaving Paige alone with her thoughts.

Paige shifted in the seat, her panties still very damp. Holy crap, she had never been this turned on in her life. Why couldn't she just feel instead of overthinking it?

Because, her voice of reason answered, *you need to be sure.*

Paige looked at Val's profile as she drove, and a wave of tenderness washed over her. This woman was worth so much more than a fling.

As if sensing Paige looking at her, Val turned. Again, she offered a gentle smile and linked her fingers with Paige's, then returned her attention to the road. Paige couldn't shake the sense that something major had shifted in Val's life, and she hoped Val would let her in and share it. Giving Val's fingers a squeeze, she laid her head back on the seat and allowed herself a few moments to just feel their connection. Because, good God, it felt amazing.

Chapter Twenty-nine

True to her word, Val kept her distance when she let Paige into her home. She switched on some lights and got Paige a water before excusing herself.

"I've got to get out of these boots. Make yourself comfortable, and I'll be right back."

Val went to her room, closed the door, and rested her forehead against it for a moment. Even after months apart, Paige had awakened things in her that she wasn't sure she'd ever feel with a woman, and honestly, she was kind of scared. Paige wanted to slow things down, which was probably a good call. Val shed her outfit and slipped into her most comfortable yoga pants and an oversized sweatshirt. She went to the bathroom, then joined Paige on the couch.

"I figured it would be a good idea to show less skin," she said with a grin.

Paige laughed. "A noble gesture, but ineffective, because you pretty much rock yoga pants."

Val shook her head. "Whatever."

Paige sipped her water and studied Val, tilting her head to the side. "Can I make an observation?"

"Sure."

"You look...different. I don't know if I can explain. It's just that, last time we saw each other..."

"I was a hot mess?" Val said. "I was, and I told you I had a lot to figure out. I've been working with my therapist weekly, and I've had some pretty major breakthroughs."

Paige flashed her warm smile. "That's fantastic, Val. You're happy with your progress?"

"Very. We've gotten to the bottom of my nightmares, and they've almost completely disappeared. It was like my mind knew I was ready to face some memories and experiences that were holding me back, and the nightmares just forced me to take that step."

"I guess that's why you look different, like you're rested, lighter somehow," Paige said.

"That's how I feel. The first night that I slept straight through felt so amazing. I'd been walking around like a zombie for weeks."

"I'm so glad you're doing better, Val," Paige said, reaching over to touch her hand in her typical affectionate way.

Val captured her hand and held it. "We've also been working on my trust issues. You see, I met a woman who made me realize I didn't want to push people away anymore."

Paige's smile faltered. "Oh?"

"Yeah. She's this gorgeous blonde with kind blue eyes and a killer smile that just melts me," Val said, rubbing her thumb over Paige's knuckles.

"It does?"

Val watched the flush climb Paige's cheeks, and she moved closer. "Yep, and you know what else?"

"Hmm?"

"She kisses like a freaking goddess."

Paige let out a tiny whimper as Val closed the distance between them. She gently traced a finger along Paige's jaw, then lightly grazed her bottom lip. "I know you wanted to slow down and just talk, but my God, Paige, you make it hard."

Paige closed her eyes as Val caressed her cheek. When she opened them, she took a deep breath and stopped Val's hand with hers. "I don't want a little fling, Val. If that's what this is…"

Val felt a stab of self-doubt—was she at all capable of a relationship? Paige was unlike any of the women she'd been with before. As she gazed into Paige's eyes, she understood that if there was ever a time to take a chance, this was it. "Paige, you deserve much more than that, and I'm starting to believe that I do, too. I can't promise you I'll be any good at this, but you make me want to try."

Paige's eyes filled with tears. "No one has ever made me feel as wanted as you just did." Her tears spilled as she held both of Val's hands in hers. "I've only had one serious relationship, you know. I spent a lot of my time trying to be who she wanted me to be, but I never quite measured up. She was just a repeat of my parents, actually. That was nine years ago. Since then, I've found happiness with Emma and my work, but I've stayed away from dating. It was just easier than always feeling like I wasn't good enough. Now here you are, beautiful, incredible you, and I'm scared."

"I get being scared. If I could, I'd find your ex, and your parents, and smack them upside the head for not seeing what a wonderful person you are."

Paige giggled. "I'm just picturing how awesome it would be to watch you mess up my mother's perfect hair. They are all such judgmental people—I can't imagine any of them are truly happy, you know? When I told my parents I wanted to be a social worker, they were horrified, like I'd said I was going to be a serial killer. Apparently social work is well below someone of my family's social standing. They never understood that their lifestyle was suffocating me."

"Do you ever see your parents?"

"Not anymore. For the first couple of years after I left New York City, I would drive down for holidays. I felt like I had to because they were my family. But when they barely acknowledged Emma, I was done. I couldn't let them suck the soul out of me anymore."

"I get it. Some people are so caught up in the idea that biological family relationships matter more than anything, but you know what? Those relationships are no different than any others—if they're toxic, a person shouldn't feel guilty for letting them go."

"Exactly." Paige reached up to brush Val's hair back. "You don't have to answer this, but do you ever want a family of your own?"

Val was silent for several moments, which Paige had learned meant she was processing the question. "I never thought so. Family equaled pain for much of my life, but I know that as an adult I have control over who I allow into my life. When you're a kid, everything happens *to* you, and you can't do much about it. As an adult, I can finally choose not to let the past continue to victimize me." Val shook her head and laughed. "I just channeled Susan, my therapist."

"Sounds like she's a smart woman."

"She really is. I think I wasn't ready to learn what she had to teach me until now. The kids—and you—unlocked something inside me." Val's eyes grew moist. "So to answer your question, I think I would like to build a family, the kind that really matters."

Paige pulled Val into a hug, rejoicing at how far they'd come in just one night. They simply held each other, drawing comfort and strength, two hearts finding their way to one another. After a while, Paige reluctantly pulled away.

"Val?"

"Hmm?"

"I hate to say it, but I have to go."

Val glanced at the clock on her cable box. "Damn. It's almost midnight."

"Yeah, and I can't impose on Connie to stay with Emma any later. Please know that I really don't want to go."

"I know. This has been an amazing night, Paige. Never in a million years did I think it would turn out like this."

Paige dropped her gaze, her feelings of vulnerability warring with her happiness. "We're on the same page here, aren't we?"

Val tipped up Paige's chin with her finger. "If the page says that we want to see where this road takes us, then yeah."

Paige smiled and gently touched her lips to Val's for a long, sweet kiss. "Thank you," she whispered, "for letting me in."

"Thank you for making me feel safe. This talking about myself stuff is new territory, but it's helping."

"I'm glad." Paige sighed. "I have to go."

"I know." Val placed a gentle kiss on Paige's forehead. "Good night, Paige. We'll talk tomorrow?"

Paige nodded. "I'll look forward to it. Good night." She pulled away and put on her coat.

"Drive safe, okay?"

"I will."

As she drove home, the evening's events went through Paige's mind like a film loop, and she felt an odd combination of exhilaration and fear. Staying single had been safe, but her feelings for Val were way too strong to ignore. She'd just have to take it one day at a time.

Chapter Thirty

I have no fucking idea how to date," Val moaned into her phone. Sasha laughed on the other end.

"It isn't rocket science, chica. You just hang out, do stuff together."

"You are the only person I've ever hung out with like that, Sash. I'm so used to being alone. What if it turns out that I'm lousy company, or boring?" The fact that she even cared was starting to freak her out.

"You're not boring. Just be you. I'm pretty sure Paige likes you just the way you are."

"I guess. I really am sorry I ditched you guys last night," Val said.

"Are you kidding? I've been waiting for you to have a good reason to ditch me. I like Paige. She seems like good people."

"She really is. So why am I so scared? Did you feel like this when you met Jen?" Val said.

"Oh my God, you have no idea. You're scared because she matters, Val. Take the risk."

Val felt warm all over as she thought of Paige's beautiful smile and their incredible kisses. "Yeah, I think I will."

❖

Paige sat in front of Connie's desk, sipping her mug of tea and waiting for her friend to return from the copy machine. When she did, she plopped into her chair and leaned forward, chin in hand, giving Paige her undivided attention.

Paige squirmed under the scrutiny. "What?"

"You had a good weekend," Connie stated.

"Yeah, I did," Paige replied, smiling.

"As in, a much better than average weekend."

Paige still hadn't gotten used to being read so easily by her freakishly intuitive friend, and she felt herself blush. "You could say that."

"Well, I just did," Connie said with a smile. "I'm getting a good vibe from you."

"I reconnected with Val Saturday night."

"Aha! I knew that look you had when you got home wasn't just from hanging out with Joe and Charlie. So this reconnection—it was positive?"

Paige nodded. "We've decided to start seeing each other." She had no idea why her cheeks caught on fire with that admission.

Connie grinned. "That's great, right?"

"Yeah, but if I'm honest, it's also scary. I mean, I feel like a clueless kid here." Paige fiddled with the handle of her mug.

"Why is that?"

"I have a pretty limited history when it comes to relationships. My last one was years ago, and it made me kind of gun-shy."

"Every relationship has its purpose. Did you learn anything from it?" Connie said.

Paige nodded. "I guess I learned a lot about how I *didn't* want to be treated," she said wryly.

"A valuable lesson, then. And this new thing with Val—does it feel like the last one?"

"Not a bit," Paige said, unable to hold back a smile. "It's like the complete opposite."

Connie smiled. "Sounds like you found something worth pursuing."

Paige's heart fluttered in her chest. "Hope so. I always feel better after I talk to you."

"Hey, I live to serve."

"Unfortunately, my social life isn't what I needed to talk to you about."

"Oh?"

"I got a call from Sheryl Watkins. Seems that Lily and Ian are not adjusting as well as we had hoped. She said Lily constantly talks about wanting to come home, and that Ian barely speaks. Lily has even begun to have trouble in school." For the first time, Paige was worried that this placement was going to fail. She was relatively new to the foster care job, and she had yet to have a foster family send a child back because of problems. Her heart ached to think of Lily and Ian being so unhappy, but she'd had to do her job and send them there.

"What did you say to her?" Connie asked.

"I just told her that all kids adjust differently, and to be patient. I also made sure she's keeping up with their therapy appointments."

"Good. Sometimes it takes a while, but I am concerned that Lily is still asking to come *home*. You made it clear that staying here wasn't an option?"

"Yes."

"Just continue to monitor the situation. Things will work out," Connie said.

Back at her desk, Paige's thoughts went to Val, as they so often did now. She wanted her input, but this case was way too close to Val, and it would upset her to hear that the kids weren't doing well. There was nothing to be done but hope for the best. Paige felt powerless, and it sucked.

❖

"Emma, I'm done folding the laundry. Come help me put your clothes away."

"Hold on, Mommy. I'm almost done with my picture."

A couple of minutes later, Emma joined Paige and started sorting out her clean clothes. She was in a good mood, humming to herself as she put away socks and pajamas.

"What are you working on out there?" Paige asked.

"A picture for Lily," she replied.

A thought struck Paige then, and she felt it like a punch in the stomach. What if maintaining contact with Emma was keeping Lily from moving on? She'd glanced at some of their correspondence, which was mostly eight-year-old chatter and artwork, but maybe she needed to take a closer look.

"How's Lily doing?" she asked.

"I don't know. I think she's sad because nobody's listening to her."

"Oh?" Paige said, feigning ignorance. "What do you mean?"

"She wants to come home, but they won't let her."

"Well, honey, that is her home now," Paige said.

"It was supposed to work!" Emma said, her voice suddenly distraught. She looked at Paige as if she'd been caught being naughty, then bit her lip and turned away.

"What was supposed to work?" Paige asked warily. Something was definitely up.

"Nothing," Emma mumbled.

"Emma," Paige said, in her no-secrets-from-Mommy tone.

Emma started to cry. "We made a plan," she said, "before Lily left. We thought that if she fussed a lot and acted sad, they'd give her back to Miss Val. And then maybe you'd be happier, too, cause we could all be together. Like a family."

Well, shit. "Emma, come here." She sat on Emma's bed and stood her daughter before her. "I know you and Lily are good friends, but you should not have made a plan like that. Lily should be working on making a new life and new friends there. You want her to be happy, don't you?"

"Yeah, but she was happy here," Emma said, sniffling.

"Listen, Em, I know you don't understand all this, but if you want to be a good friend to Lily, you should help her to be okay in her new home." Paige's head hurt—how could she have been such a complete idiot not to foresee this problem? And what the hell did Emma mean about them all being a family? Had she really been so transparent that her child could see how she felt about Val?

"Mommy, please don't say anything. I don't want Lily to get in trouble." Emma looked deeply worried, and Paige felt a rush of affection for her compassionate little girl.

"I won't, but I'll be helping you with your letters from now on. Got it?"

"Okay." Emma threw her arms around Paige, a fresh round of tears threatening. Paige held her and rubbed her back, but her mind was on the hot mess she might have inadvertently helped create. *Way to go, dumbass.*

CHAPTER THIRTY-ONE

Val glanced at her ringing phone and smiled as she picked it up. "Hey, I was just thinking about you."

"Perfect," Paige replied, "because I was just thinking about you plus me plus lunch. Could you meet me in half an hour?"

"I think I could make that happen. Where?"

"Well, I have to be in court all afternoon, so somewhere close. How about Panera?" Paige said.

"Sounds good. I'll see you soon," Val said.

"Looking forward to it."

Val hung up, amazed at how just the sound of Paige's voice could improve her day dramatically. She finished up what she'd been working on and walked out to the circulation desk.

"Hey, Linda, I'm going to step out for lunch."

Linda looked at her, head tilted to the side. "Excuse me, but I thought I heard you say you were stepping out for lunch."

"That's what I said," Val replied.

"You, who have eaten lunch in that office every day for years, are stepping out for lunch."

"Hey, maybe I want to shake it up a little," Val said, only a little defensively.

Linda tilted her head the other way, then her eyes opened wide. "You're meeting someone."

Val tried to smother her smile but failed miserably. "Maybe."

"Oh my God, you have a lunch date. Who is she?" Linda looked like she'd just won the lottery.

"Relax, would you? I'm just meeting a friend. I'll be back in time for your break. Bye." Val waved at Linda over her shoulder and headed to the door.

"Don't hurry back on my account," Linda called after her. Val shook her head, laughing.

On the short drive to the restaurant, Val felt a little tingly in anticipation of seeing Paige. They hadn't had the chance to truly be alone since the weekend, but Val felt no pressure. They spoke every day, and their conversations were easy and light. So far, so good.

She parked and entered the restaurant but didn't find Paige. Taking a seat by the nearest window, she watched the lunch hour crowd coming and going until she saw her. Paige was walking across the parking lot, looking sophisticated and sexy in a navy blue skirt and jacket, a coral pink blouse adding a splash of color. Val's work attire was far less elegant, and she felt momentarily underdressed in her khakis and black sweater. When Paige walked in the door, she found Val almost immediately and smiled—and at that moment, nothing else mattered.

Val stood and accepted Paige's quick hug, wishing everyone would leave so she could hold on a whole lot longer. She was still able to catch Paige's scent of lavender, and it soothed her senses.

"If this is what you wear to court, how does anyone pay attention to the case?"

"Ha ha," Paige said, but Val could tell she was pleased. "Thanks for meeting me, Val. I had a crazy morning, and I had to get out of there for a bit. Seeing you is just the bonus I needed."

"My pleasure," Val replied. "Know what you want to eat?"

They ordered salads and found a booth in the far back corner. Val reached over the table and held Paige's hand. They just looked at each other, fingers lightly caressing.

"What have you got going on the rest of the day?" Paige asked.

"I'm planning for a fundraising contest. Kids will get pledges for how many books they can read in a month, and the money will be used to buy books for the library at the children's hospital. Would Emma like to do it?"

"Probably. It's a great idea, and she loves to read," Paige said.

"You know what I love to see, besides you in that suit?" Val said. Paige grinned. "What?"

"Kids reading instead of staring at electronics. Call me crazy."

"I happen to agree with you wholeheartedly. You and I were both avid readers, and look how fabulously we turned out," Paige noted.

"You definitely did," Val said. She beckoned Paige to lean closer and whispered, "I want to kiss you senseless right now."

A powerful blush colored Paige's cheeks, and Val wanted to follow it with her fingers as it crept down her throat and into the vee of her blouse.

"Eyes up here," Paige murmured, and when Val met her gaze, the connection shot straight to her groin. Just then, the server arrived with their food, thankfully giving them something else to focus on.

"Maybe this wasn't such a good idea," Paige said casually, as she pulled a hunk off of her baguette. "Now I have to sit in court all afternoon in damp panties and pretend I'm paying attention."

Val almost choked on her salad. Recovering, she said, "And to think I had you pegged as uptight when we first met."

Paige drew in a dramatic breath. "You did not."

"Did too, but I've amended my first impression."

"And now?" Paige asked, the tines of her fork gently pulling down her bottom lip.

"And now you're so hot you're driving me crazy." Val fanned her face with her napkin. "Hurry up and eat. This place is way too crowded."

"It's not like we can go anywhere. I have to be in court in half an hour," Paige pointed out.

"After work?"

"I'll have Emma," Paige said, looking very amused.

"The universe is conspiring against me," Val lamented, throwing up her hands.

"Emma will be in bed by eight."

"You totally just batted your eyelashes at me. Was that an invitation?" Val said.

"Would you like it to be?"

"Hmm, let me see—is the pope Catholic? Do bears shit in the woods? Is Donald a colossal asshole on Twitter?"

Paige laughed out loud, then covered her mouth with her hand in embarrassment. "I'll take that as a yes."

"You're adorable when you laugh," Val said, as she stood to clean up their plates. "And I'll be seeing you later."

❖

Paige heard the car in the driveway and was waiting at the door when Val knocked gently. She counted to ten so she didn't seem too eager, then opened the door.

"Hey," Paige said softly. "Come on in." Val had changed into a soft blue pullover and jeans that fit like they were made just for her. She was gorgeous.

Val looked her up and down. "I was hoping you'd still have that suit on, but this is even better."

Paige looked down at her favorite jeans and off the shoulder sage-green peasant blouse. "I'm all about comfort by the end of the day."

"Comfortable looks good on you," Val said, stepping closer. She slid her hand into Paige's hair, cupping the back of her head.

Paige's pulse quickened as they stared into each other's eyes. Val pulled her close, and everywhere their bodies touched tingled in anticipation.

"Can I kiss you senseless now?" Val whispered.

Paige nodded. "You'd better."

Val claimed her mouth eagerly, her lips soft yet demanding, and the result was intoxicating. Paige felt like she couldn't get close enough, but she tried, burying her hands in Val's thick hair and pressing their bodies together. She moaned as Val's tongue traced the inside of her lips, then plunged inside her mouth. Val slowly walked her backward until her back met the wall, and taking her hands, she raised Paige's arms over her head. Holding them there, Val began a delicious assault on her neck, licking and sucking before claiming her lips once again.

Paige's legs trembled, and when Val pressed her thigh between them, her knees nearly gave way.

"Couch," she managed to say between kisses.

They stumbled to the living room, kissing and giggling. Val sat and pulled Paige down to straddle her lap, her mouth resuming its exploration of Paige's throat and bare shoulders. Paige's hands were braced on Val's shoulders, and she had thrown her head back to give Val better access. She was intensely wet, and her hips began to move of their own accord.

"Mommy?"

Val froze, then in one fluid movement, flipped Paige off to sit beside her on the couch. Paige adjusted her blouse and tried to keep her voice normal.

"What are you doing up, Emma?"

Emma emerged from the hallway, rubbing her eyes, then stopped when she saw Val.

"Miss Val came over to watch a movie with me," Paige said with what she hoped was composure, and Val quickly grabbed the remote from the coffee table and turned on the TV.

"Hi, Emma," Val greeted with a wave.

"Hi. Mommy, can I get some water?"

"Sure, honey, but then you need to get right back in bed. It's a school night."

"Okay." Emma trudged sleepily into the kitchen, got herself a glass of water, and headed back to the hallway. "G'night."

"G'night," Paige and Val responded in unison. Once they were sure Emma was out of earshot, they collapsed into laughter.

"Holy crap, that was close," Val said.

"Why do I feel like I just got busted by my parents for inappropriate behavior?" Paige said, still giggling.

"I don't know. Was that a common occurrence when you were a teenager?" Val teased.

"Totally the opposite. I guess this is what it *would* have felt like if I hadn't been such a good girl."

Val started at Paige's knee and slowly ran a finger up her thigh. "I kinda prefer your bad girl side."

Paige stopped her hand. "Quit it. I am totally paranoid now."

"Ugh. Well, we do both have to work in the morning, so I guess I should go," Val grumbled.

Paige shrugged apologetically. "Life with kids."

"No worries." Val stood, then offered her hand to help Paige up. "For the record, that was the best make-out session I've ever had."

Paige touched a finger to Val's lips. "Agreed. Let's do it again soon."

Val laughed. "You're on." She held Paige's hand as they walked to the door, then lifted it for a kiss. "Until then, beautiful. Sweet dreams."

"They will be if I'm dreaming of you," Paige replied. She felt her cheeks flame. *Did I really just say that?*

Val grinned. "You're adorable. Bye, Paige."

"Good night, Val."

Paige watched through the window as Val flashed her lights and drove away. She felt giddy, and awesome, and still very aroused. Paige touched a finger to her swollen lips. *She called me beautiful.* An old familiar pang of trepidation erupted in her chest, but she shook it off. *Quit worrying. Just enjoy this.* She headed to bed and eventually drifted off to sleep, smiling all the while.

CHAPTER THIRTY-TWO

Val shut her office door and sat down for a much needed mental break. She'd been extra busy at the library getting ready for the hospital fundraiser and writing a grant for additional funding. She hadn't seen Paige in three days and missed her. The last three weeks had been a whirlwind of coffee dates, stolen kisses, and the occasional dinner, but Val was happy. No matter how crazy their days were, she and Paige ended each one on the phone, sharing a few moments before they drifted off to sleep. That had become the best part of Val's day, and she thought about how strange and different her life was now. She'd gone years with barely a connection to anyone, but now she craved her moments with Paige. It was incredible, and scary, but they were taking things slowly and getting to know each other. This was what she'd been missing, and it was already beginning to fill the emptiness inside her.

Val pulled her phone out of her pocket and sent off a text to Paige. *How's your day going?*

Her phone dinged a few moments later. *Slowly. How about yours?*

Same. Weekend can't come soon enough.

Can't wait for Saturday, Paige replied. Val couldn't, either. Saturday was her birthday, and Paige had planned a special evening. No matter how much Val pestered her, Paige wouldn't give up the details. Val hadn't been this excited for her birthday since she was a little kid.

Just one more day.

Yep. Gotta go. Meeting. TTYL. Paige had ended her text with a little kissy-face emoji, and Val smiled. Everything with Paige was simple, sweet, and easy—completely different from any other experience she'd had. The few women she'd been with had been all about shallow attractions and quick hookups. Paige was genuine, kind, and above all, a friend. Val was scared to death she would screw it up.

Lately this had been the topic of her sessions with Susan. Val's tendency was to distrust good things—she was always waiting for the other shoe to drop, because in her experience, it often did. Susan was working with her on reframing her experiences and beliefs about life in positive terms, and it was freaking hard sometimes. She was sure of one thing, though—Paige made her want to keep trying.

Val got up and headed back into the library area. She looked to her left and stopped dead in her tracks. *Ian?* A little boy who looked just like Ian from behind was pulling a book off the shelf. He turned, and the urge to cry squeezed Val's throat. Not him.

God, I miss them. Though she'd made it through the roughest patch emotionally since they'd left, she still thought about them all the time. Every night, she sent up a little prayer for their safety and happiness. Several times she'd wanted to ask Paige to find out how they were doing, but she knew it wouldn't help her let go. She had no idea how other foster parents did it, over and over. This job was hard. And the county could call again at any time.

Val went over to the circulation desk, and a moment later, her phone rang.

"Hello?"

"Hey, kiddo. How are ya?" Connie's cheerful voice made Val smile.

"I'm good. You?"

"Fabulous, as usual. Listen, I've got to ask you something—do you think you're ready for another placement?"

Oh, for fuck's sake. Could she read my mind from across town? "I'm...not sure."

"Now, I know you've been working through some things, but I just want you to think about it," Connie said. "You did a great job last time."

"Thanks."

"So you'll let me know?"

"Yeah, I will," Val said.

"Thanks, honey. By the way, Paige is smiling around the office a lot more these days—wonder why?"

"Connie!" Val heard her friend's laughter before the call disconnected.

Val fanned her face—judging from the heat, she must be red as a tomato. Her embarrassment turned to pleasure as she imagined Paige's amazing smile.

❖

Paige was giddy with excitement as she pulled into Val's driveway. She'd arranged for Emma to have a sleepover at a friend's, so she could be free to pull off her surprise. If everything went according to plan, tonight would be very special, and Paige hoped Val would enjoy it. She parked and checked herself in the mirror, then went to get Val.

When the door opened, Paige felt the flutter of intense attraction she always experienced when she saw Val. Tonight, she was wearing low-slung black pants and a high-necked, sleeveless white top, cropped to show a glimpse of her smooth flat belly. She wore a chunky black and silver belt and black boots, and silver bangles and earrings joined her eagle necklace to round out the ensemble. Val had the sides of her hair pulled back in a clip while the rest hung over her shoulders in dark waves.

Paige only realized she had been staring, transfixed, when Val touched a finger beneath her chin and closed her mouth for her. Val's smile was amused, but her dark eyes flashed with desire.

"Hi," Paige said. "You look...criminally sexy."

Val laughed, then looked her slowly up and down. "And you are gorgeous."

Paige had worn a short-sleeved sapphire-blue minidress and heels that brought her even with Val's height. She'd put her hair up in a loose French twist and accessorized with silver jewelry. She hadn't dressed up purposely to impress someone in a long time, but it seemed to be working. "Thank you," she said, smiling.

"So are you going to tell me where we're going?" Val asked.

"Nope. You'll have to wait and see. Let's go."

Paige drove downtown, laughing at Val's attempts to figure out the plan. "You're relentless, you know that? Do you not like surprises?"

"Well," Val said, "I guess surprises kind of stress me out. Must be another one of those leftover issues from my childhood, right?" She smiled, letting Paige know she wasn't upset.

"Okay, I'll tell you this much—we're going to dinner."

"Judging from your outfit, we can rule out McDonald's, Taco Bell, Burger King, Wendy's…"

"Stop." Paige laughed, whacking Val on the knee. Val captured her hand and held it to her thigh, stroking lightly. The contact immediately sent a shiver of pleasure down Paige's spine.

They spent the drive chatting and laughing, but when Paige pulled into the parking lot of Paolo's, Val's eyes went wide.

"No way," she said, looking at Paige in shock. "Paolo's? As in the best restaurant in the city?"

"Hey, you only turn thirty once, right?" Paige replied, pleased. "Gotta make it special."

Val squeezed Paige's hand. "Just being with you makes it my best birthday ever." She leaned over and kissed Paige lightly on the lips, then touched their foreheads together. "If I forget to say it later, thank you."

Paige's eyes moistened as a powerful surge of happiness coursed through her. "You're welcome. Ready?"

"Absolutely," Val replied, her beautiful face alight with a smile.

"By the way," Paige said, as they walked to the restaurant's entrance, "if you limit your order to a side salad or something, I'll smack you."

"Warning noted. Besides, it would be a crime to order a salad in a place like this."

They approached the hostess station, and Paige gave her name. "We have reservations for seven o'clock."

"Ah, yes. Right this way, please," the woman said. The restaurant was busy, and it wasn't until they got right to their table that Val realized the next phase of her surprise.

"Happy birthday, chica!" Seated at the table, all smiles, were Sasha, Jen, and Connie.

"Oh my God, you guys," Val said, her hand on her chest in surprise. "I can't believe you're all here." She turned to Paige. "How did you get ahold of them?"

"I am very resourceful," Paige replied.

"She just called up to the base and asked for me by name," Sasha said, standing to give Val a hug. "I traded shifts with someone so we could be here—didn't want to miss your big three-oh."

"That's so awesome. Thank you. Hey, Jen," Val said, giving her a hug, then she turned to Connie. "And you, too? I seriously can't believe it."

"When Paige has a plan, you don't mess it up," Connie said with a wink. "Besides, I didn't want to miss out on a steak at Paolo's." Her words were teasing, but the warm hug she gave Val conveyed her affection.

"Wow." Val gave Paige a hug filled with gratitude and emotion. "You're something else."

"Just enjoy," Paige whispered in her ear.

The food was phenomenal, and they had a wonderful time. Val and Sasha entertained the table with crazy stories of their teen years, and Jen and Paige threw in a few of their own. Connie kept them all laughing with her dry wit, and the time flew by. Throughout the meal, Val kept smiling at Paige, her dark eyes shining. So far, the evening was perfect.

As they finished their after-dinner coffee, Paige turned to Val. "So now that you're fed, we need to discuss the remainder of the evening's activities."

Val arched an eyebrow at her. "There's more?" The look that passed between them gave little doubt as to what Val was hoping for.

"You have three options to choose from. An LGBTQ film festival is going on at the university, and there's a ten o'clock showing. Or we could go over to the Pavilion for live jazz. Or tonight is Latin Dance Party Night at Pony's."

Val pretended to consider, but Paige was pretty sure she knew what Val would choose. She was right.

"I want to teach you how to salsa," Val said. "Let's go to Pony's."

"Well, I'll leave you kids to your twerking or whatever it is people do these days," Connie said, laying down some money for her part of the bill.

"Connie, you're crazy," Val said, shaking her head and laughing.

"So I've been told." Connie got up and gave Val a kiss on the cheek. "Happy birthday, kiddo. Don't do anything I wouldn't do."

"What options does that leave me, exactly?" Val teased.

Connie winked as she gave Sasha's shoulder a squeeze. "Jen, it was great to meet you. And Paige, thanks for inviting me along tonight. I'll see you Monday."

"G'night, Connie," they all said, smiling as she took her leave.

"You were right, Sasha," Jen said with a grin. "She's a riot."

"She's a very special woman, right, Val?"

"Yep, she really is. So, who's ready to dance?" Val flashed a smile at Paige.

"Can't wait," Paige replied.

❖

By ten o'clock, Pony's was already packed. Latin Night was a favorite, and people came from all over the area. Holding Paige's hand, Val led the way in and found them a spot to stand near the dance floor.

"Want a drink?" she asked.

"No, I'm fine for now. Look at those people. They're really good dancers," Paige replied, sounding a little anxious.

Val looked out at the dance floor. Several couple were dancing salsa and bachata to an upbeat Shakira song. The energy was electric.

"I don't think I can do that," Paige said, gripping Val's hand tightly.

"Sure you can. We'll wait for a slower song, and I'll teach you." Paige was biting her lip, and she looked sexy as hell. "I'm having an amazing time tonight. I still can't believe you did all this for me."

"Why is that so hard to believe? You deserve it," Paige replied, gazing into Val's eyes.

Their connection was undeniable. "You make me feel so much," Val said, pulling Paige close. She nuzzled her neck, breathing in her warm scent, and placed both hands on Paige's lower back. Paige draped her arms over Val's shoulders, burying her hands in the hair at the nape of her neck. Holding Paige's gaze, Val began to move her hips to the music, leading Paige in a sensual dance that was intoxicating and incredibly hot. She saw her own desire mirrored in Paige's eyes, and she suddenly wanted to take her right there.

Paige moaned, and though the lights were dim, Val saw the flush spread from her face to her throat. Someone nudged Val's shoulder, and she looked up to see Sasha's amused grin.

Sasha leaned in to speak low in her ear. "You two can stand there and continue with the fireworks show, or you can come dance with us."

Val felt herself flush hot, then noticed that the music's tempo had changed. She smiled at Paige. "Ready to salsa?"

Paige nodded, and Val led her onto the dance floor. Paige stood, unsure, and Val took her hands. "Let me lead," she said, placing Paige's hands on her body in the correct positions. "Just feel the rhythm."

Val began to move, whispering instructions and encouragement to Paige. She was a fast learner, and soon they were moving almost as one. Val felt the music flowing through her as she moved, and she let herself go as if no one was watching. She twirled Paige around and dipped her backward, placing a kiss on her throat before bringing their bodies back together.

Nearby, people were clapping and catcalling, and other dancers were giving them a wide berth. Val realized that they were putting on a show, and she felt a rush of pride as she looked at Paige. She was beautiful, her dress hugging her curves and showing off her long shapely legs. A couple of strands of golden hair had escaped their confines and gracefully framed her face. Paige's blue eyes had darkened to indigo, and her lips were parted in a breathless smile.

Val pulled Paige close. "They're watching us," she whispered. "You're incredible."

Paige shook her head in disbelief, glancing around. Her blush deepened, but Val cupped her cheek and gently made Paige look her in the eye. "So beautiful. Let's finish this...follow me." She took Paige's hand and spun her out before her, then pulled her in close, insinuating her thigh between Paige's legs as they moved their hips. As the song ended, Val dipped Paige once more, this time kissing her lips. They came together again without breaking contact, and Paige took Val's face in her hands, deepening the kiss with her tongue.

A moment later Paige broke away breathlessly, clutching Val's shoulders. "Oh my God," Paige murmured.

"Yeah," Val replied, smiling.

"Damn, you two," Sasha said, as she and Jen came up alongside them.

"Yeah, you about set the place on fire," Jen added. "You guys can really dance."

"I've never done that before in my life," Paige said, eyes wide.

"Then you're a natural, and a perfect partner for J.Lo here," Sasha replied.

"Would you stop?" Val said, rolling her eyes. "I am so not like J.Lo."

"Actually, you're hotter," Paige said with a sexy smile, "and I need a drink." She turned and headed toward the bar.

Sasha clapped Val on the back. "Girl, you've got to hang on to that one."

"I plan on it," Val replied. She took a couple of moments to catch her breath, then followed after Paige.

❖

Finding a few inches of space to claim, Paige eased up to the bar. She managed to wave down one of the busy bartenders and ordered a White Russian. As she waited, she looked at the slightly distorted reflections of people in the mirror that covered the entire back of the bar area. She felt her before she saw her, as Val placed her hands on her hips and pressed up against her back.

"Hey," Val said, putting her chin on Paige's shoulder.

"Hey, yourself. What would you like for your birthday drink?"

"I don't know—how about a hard cider?"

"You got it." When the bartender returned with Paige's drink, she placed Val's order, then turned to place her back against the bar rail.

"Thanks for teaching me how to dance. That was so much fun."

"I hate to tell you this, but your secret is out. There's no way you haven't danced like that before," Val said.

"I swear I haven't. I mean, I used to go clubbing once in a while in college, but all my dancing was in front of the mirror in my room when I was in high school." Paige giggled. "How's that for embarrassing stories?"

"That was one lucky-ass mirror. Whatever. You are a perfect dance partner, so I'm the lucky one tonight."

Paige smiled. "Thank you." She gave Val a hug, and behind her, Paige suddenly saw a familiar face glaring back. Paige had a vision of glowing red eyes shooting out daggers at Val's head.

"Don't turn around," Paige whispered, "but Lisa the Lawyer is here."

"Oh, fabulous."

Paige laughed. "Exactly. At least she's staying over there." Paige felt a flash of possessive pride. "I don't think she's very happy that you're mine."

"I'm yours, huh?" Val nuzzled her throat. "That sounds really good to me."

"It does, doesn't it?" Paige put her hand into Val's hair, drawing the silky strands through her fingers. Their attraction was off the charts, but something deeper passed between them in that moment. "Let's go hang out with Sasha and Jen for a while longer and get out of Lisa's firing range."

For the next two hours, they had a blast dancing and laughing with their friends, but in the back of Paige's mind were thoughts of what would happen when they left the bar. She wanted Val, wanted to bring her home and make love for days. All signs pointed to Val feeling the same way, but were they ready to go there? Would their relationship withstand a move to the next level?

"You looked really serious there for a minute," Val said, interrupting her thoughts. "Everything okay?"

"Yeah," Paige lied, "it's just that my feet are killing me in these heels."

"It's crazy crowded in here. I'm ready to go if you are," Val said, gently rubbing her hand up Paige's arm.

Paige looked away. "Tonight's been incredible. I'm just not sure where to go from here." There, she'd said it. Now it was up to Val.

Val ducked her head to meet Paige's eyes. "I'm not ready for our night to end, if that's what you mean."

"Are you sure? I mean, Sasha and Jen…"

"Are going to crash at my house and head home in the morning."

"Do you want to come back to my place?" Paige held her breath, waiting for the answer.

"More than anything, if that's okay." Val's expression was open and honest, and Paige could see the desire simmering in her eyes.

"Then let's go home."

Val gave Sasha her house key, and the four women hugged good-bye.

"Thanks again, you guys. This has been the best night I've had in forever," Val said.

"Glad we could be a part of it," Sasha replied, clasping Val's hand. "Love you, chica. Happy birthday."

"Love you, too," Val said, her eyes glistening.

"Ready?" Paige said. They linked fingers and headed to the parking lot.

On the ride home, Val rested her head on the seat back and sighed. "Thank you, Paige. I can't believe you planned all this tonight. No one's ever done anything like that for me before."

Paige heard the break in Val's voice, and her heart swelled. "I'm so happy you had a good time."

"And I'm so happy I shared it with you. You are very special to me, Paige. I hope you know that." Val's fingers gently stroked the back of Paige's neck.

Paige blinked back tears. "I feel exactly the same way."

Minutes later, she pulled into her driveway, her stomach trembling with nerves and anticipation. They walked to the door, her hand shaking as she fit the key into the lock. Once inside, she flicked on the light and turned directly into Val's arms.

Val caressed Paige's cheeks with featherlight strokes of her thumbs. "I've needed to do this properly all night." She touched her lips to Paige's forehead, her eyes, her jaw, then claimed her mouth, hard.

A dam broke inside Paige. Powerful feelings swirled through her as Val ignited her with kisses. "God, I want you," she gasped. "Come to bed with me."

They kissed and touched as they hurried to Paige's bedroom. She switched on the bedside lamp and stood, weak with need. She held out her hand, and Val closed the distance between them in one long stride.

They kissed deeply with a passion Paige had never felt before. Val thrust her hands into Paige's hair and removed the pins, then ran her hands through it until it fell loosely to her shoulders. Moaning, she nipped at Paige's neck then soothed it with her tongue, before once again kissing Paige breathless.

Val ran her hands down Paige's sides as she fell to her knees before her. Pushing gently at her hips, she made Paige sit on the edge of the bed. Running her hands down her calves, she removed Paige's shoes.

She cradled one foot in her hands, massaging with her thumbs, then rubbed the other. That was a first for Paige, and she groaned in pleasure. Val then trailed her fingers up the backs of Paige's legs until she reached the hem of her dress. Standing, Val took Paige's hands and pulled her up again. Reaching around to her back, she touched the zipper of Paige's dress, her eyes asking for permission. Paige nodded, and Val slowly pulled it down.

Thank God I had a halfway decent set of matching lingerie, Paige thought, before Val's mouth on her made further thinking impossible. Val slowly slid the dress from Paige's shoulders, kissing each new expanse of skin as it was revealed. Soon the dress was in a puddle at her feet, and she stepped out of it, kicking it away.

Self-conscious about her body, Paige pulled Val close. She buried her face in Val's hair, inhaling the warm tropical scent of her. Releasing the clip that held it back, she sank her fingers into the silky waves, holding Val's head still while they kissed. Paige trailed a finger down Val's throat, between her breasts, and down to her exposed midriff. She let her fingers play over the smooth skin before grasping the hem of the shirt.

"Off," she whispered and lifted it over Val's head. Val stepped back and made short work of removing her boots and pants, until they stood before each other in only bras and panties.

Val's eyes traveled Paige's body from head to toe. "You're so beautiful," she said. "I love how your skin blushes everywhere when you're turned on."

Paige's self-consciousness slowly faded away under Val's worshipful gaze. Things she had always thought of as flaws suddenly weren't in Val's eyes. Val kissed her freckled shoulders, slowly easing down the straps of her bra. She nuzzled the little mole at the top of her left breast before unclasping her bra and tossing it aside. Val lifted Paige's breasts in her hands as she leaned in for a searing kiss. Her thumbs played over Paige's nipples, making her moan aloud.

"God, that feels so good," Paige said, her voice catching. "I need to feel you, too." She tenderly stroked between Val's lovely breasts, their dusky nipples visible through the white satin, then reached around to unclasp her bra and free the warm flesh into her waiting hands. "Oh," she breathed, caressing them, then dipped her head to capture a firm nipple between her lips.

Val moaned, holding Paige's head to her breast as Paige bathed the nipple with her tongue, then sucked it gently into her mouth. Paige circled the other nipple with her fingers, teasing it into a hard pebble. Putting her hands on Paige's shoulders, Val pushed until Paige fell back onto the bed. Straddling her, Val leaned down for another hot marathon kiss. She released Paige's mouth and leaned forward, giving Paige access to her breasts, and Paige took full advantage, licking and sucking until Val cried out in need.

Val grasped Paige's hands and pushed her arms up over her head, then scooted back to lavish her breasts with attention. Paige could feel Val's hot wetness through her panties as she moved against her thigh. She ran her hands down Val's back and underneath her panties, cupping her ass.

"Take these off," she demanded, and Val complied.

"Now yours," Val said and slid Paige's soaked panties down her legs.

Paige scooted up until her head lay on the pillow, and Val stretched out beside her, molding their bodies together. Paige sought Val's mouth once again, and as they kissed, Val ran her hand in slow, teasing circles down Paige's body. Nudging her legs apart, Val continued to stroke and tickle Paige's thighs, avoiding her center in a dance of sweet torture.

"Please," Paige begged when she couldn't stand it any longer, and Val finally touched her.

"You're so wet," Val murmured, sliding her fingers through Paige's silky heat. She drew a nipple into her mouth as she stroked, building Paige up until she was writhing with pleasure.

"Inside," Paige moaned, and Val entered her in one smooth stroke. The powerful sensations soon took Paige over the edge, and she cried out as her trembling thighs clamped together, holding Val inside. Several moments elapsed before the aftershocks subsided and Paige released Val's hand.

Paige couldn't stop the tears, and she flung an arm over her eyes, mortified that she was crying. This had been the most incredible sexual experience of her life, and she was overwhelmed with emotion.

"Paige, what's wrong? Did I hurt you?" Val leaned over her, frowning with concern.

Paige reached up and cupped Val's cheek, running her thumb lightly over her bottom lip. "Oh God, no." Paige didn't know how to put her feelings into words without sounding stupid, but the tenderness in Val's eyes eased her fear. "I've just never felt so amazing before. You made me feel...beautiful."

"Well, you are, so mission accomplished," Val said, smiling. She gently brushed Paige's hair away from her face, then leaned down and kissed her lips. "You are very beautiful, and it boggles my mind that you don't know that."

"Guess I've got my own baggage, but you're helping," Paige said, smiling. She pushed Val down and rolled over to straddle her thighs. "You, on the other hand," she said, taking in the sight before her, "leave me at a loss for words."

Val's dark hair was fanned out on the pillow, and her golden brown skin shone in the lamplight. Her face was perfection, and Paige leaned down to claim those full lips once again. "You're incredible," she whispered, as she moved her lips along Val's jaw to nuzzle her earlobe, then nibbled her way down her throat. She filled her hands with Val's breasts, kneading them gently before pushing them together so she could lick both nipples at once.

Val groaned. "Yes, so good."

Paige took her time, slowly moving down Val's body. Her hair brushed Val's flawless skin, raising gooseflesh as she kissed and tasted her way to her destination. Val moaned softly, her hips undulating beneath Paige. Easing herself down, she spread Val's legs and lay between them, kissing along one thigh, then the other.

Val buried her hands in Paige's hair and stilled her hips in anticipation. "Touch me," she whispered.

Paige spread her open, reveling in the slick heat of her arousal. She stroked her, circling, until Val's legs began to tremble and her moans grew louder. At the first touch of her tongue, Val jerked and whimpered, and Paige rubbed her belly in soft, soothing circles as her mouth tasted and explored. When Val's thighs tightened and her hips came off the bed, Paige entered her, thrusting as she sucked her into her mouth. Val came hard with a low keening cry, and Paige felt a rush of satisfaction, like she'd just summited Everest.

"Oh my God, oh my God, oh my God," Val said, pulling weakly on Paige's hair. "Come here." Paige crawled up to lay her head on Val's shoulder. Pulling her close, Val pressed her lips to her forehead.

"That was beyond amazing," Val said quietly. "You are unbelievable."

"Glad you think so," Paige replied, lightly tracing Val's collarbone with her fingers.

"I know so, because I can't move. You shattered me."

"Uh-oh, that sounds serious," Paige teased, kissing Val's shoulder. "Is there a remedy for that condition?"

"Yeah. Falling asleep with you in my arms ought to do the trick."

"Good plan. Let's get under the covers."

They snuggled together, limbs entwined, and drifted off to sleep.

CHAPTER THIRTY-THREE

Val dreamed she was floating, surrounded by softness and warmth, seeing nothing, but feeling completely at peace. A warm weight lay across her chest, and every breath in brought the scents of lavender and vanilla. The sensations were foreign but not unpleasant, and she let herself drift.

She awakened with a start to find a warm head tucked beneath her chin and a hand cupping her breast. For a moment she didn't know where she was, but then Paige stirred against her. Memories of their night together flooded back, and she stroked Paige's soft hair in wonder.

She had shared a beautiful, incredible night with a woman she cared deeply for, which put her solidly in uncharted territory. She had no clue what to do next, and little stabs of anxiety prickled in her chest. The warm hand left her breast and softly caressed her cheek.

"Are you okay?" Paige lifted her head to look at Val.

"Yeah, why?" Val replied, trying to play it cool.

"You tensed up, that's all." Paige sat up, and the sheet fell from her naked breasts.

Val's groin tightened with arousal. "I'm fine. Just reliving last night." She reached out to touch Paige's nipple, and it hardened immediately.

"That'll be my favorite daydream for quite a while," Paige replied, biting her lip as Val's hand moved to her other breast.

"I don't suppose we can stay in bed for the rest of the day," Val said.

"Unfortunately, no. I have to pick up Emma by eleven." Paige glanced at her alarm clock. "That does, however, leave us with three more hours to ourselves."

"I have some ideas on how to spend that time, if you're up for it," Val replied, throwing off the covers.

"Race you to the shower."

❖

They'd made love twice that morning, and Val had been just as attentive as the night before, but now Paige could feel her pulling away. As they drove back to Val's house, she was quiet and Paige didn't press, but once in the driveway, she named the elephant in the room.

"Val," she said, putting her hand on Val's arm, "we don't have to pretend that this was business as usual for either of us. I get the whole morning-after awkward thing, but it's more than that, at least for me."

Val stared at her lap for several moments, then looked sidelong at Paige as if she was embarrassed. "You're right. I'm kind of at a loss here. We just shared the most amazing night of my life, and I want more. Not just more sex, though that would be awesome, but more of you. That's never happened to me before."

"I understand," Paige said, "because being with you is completely different, and better, than anything I've ever experienced. So would it be fair to say that we're both scared shitless?"

Val laughed. "That about sums it up."

"Okay. Now that we know that, we can work through it."

"You want to work through it? I told you before, Paige, I'm damaged goods when it comes to relationships. I know you've been hurt before—I don't want to hurt you again."

Paige sighed. "Let me tell you about that past relationship. I was young and had just gotten away from my parents for the first time. Maura was older and everything I wanted to be—confident, beautiful, in control, successful. I thought the sun rose and set on her. Looking back now, I was beyond stupid, but I had no idea then.

"She basically picked up where my parents left off, trying to mold me into whatever it was she thought I should be. Guess I never quite measured up, and she made sure I knew it. She criticized everything— my clothing choices, my hairstyles, how I expressed my emotions.

With sex, she acted like she was doing me a favor by allowing me to touch her."

"What a bitch," Val said, frowning.

"You know what the kicker was? She cheated on me and blamed it on my inadequacies as a girlfriend."

"I pretty much want to go find this woman and kick her ass," Val declared. "I can't believe she treated you that way."

"I can't believe I let her. My self-esteem was in the toilet for so many years, and it took therapy, being alone, and raising Emma to make me see my worth. If I had met you back then, no way in hell would I have even spoken to you."

"Are you kidding me? You're a better person than I'll ever be."

"Not true, but anyway, my whole point is this—we've both had bad experiences, but we are not damaged goods, and we both deserve to be happy." Paige put up both fists like a boxer. "I dare you to disagree with me."

"And here I thought you didn't have a violent bone in your body," Val teased. Then she sobered, looking Paige in the eye. "You're happy with me?"

"I am, very much so, and I don't want to ruin this chance with you by thinking about past history." Paige leaned over and gave Val a long, sweet kiss. "I've got no plans, no expectations. Let's just do this one day at a time."

Val's eyes welled up with tears. "I stopped wishing for good things a long time ago, because losing hurts too much, and I can't lose what I don't have. Then the kids came and unlocked something in me, but now they're gone, too." Tears streamed down Val's cheeks, and Paige's heart broke for her, for all she'd been through.

"You slipped past my defenses before I even knew I'd let you in. I'm afraid to want you, Paige. And I don't know what to do with that."

"Just give it a chance. Whatever is happening with us is too special to run away from." Paige held Val's face in her hands. "Okay?"

"Okay." Val sniffed and wiped her eyes. "You are the most amazing person I've ever met, and that Maura chick was a complete idiot not to realize it."

"Lucky for me she didn't, or I might not have met you. Plus, I am fully confident that karma will kick her ass someday."

"Good attitude."

Paige glanced at the time. "I've gotta go. Are we okay?"

Val nodded. "We're good. I'll be thinking about how good all day." She waggled her eyebrows suggestively.

Paige laughed, relieved that the mood was lighter. "I'll call you later."

Val leaned over for a quick kiss and got out of the car. "Paige?" she said, before shutting the door.

"Hmm?"

"Thank you, for everything. I mean it."

"I know." Paige smiled and blew Val a kiss, then watched as she walked to her door and went inside, waving one last time before closing the door.

The tears that had been threatening finally spilled from Paige's eyes. *Please, baby, just give us a chance.*

"Tell me about her," Susan said.

"Well, she works for the foster care unit, she's my age, and she has a daughter..."

Susan waved her hand impatiently. "No, no, no—that's just demographics. Tell me about *her*."

Val couldn't keep from smiling. "She's beautiful, and smart, and her smile takes my breath away. She's funny, and honest, and incredibly kind. How's that for descriptive?"

"Great, but your body language told me even more. You really care about this woman."

Val nodded. "I do."

"You feel safe with her, grounded," Susan said.

Val looked at her, surprised. "What makes you say that?"

"When you talk about her, your whole body relaxes, which I'm not sure I've ever seen with you before. I think this is a pretty big deal, actually."

"That's why I'm worried. I've never let anyone get so close to me, but I wanted to with her. Now my emotions are all over the place, and I feel kind of, I don't know, out of control." Val's knee started bouncing as her anxiety grew.

"Let's explore that. What do you feel?" Susan said.

Val blew out a breath. "Excited and happy one minute, then scared the next. When I'm with her, she calms me. When I'm not, I feel agitated. I want to let myself feel everything with her, but there's something in the way. It's like I'm trying to swim to her, but the current keeps pulling me back. And that makes me angry." Val threw her hands in the air. "See? I'm a hot fucking mess."

Susan chuckled. "What you are is a very passionate woman who needs to let go of the past to fully embrace the future. I think you need to give yourself permission to care about her."

"Yeah, well, easier said than done."

"We'll get you there. Remember you told me that you feel guilty for not caring about others in your past the way you thought you should have?"

"Yeah, some of my foster siblings. I think they loved me, but I didn't let myself love them," Val replied, staring at the floor.

"Why?"

"I know you're going to say it's about loss, because I loved my mom and my grandma and my brother, but I lost them."

"And?"

"And I didn't let myself love people because it would hurt too much if they left, too," Val recited. "I get all that in my head, but it's still hard to keep the fear from taking over."

"You mentioned your grandma. Tell me about her," Susan said.

"She was a tiny Puerto Rican woman, but she filled a room. She was just full of wisdom and love, and very protective of my brother and me. When Abuelita said something, we listened. She always told me stories and taught me about life. She encouraged me to read and do well in school. She was basically everything my mother wasn't." Tears stung Val's eyes as she remembered.

"So did having your grandmother improve your life?"

"Well, yeah. She was everything to me."

"And even though you lost her, was loving her worth it?"

Val looked up at Susan as her point hit home. After a moment, she said, "I see what you did there."

Susan smiled. "Playing it safe is an option, but so is going after what you want. Nothing is guaranteed, and nothing lasts forever, no matter which way you go. The way I see it, we can choose to avoid life, or we can truly live it."

Val nodded. "Valid point, Doc."

Susan checked her watch. "Time's about up for today, so I'll send you home with one more question to think about."

Val rolled her eyes. "My brain's already scrambled, but let me have it."

"Is Paige worth the risk?"

CHAPTER THIRTY-FOUR

Four days without touching you has been a new kind of torture," Val murmured, as she and Paige fumbled through her front door after work. Emma was at her Brownie meeting, and they were taking full advantage of their kid-free time.

Paige had her up against the door as soon as it shut, her mouth on her neck. "I completely agree," she replied, nuzzling Val in the velvety soft spot beneath her ear.

"So do you want to watch TV?" Val teased.

"Hell no," Paige growled, pulling Val's shirt from her pants and touching the warm skin of her back.

"How about a game of Scrabble?"

"Nuh-uh." Paige brought her hands to the front and frantically began undoing shirt buttons. She opened Val's shirt wide and buried her face between her breasts.

"Go for a walk?" Val's voice was getting a little breathless, and Paige grinned.

"Maybe later." She cupped Val's breasts, massaging her nipples through the fabric of her bra.

"Perhaps," Val said, moaning, "you'd like to have wild, passionate sex?"

"Bingo." Paige pushed Val's shirt off her shoulders, trapping her arms, and moved in for a fiery kiss. Five minutes later, they both stood naked in Val's room.

"You smell so good," Val whispered as she buried her face in Paige's hair from behind.

She wrapped her arms around Paige and pulled her back against her body. Paige moaned at the exquisite contact of Val's nipples on her back, her heat pressed against her ass. Val's soft lips caressed her neck, and when she cupped her breasts and squeezed, Paige nearly came.

"I can't believe what you do to me," Paige said, taking Val's hand and pressing it to her center. She turned her head to capture Val's lips, and they kissed deeply as Val stroked her. Too soon, the orgasm rolled over her, sweet and slow, and Paige's trembling legs nearly gave out.

Val's strong arms held her close. "Lie down," she said softly.

Paige lay back on the bed, and Val lowered herself, hips to hips, breasts to breasts. The sensation of Val's satin skin on her body was intoxicating, and Paige let her hands roam. She stroked Val's back as they kissed, and when she grasped her hips, Val began to thrust against her. Paige slipped her hand between their bodies and gasped when she felt the intensity of Val's silky heat. Eyes closed, lips parted, Val moved against Paige's hand, moaning softly. It was the most beautiful image Paige had ever seen.

Val threw her head back and cried out when Paige entered her. Thrusting faster, she rode Paige's hand to an explosive orgasm. Paige stayed inside, feeling Val's body clench around her fingers over and over. Val collapsed onto Paige's chest, her thick hair blanketing her skin, and whimpered as Paige withdrew her hand.

"Wow," Val said, her voice husky.

"You're breathtaking," Paige said, sweeping Val's hair back and kissing her forehead.

"Can I tell you something?"

"Of course," Paige said.

"My whole life, people have made comments about how I look, saying I'm hot or whatever. I always hated that, because I felt like an object. They never looked past the outside to see *me*." Val brought her hand to Paige's cheek, caressing gently. "With you, I actually feel beautiful, for the first time in my life."

Paige couldn't speak. She held Val close and they both cried, finally releasing some of the pain and insecurity they'd carried for years.

❖

Three weeks later, Paige was still on cloud nine. Things between her and Val were amazing, and she'd never been happier. She was walking down the corridor, humming to herself, when someone called her name. Connie caught up to her.

"Hey, Paige, come talk with me for a minute?"

"Sure," Paige said, curious. She followed Connie to her desk and sat down. "What's up?"

"So, how are things going with Val?"

Paige smiled. "Really good."

"And you're serious about developing this relationship?" Connie pressed.

"Well, yeah. Why? Did Val say something?" Paige's heart skipped a beat.

"No, no, nothing like that. I just wanted to check to see if my intuition was right about you two."

"We're in a good place. I'm a little curious about why you're asking, though," Paige said.

"Well, it's like this. I received a call this morning from Sheryl Watkins."

"Really? Huh. She usually calls me," Paige said.

"She said that you had been very helpful and kind, but she felt like her news would disappoint you, so she called me instead," Connie explained. "Her husband's company is downsizing, and he has to move to Indiana or he'll lose his job. They've decided to go, but they do not want to bring the foster children with them."

Paige was stunned. "The kids were having trouble adjusting, but I didn't expect this. Wow."

"Mrs. Watkins asked if they could go back to Valerie. We will need to ask her if she is willing to take the children, although I'm fairly certain of the answer. Typically, in a situation like this, the case would also transfer back to the original worker."

"I see." A flurry of emotions took up residence in Paige's stomach. What would this mean?

"So you see why I needed to officially ask about your

relationship," Connie said. "Since there is now a conflict of interest, our supervisor needs to know. I'll ask Sandra to assign the case to someone else."

The only people at work who knew Paige was a lesbian were Connie and Joe. Guess that was about to change. She looked at Connie. "That pretty much outs me to the boss, then, doesn't it?"

"You don't need to worry about that, kiddo. Sandra is as open-minded as they come," Connie replied.

Paige breathed a sigh of relief. "Thank you."

"Not a problem," Connie said, smiling. "Now, I'm guessing you'd like to let Val know of this new development." She winked, and Paige just looked at her as the news finally sank in. Then she grinned.

"Yes, ma'am, I will."

"Hey, hon. How's your day going?" Paige said.

Val smiled. She loved that Paige called on occasion just to say hi. "Hey, yourself. My day just got better."

"Sweet talker. Listen, could you come over for dinner tonight? I've got some news."

"Sure. Is everything okay?"

"I think it will be," Paige replied. "I've got to go. See you at six?"

"I'll be there. Can I bring anything?"

"Just you."

She pulled into Paige's driveway a little before six, her curiosity piqued. Why hadn't Paige just told her over the phone? She tried to tamp down her tendency to catastrophize. News didn't have to be bad, she reminded herself, and Paige hadn't sounded upset. She shook her head at her own impatience and headed to the door.

Paige opened it with a smile, and Val stepped into her arms. Paige didn't mess around when she gave hugs, and Val instantly felt good all over.

"Hi," Paige said, giving Val a kiss on the neck before releasing her. "Thanks for coming over on such short notice."

"It's not like I had to fit you into my vast calendar of social engagements or anything."

"Thank goodness. Dinner's about ready."

"What's your news?"

"We'll talk after dinner. Emma, come and eat."

Emma walked slowly into the room, her nose in a book.

"Hey, kiddo," Val said. "Whatcha reading?"

Emma looked up and smiled. "Hey, Miss Val. It's *A Wrinkle in Time*. I got it at the book fair at school."

"That was one of my favorites when I was a kid."

"Really?" Emma said.

"Yep. I love books about smart, brave girls."

"Me, too. Mommy, what's for dinner?"

"Why don't you two come sit down and see?" Paige replied.

❖

After dinner they cleaned up the dishes, and Paige still hadn't said anything about her news. Val couldn't stand it any longer.

"*So*...what's your news?"

"Let me finish washing the dishes, and then I'll tell you," Paige replied.

"You know you're killing me here, right? Patience is not my forte. What if I guess? Will you tell me then?"

Paige laughed. "Guess away."

"You're pregnant."

Paige snorted. "Yeah, right."

"You won the lottery?"

"I wish, but no."

"You want to move to Montana and live off grid in a yurt," Val said.

"You have a very vivid imagination, Val."

"Yes, I know."

Paige rinsed the last dish and set it in the drainer. "Okay, you big baby, come on." She went to the living room and sat on the couch, patting the cushion beside her.

Val sat down, her chest fluttering with anticipation.

"Connie sat me down for a chat today."

"Okay. What about?"

"She wanted to know, officially, if you and I are serious," Paige said.

"I don't get it," Val said. "She knows we're together." Her eyes suddenly widened. "What did you tell her?"

Paige laughed. "I said yes, we are happily pursuing a serious relationship. The thing is, she received a phone call that made her have to ask me in the first place. Turns out I have a conflict of interest with a case coming in, and she needed to let my boss know that we're together."

"Your boss. Will that make trouble for you?"

"Connie assured me it wouldn't, but there's more."

Val's leg started bouncing as her anxiety kicked in. "I'm not sure I want to hear this."

She stilled under the gentle pressure of Paige's hand. "I think you do. Sheryl Watkins and her husband are moving to Indiana for his job. They don't want to take Lily and Ian."

Val felt like she couldn't breathe. "What?"

"They're coming back, Val, and we'd like them to be with you."

Val's emotions spun like a pinwheel in a stiff breeze. "With me?"

"Honey, do you want them to be with you?" Paige asked.

"Yes! I mean, of course I do, but what happens next? What if someone else steps up and wants to take them again?" The idea of losing them twice made Val sick.

"Here's the thing—I already went through everyone related to the kids, and no one else came forward. The county is going to seek termination of parental rights, so if the judge agrees, the kids would be available for adoption," Paige said, squeezing Val's knee.

"Oh my God. You mean that they could stay with me... permanently?"

"It's a very good possibility." Paige was smiling broadly now, and Val's heart soared.

"But what about you? Your boss knows we're together."

"Yes, so she gave the case to Joe. No more conflict of interest," Paige said, wrapping her arm around Val's shoulder.

"This is incredible." Val's eyes filled with tears. "I'm afraid to really believe it."

"Believe it, babe. Good things really do happen." Paige turned and looped her arms around Val's neck, her own eyes moist. "And I can't think of a better person for them to happen to."

Val was too choked up to speak. She pulled Paige into her arms and held her close, letting her tears of happiness flow. After a few moments, a thought occurred to her, and she pulled back suddenly.

"When can they come home?"

"Whenever you're ready," Paige replied, caressing her cheek.

"How about tomorrow?"

CHAPTER THIRTY-FIVE

They'd decided to let Lily and Ian finish the school week and come back on Saturday, and the day was finally here. Val was so excited she had barely slept the night before. She'd spent the last couple of days preparing for the kids' return—getting their room ready, stocking up on their favorite foods, and reenrolling them in school. Paige was going to drop Emma off in a little while, then accompany Joe when he picked up the kids.

Val's emotions had been on a roller-coaster ride since Paige told her the news. She was hoping that she would be able to adopt Lily and Ian, but nothing was certain yet. Connie had stopped by on Thursday to check in, and Val told her about her nagging worry that something might go wrong. Connie reminded her that she was the main constant in the children's lives since they'd entered the system, and by summer she would have had them for the better part of a year. If anyone else came forward after the year mark, she would have rights to custody.

Yesterday, she and Susan spent the whole session talking about those damned what-ifs that kept popping into her head. So far today, she was doing a much better job keeping her anxiety in check. Sometimes, when she thought of everything that had happened in her life since last summer, it was a little overwhelming, but she now knew she wouldn't trade it for anything.

Val heard a car in the driveway and went to the door. Emma came running up to her, surprising her with a big hug.

"This is the best day ever," she exclaimed, bouncing up and down. "Aren't you excited, Miss Val?"

"Yep, I'm very excited," Val said, exchanging a warm look with

Paige over Emma's head. "Morning," she said, and Paige's answering smile settled over her like a soft blanket, soothing her nerves.

"Did you sleep?" Paige asked.

"Not much," Val replied. "I just couldn't shut off my head."

"I figured as much. Put Emma in front of the TV, and maybe you can catch a quick nap."

"I can try."

"Emma brought some things to occupy herself, right, Em?"

"Yeah. I'm gonna make Lily and Ian a welcome home poster," Emma replied.

"Great idea, kiddo. Why don't you go to the kitchen table and get started?" Val replied. When Emma was out of sight, Val pulled Paige into a tight hug. "I think I'm going to burst. I feel like dancing, singing, and throwing up all at once."

Paige laughed. "I'm so happy for you guys. I couldn't have imagined a better outcome."

Val tipped up Paige's chin and kissed her softly. "I don't know how I would've managed without you through all of this."

"You would've done just fine, but I am very happy to be a part of it." Paige kissed Val more thoroughly, then reluctantly pulled away. "As much as I'd like to stand here and kiss you all day, I've got to go meet Joe. We've got some kids to pick up."

"Go on, then. When do you think you'll be back?"

"It's about three hours round-trip, and we'll probably need to stop along the way. I'm thinking by two?" Paige replied.

"Can't wait. Tell Joe to drive safely, okay? He's going to be transporting some very precious cargo."

Paige smiled. "Will do. Emma," she called, "you behave for Miss Valerie, okay? Be back soon."

Emma came out of the kitchen. "Okay, Mommy. Bye."

After Paige left, Val turned to Emma. "Want some help with your poster?"

"Yeah, sure! Come on, I'll show you all the stuff I brought."

Seeing that there were glitter and glue involved, Val covered the table with newspaper, and the two of them got busy. Val was coloring in some block letters when Emma abruptly spoke.

"I know you and Mommy are girlfriends."

Val tried to hide her shock. "You do?"

"Yeah. I asked Mommy because I saw you kissing. It's okay, though. Mommy really likes you, and so do I," Emma said.

Val's heart melted, even as her cheeks flamed. "Aw, thanks, Emma. I really like both of you, too."

Emma smiled. "Good." They continued their project while she chattered on about school and why she thought the book version of *A Wrinkle in Time* was better than the movie. Soon they had two colorful, sparkly posters, one for Lily and one for Ian.

"Do you think they'll like them?" Emma asked as they cleaned up.

"I know so," Val replied. "Are you hungry?"

They had some lunch, then watched a movie. Emma was a great kid to hang out with, and Val was enjoying herself. Her relationship with Paige wasn't mentioned again, but Val was relieved that Emma seemed fine with it.

By one thirty, Val was getting antsy. Paige had texted an hour ago when they'd gotten back on the Thruway. They should be here any minute now. Emma was engrossed in her book, oblivious of the time or that Val kept checking out the front window.

Finally, Val heard a car. "Emma, I think they're here."

Emma let out a squeal, and they both rushed to the door. Val made it out onto the front step just in time to be tackled by Lily, who was crying hysterically. Val held her and rubbed her back, her own tears flowing unchecked.

Ian ran up the stairs next and threw his arms around Val's waist. "Mama, I missed you," he said, and buried his face in her side. When Lily realized Emma was there, she let go of Val and bear hugged her best friend, both of them laughing and crying at the same time.

Val looked up to see Paige and Joe standing at the bottom of the porch steps, holding the kids' bags and grinning from ear to ear. This ranked right up there among the happiest moments of her life.

❖

Two hours later, the kids were all playing in their bedroom. Val demanded a play-by-play of the events of the day.

"When we got to the house, Lily and Ian practically ran to the car. I had to make them go back and thank Sheryl for taking care of them," Paige said.

"Oh no. How did Sheryl react to that?"

"She looked just as relieved as they did that they were leaving."

"Do you think she treated them okay?" Val asked.

"Yes, but she and her husband are in their fifties. They didn't really spend time or play with the kids, and I think Lily's refusal to accept things made it tough for them to bond," Paige said.

"Hopefully everyone will be happier now," Val said. "Right now, I feel like life is pretty damn close to perfect."

Paige took Val's face in her hands. "You glow when you're happy. It's a pretty awesome sight, I must say." She kissed her then, a slow, sweet kiss full of promise.

Val moaned. "You should win an award for kissing." Then she grinned, remembering. "Guess what Emma told me earlier?"

"God only knows with that kid. What?"

"She said she knew we were girlfriends, then proceeded to give her blessing. She said that you really liked me and so did she."

Paige jaw dropped. "Shut up. She just asked me this morning. Remember that night she walked in on us on the couch? She saw more than we thought, and she's apparently been putting two and two together. What did you say?"

"I told her that the feelings were mutual."

Paige smiled. "The feelings are definitely mutual." They kissed again, then embraced.

Val wanted to share how she was truly feeling, but her anxiety was getting in the way. Finally, she won the battle. "Paige, I need to say something, and I hope you don't freak out."

Paige frowned at her. "Way to go—now I'm expecting to freak out."

"Hope not." Val held both of her hands and looked down at them as she spoke. "It's just…having all of us here together, it feels right. We've all taken so many chances to get to this point, but it was worth it. I feel like I have a family."

Paige didn't respond, and Val glanced up to find tears coursing down Paige's cheeks. Val's stomach clenched. "Did I upset you?"

Paige smiled and wrapped her arms around Val's neck. "No, baby. There is nothing I'd like more than making a family with you. I just needed you to be ready."

Val pressed her lips to Paige's, trying to convey everything she felt. "I'm ready. I love you."

Paige smile spoke right to Val's heart. "I love you, too."

They held each other, simply staying in the moment and basking in their love.

❖

The giggles from down the hall grew louder as the girls came from the bedroom into the living room.

Paige looked at Val. "Wanna tell them?"

Val got a sudden case of nerves, but Paige just rubbed her back, calming her.

"So, listen, you guys," Val began, "how would you feel if we all spent a lot more time together?"

Lily tilted her head. "You mean like best friends?"

"Even better than that," Val replied, smiling at Paige.

"I told you, Lily. They love each other," Emma exclaimed, grinning widely.

"Does this mean we can all stay together?" Lily asked.

Val nodded, knowing in her heart that everything would work out, that this was meant to be.

"That means we can be sisters *and* best friends," Emma said, high-fiving Lily.

Ian poked his head between the two girls and looked at Val. "We're a family, Mama?"

Val looked at Paige and saw her future clearly. "Yeah, buddy, we are."

A huge grin spread across his face and he threw both hands in the air. "Yay!"

Epilogue

Eight months later

"Mama, can you put this thing on me?" Ian held up his blue plaid bow tie.

"Sure, buddy. Come here." Val clipped the tie onto his white shirt collar, then tucked the shirttail into his navy blue pants. Holding him by the shoulders at arm's length, she looked at her boy. "You are a very handsome little man, Ian."

Ian blushed and smiled. "Stop it, Mama."

"Well, it's true. Are your sisters ready?"

"Probably not. They take forever."

Paige came into the room, looking gorgeous in the new floral print dress that she'd bought for the occasion. "They're braiding each other's hair. They're almost done." She walked over to Val and looked her up and down. "You look great, babe."

Val had also purchased a new outfit for today, to match Ian. She wore a dressy white peasant blouse embroidered in a blue and green floral pattern, and loose navy blue linen slacks. "Thanks. So do you."

The girls came out in their matching pink flowered dresses, their hair in neat French braids. "We're ready," Lily said.

"Did everybody brush their teeth?" Val asked. Three little heads nodded. "Okay, then. Let's go."

They headed downtown for their nine a.m. appointment. Val felt almost giddy with excitement, but Paige was holding her hand, caressing gently, grounding her. She parked in the city lot, and they all walked across the street. There, on the courthouse steps, stood Sasha, Jen, Connie, Joe, and Charlie, all smiling broadly.

Val's heart was full. "Hi, everyone. Thanks for coming."

"Wouldn't have missed it for the world. It's a very important day, right, Ian?" Sasha said, ruffling his hair. He nodded, smiling shyly.

"Well, don't you girls look pretty," Connie said to Lily and Emma.

"Thank you," they replied in unison, grinning at each other.

"We'd better go in. Judge Foster is waiting," Paige said.

In the courtroom, Val and Paige sat at an attorney's table with Lily and Ian while the others took seats in the gallery. Val looked around, still in awe at the turn her life had taken. She had last been here four months ago, when Paige had become her wife. Now, in the eyes of the law, they would finally all be a family.

"All rise," the clerk said, and they stood as Judge Foster entered the chambers. He was generally an imposing, no-nonsense man, but today he had a kind grandfatherly air about him.

"Please be seated." He made a show of shuffling papers as the kids looked on, wide-eyed. "Now, let's see. I believe there are two children here that I'd like to meet. Lily and Ian, please approach the bench."

Val nudged them forward, and Lily took Ian's hand as they walked up to the judge.

"I understand that you two are ready to become part of your forever family, is that right?" The children nodded solemnly. "Well, I've reviewed the case and am in full agreement that we should make that happen right this minute," Judge Foster said. "Come here, children. I have important documents to show you."

Lily and Ian walked up the step and around the judge's bench to stand beside him. Paige and Sasha began taking pictures of the children looking so adorably serious.

"See these papers?" the judge said. "These are legal documents. They say that you will be known from this moment forward as Lily and Ian Wellington-Cruz, because your moms love you and want you to be their forever children. Ian, take this little hammer here." Judge Foster handed Ian the gavel. "On the count of three, I want you to use that hammer to hit this wooden circle right here."

Ian held the gavel with both hands, looking at the judge expectantly.

"Okay, everyone, let's count."

All in attendance chanted, "One, two, three!" and Ian swung the gavel as hard as he could, making a resounding *thwack* that echoed in the courtroom. Everyone laughed, and Ian grinned widely.

The judge stood and put his hands on Lily's and Ian's shoulders. "By the powers vested in me by the State of New York, I hereby declare that Lily and Ian are officially adopted." He reached beneath his bench and pulled out two white teddy bears for the children. Lily and Ian hugged their adoption bears tightly, and everyone cheered.

The next few minutes were a flurry of hugs and picture-taking, but finally, Val stood with Paige and the three children in a group hug. Val kissed Paige, then touched her lips to the top of each child's head.

"I love you guys with all my heart," she said. The girls squeezed tighter, and Ian's muffled voice rose from the center.

"Love you, too!"

❖

Paige gently played with Val's hair as she lay with her head pillowed on Paige's breast. Tears came to her eyes as she relived how exquisite and deeply emotional their earlier lovemaking had been. Paige had never connected so completely with another person in her entire life, and the feelings coursing through her were overwhelming, but in a good way.

Val lifted her head and looked up at her. "Baby, what's wrong? You're trembling."

Paige laid her hand on Val's cheek and smiled. "Nothing's wrong. I was just thinking about how blessed I am that everything is so right."

Val moved up and kissed Paige slowly and tenderly, her own tears mingling with Paige's. When they parted, Val placed her hand over Paige's heart.

"I never in my life thought this could happen to me. In fact, I spent a lot of time and effort ensuring it wouldn't." Val smiled and shook her head. "But you—kind, giving, wonderful you—taught me how to love again. You and the kids have given me a family, and I swear to you that I will do everything I can to protect that for the rest of my life."

Paige's tears flowed freely now as her heart surged with love for Val. "You're incredible. You just put everything I've been thinking and feeling into the perfect words. How do you do that?"

Val grinned. "What can I say? I've got it going on."

"Oh, I can attest to that." Paige laughed and pulled Val close. She held her, stroking her hair for several long moments, adrift in bliss.

"Paige?"

"Hmm?"

"Does the county keep records of past foster placements and adoptions?"

"I believe so, but I'd have to ask Connie what's kept and for how long. Why?"

Val didn't answer right away, and Paige waited, caressing the bare skin of her shoulder and giving her time to gather her thoughts.

"I think," Val said quietly, "I'd like to try and find Enrique."

"Wow, sweetie," Paige said, surprised. "That's huge. So you're hoping the county has a record of him?"

"Yeah. I mean, all I know is that he supposedly went to live with his father somewhere out West. I don't know if he still has my last name or not, and I feel like I'd be looking for a needle in a haystack."

Val took a deep breath and let it out slowly. Paige knew that this was a giant risk for Val to take after all she'd been through, and Paige was amazed at her courage.

As if reading Paige's mind, Val said, "I know trying to find him could be a total bust, but for so many years I've wondered if he's okay. I want to know if he graduated from high school, if he's happy, how tall he's grown. Ian is the same age my brother was the last time I saw him. Now Enrique is twenty-five years old—I've missed so much."

Val sniffed, and Paige gave her a squeeze. "Whatever you need, I'll help, okay?"

Val sat up and looked into Paige's eyes. "Thank you. Because of you, I'm ready. I already feel like I have the perfect sundae—Enrique would just be an extra cherry on top."

Paige laughed through a fresh flow of tears. "Great. Not only have you made me cry again, but now I want ice cream."

Val grinned. "That could be arranged."

"It's two o'clock in the morning, you goof."

"True. Is there perhaps something else I could do to satisfy your craving?" Val said, touching a fingertip to Paige's bottom lip.

"Hmm, let me see," Paige replied, feeling her body ignite. She put her hands on Val's shoulders and pushed her onto her back, then lowered her body until they were breast to breast. The love and trust she saw in Val's eyes made her heart sing. "Thanks for taking a chance on me," Paige whispered.

"Hey, I think that's my line," Val said with a smile. She pulled Paige down for a kiss that felt like a thousand promises. "My beautiful woman, I love you."

Paige felt like she might explode with joy. "Oh, baby, I love you, too."

About the Author

Erin McKenzie has been a lover of words since she first learned her ABCs, sparking a lifelong passion for reading, writing, and of course, word games! She is a professional school counselor, mom to her three young children, partner to her wife of seventeen years, chief dishwasher and laundry folder, soccer mom and homework checker. She and her family live in the Finger Lakes region of New York State and share their home with several furry friends.

Taking Chances is Erin's second novel and features a topic that is near and dear to her family's heart. She hopes you enjoy the story!

Books Available From Bold Strokes Books

A Wish Upon a Star by Jeannie Levig. Erica Cooper has learned to depend on only herself, but when her new neighbor, Leslie Raymond, befriends Erica's special needs daughter, the walls protecting Erica's heart threaten to crumble. (978-1-163555-274-4)

Answering the Call by Ali Vali. Detective Sept Savoie returns to the streets of New Orleans, as do the dead bodies from ritualistic killings, and she does everything in her power to bring their killers to justice while trying to keep her partner, Keegan Blanchard, safe. (978-1-163555-050-4)

Friends Without Benefits by Dena Blake. When Dex Putman gets the woman she thought she always wanted, she soon wonders if it's really love after all. (978-1-163555-349-9)

Invalid Evidence by Stevie Mikayne. Private Investigator Jil Kidd is called away to investigate a possible killer whale, just when her partner Jess needs her most. (978-1-163555-307-9)

Pursuit of Happiness by Carsen Taite. When attorney Stevie Palmer's client reveals a scandal that could derail Senator Meredith Mitchell's presidential bid, their chance at love may be collateral damage. (978-1-163555-044-3)

Seascape by Karis Walsh. Marine biologist Tess Hansen returns to Washington's isolated northern coast, where she struggles to adjust to small-town living while courting an endowment from Brittany James for her orca research center. (978-1-163555-079-5)

Second In Command by VK Powell. Jazz Perry's life is disrupted and her career jeopardized when she becomes personally involved with the case of an abandoned child and the child's competent but strict social worker, Emory Blake. (978-1-163555-185-3)

Taking Chances by Erin McKenzie. When Valerie Cruz and Paige Wellington clash over what's in the best interest of the children in Valerie's care, the children may be the ones who teach them it's worth taking chances for love. (978-1-163555-209-6)

Breaking Down Her Walls by Erin Zak. Could a love worth staying for be the key to breaking down Julia Finch's walls? (978-1-63555-369-7)

All of Me by Emily Smith. When chief surgical resident Galen Burgess meets her new intern, Rowan Duncan, she may finally discover that doing what you've always done will only give you what you've always had. (978-1-163555-321-5)

As the Crow Flies by Karen F. Williams. Romance seems to be blooming all around, but problems arise when a restless ghost emerges from the ether to roam the dark corners of this haunting tale. (978-1-163555-285-0)

Both Ways by Ileandra Young. SPEAR agent Danika Karson races to protect the city from a supernatural threat and must rely on the woman she's trained to despise: Rayne, an achingly beautiful vampire. (978-1-163555-298-0)

Calendar Girl by Georgia Beers. Forced to work together, Addison Fairchild and Kate Cooper discover that opposites really do attract. (978-1-163555-333-8)

Cash and the Sorority Girl by Ashley Bartlett. Cash Braddock doesn't want to deal with morality, drugs, or people. Unfortunately, she's going to have to. (978-1-163555-310-9)

Lovebirds by Lisa Moreau. Two women from different worlds collide in a small California mountain town, each with a mission that doesn't include falling in love. (978-1-163555-213-3)

Media Darling by Fiona Riley. Can Hollywood bad girl Emerson and reluctant celebrity gossip reporter Hayley work together to make each other's dreams come true? Or will Emerson's secrets ruin not one career, but two? (978-1-163555-278-2)

Stroke of Fate by Renee Roman. Can Sean Moore live up to her reputation and save Jade Rivers from the stalker determined to end Jade's career and, ultimately, her life? (978-1-163555-162-4)

The Rise of the Resistance by Jackie D. The soul of America has been lost for almost a century. A few people may be the difference between a phoenix rising to save the masses or permanent destruction. (978-1-163555-259-1)

The Sex Therapist Next Door by Meghan O'Brien. At the intersection of sex and intimacy, anything is possible. Even love. (978-1-163555-296-6)

Unexpected Lightning by Cass Sellars. Lightning strikes once more when Sydney and Parker fight a dangerous stranger who threatens the peace they both desperately want. (978-1-163555-276-8)

Unforgettable by Elle Spencer. When one night changes a lifetime... Two romance novellas from best-selling author Elle Spencer. (978-1-63555-429-8)

Against All Odds by Kris Bryant, Maggie Cummings, and M. Ullrich. Peyton and Tory escaped death once, but will they survive when Bradley's determined to make his kill rate 100 percent? (978-1-163555-193-8)

Autumn's Light by Aurora Rey. Casual hookups aren't supposed to include romantic dinners and meeting the family. Can Mat Pero see beyond the heartbreak that led her to keep her worlds so separate, and will Graham Connor be waiting if she does? (978-1-163555-272-0)

Breaking the Rules by Larkin Rose. When Virginia and Carmen are thrown together by an embarrassing mistake, they find out their stubborn determination isn't so heroic after all. (978-1-163555-261-4)

Broad Awakening by Mickey Brent. In the sequel to *Underwater Vibes*, Hélène and Sylvie find ruts in their road to eternal bliss. (978-1-163555-270-6)

Broken Vows by MJ Williamz. Sister Mary Margaret must reconcile her divided heart or risk losing a love that just might be heaven sent. (978-1-163555-022-1)

Flesh and Gold by Ann Aptaker. Havana, 1952, where art thief and smuggler Cantor Gold dodges gangland bullets and mobsters' schemes while she searches Havana's steamy red light district for her kidnapped love. (978-1-163555-153-2)

Isle of Broken Years by Jane Fletcher. Spanish noblewoman Catalina de Valasco is in peril, even before the pirates holding her for ransom sail into seas destined to become known as the Bermuda Triangle. (978-1-163555-175-4)

Love Like This by Melissa Brayden. Hadley Cooper and Spencer Adair set out to take the fashion world by storm. If only they knew their hearts were about to be taken. (978-1-163555-018-4)

Secrets On the Clock by Nicole Disney. Jenna and Danielle love their jobs helping endangered children, but that might not be enough to stop them from breaking the rules by falling in love. (978-1-163555-292-8)

Unexpected Partners by Michelle Larkin. Dr. Chloe Maddox tries desperately to deny her attraction for Detective Dana Blake as they flee from a serial killer who's hunting them both. (978-1-163555-203-4)

A Fighting Chance by T. L. Hayes. Will Lou be able to come to terms with her past to give love a fighting chance? (978-1-163555-257-7)

Chosen by Brey Willows. When the choice is adapt or die, can love save us all? (978-1-163555-110-5)

Gnarled Hollow by Charlotte Greene. After they are invited to study a secluded nineteenth-century estate, a former English professor and a group of historians discover that they will have to fight against the unknown if they have any hope of staying alive. (978-1-163555-235-5)

Jacob's Grace by C.P. Rowlands. Captain Tag Becket wants to keep her head down and her past behind her, but her feelings for AJ's second-in-command, Grace Fields, makes keeping secrets next to impossible. (978-1-163555-187-7)

On the Fly by PJ Trebelhorn. Hockey player Courtney Abbott is content with her solitary life until visiting concert violinist Lana Caruso makes her second-guess everything she always thought she wanted. (978-1-163555-255-3)

Passionate Rivals by Radclyffe. Professional rivalry and long-simmering passions create a combustible combination when Emmet McCabe and Sydney Stevens are forced to work together, especially when past attractions won't stay buried. (978-1-63555-231-7)

Proxima Five by Missouri Vaun. When geologist Leah Warren crash-lands on a preindustrial planet and is claimed by its tyrant, Tiago, will clan warrior Keegan's love for Leah give her the strength to defeat him? (978-1-163555-122-8)

Shadowboxer by Jessica L. Webb. Jordan McAddie is prepared to keep her street kids safe from a dangerous underground protest group, but she isn't prepared for her first love to walk back into her life. (978-1-163555-267-6)

Racing Hearts by Dena Blake. When you cross a hot-tempered race car mechanic with a reckless cop, the result can only be spontaneous combustion. (978-1-163555-251-5)

The Tattered Lands by Barbara Ann Wright. As Vandra and Lilani strive to make peace, they slowly fall in love. With mistrust and murder surrounding them, only their faith in each other can keep their plan to save the world from falling apart. (978-1-163555-108-2)

Captive by Donna K. Ford. To escape a human trafficking ring, Greyson Cooper and Olivia Danner become players in a game of deceit and violence. Will their love stand a chance? (978-1-63555-215-7)

Crossing the Line by CF Frizzell. The Mob discovers a nemesis within its ranks, and in the ultimate retaliation, draws Stick McLaughlin from anonymity by threatening everything she holds dear. (978-1-63555-161-7)

Love's Verdict by Carsen Taite. Attorneys Landon Holt and Carly Pachett want the exact same thing: the only open partnership spot at their prestigious criminal defense firm. But will they compromise their careers for love? (978-1-63555-042-9)

Precipice of Doubt by Mardi Alexander & Laurie Eichler. Can Cole Jameson resist her attraction to her boss, veterinarian Jodi Bowman, or will she risk a workplace romance and her heart? (978-1-63555-128-0)

Savage Horizons by CJ Birch. Captain Jordan Kellow's feelings for Lt. Ali Ash have her past and future colliding, setting in motion a series of events that strands her crew in an unknown galaxy thousands of light years from home. (978-1-63555-250-8)

Secrets of the Last Castle by A. Rose Mathieu. When Elizabeth Campbell represents a young man accused of murdering an elderly woman, her investigation leads to an abandoned plantation that reveals many dark Southern secrets. (978-1-63555-240-9)

Take Your Time by VK Powell. A neurotic parrot brings police officer Grace Booker and temporary veterinarian Dr. Dani Wingate together in the tiny town of Pine Cone, but their unexpected attraction keeps the sparks flying. (978-1-63555-130-3)

The Last Seduction by Ronica Black. When you allow true love to elude you once and you desperately regret it, are you brave enough to grab it when it comes around again? (978-1-63555-211-9)

The Shape of You by Georgia Beers. Rebecca McCall doesn't play it safe, but when sexy Spencer Thompson joins her workout class, their nonstop sparring forces her to face her ultimate challenge—a chance at love. (978-1-63555-217-1)

Force of Fire: Toujours a Vous by Ali Vali. Immortals Kendal and Piper welcome their new child and celebrate the defeat of an old enemy, but another ancient evil is about to awaken deep in the jungles of Costa Rica. (978-1-63555-047-4)